# THE HYSTERIA OF BODALIS

MARCOS ANTONIO HERNANDEZ

# CHAPTER ONE

The breakfast buffet in the front lobby is the only thing I look forward to in this average hotel. I think about the pictures of the food I saw online as I ride down the elevator. I can't decide which color food to start with: red, orange, and green fruit or golden scrambled eggs. The elevator doors open and the smell of food hits me as I step out into the front lobby. My stomach lets me know how long it has been since my last meal. Come to think of it, I haven't eaten since before I took off for Phoenix last night.

I turn the corner to be greeted by the saddest display of breakfast foods I have ever seen. All the colors seep out of the picture in my head to leave a dull grey hue on the food in front of me. The apples are withered, the bananas either too green or too ripe, and the cut-up melon must be from the leftovers that didn't pass the quality control tests to be sold in supermarkets. The eggs are watery and look like they could have been left over from yesterday. The breakfast meat is the type found at a twenty-four-hour truck stop, the type I know will give me nausea the rest of the morning. I don't know why I ever believed the pictures posted online.

At the far end of the buffet is oatmeal, the one thing nobody can fuck up. I take two scoops into my bowl and add plenty of maple syrup. I pour myself a glass of orange juice and make my way around the wall that separates the food from the area where guests sit to eat their meals. Most of the tables are already occupied. Some tables play host to families and some to loners who watch the news on monitors scattered around the room. I find an unused table at the back, away from any of the monitors, and sit down. Launching the reading app on my phone I continue to read the biography of Amanda West while I take the first bite of my oatmeal.

After her successful rocket launch to Mars, Amanda turned her tremendous focus towards her final project: the ability to upload human consciousness. A surprise to shareholders but when faced with her own mortality, she decided she would be able to further the human race if her mind was able to stick around longer than her body. I am at the part of the book when she pivots to this new venture in order to prepare the world for a future without her.

I should prepare for my future as well. I set my phone down on the table. I need to give some thought to my time at the conference today, a future much more immediate than Amanda's.

While I review my plan for the day in my head, I can't help but dread the large crowds of people that will clog the aisles of the conference. I will throw a few elbows or jostle my way through if I have to, but I am not a fan of crowds in general. What if I see someone I know? Do I stop to talk to them in the middle of the aisle and hold up traffic? Do I ask if they want to step off to the side for a quick chat? And what if they say yes? I will be stuck with them for minutes of long, painful small talk. A social prison. I could always ignore them, pretend I do not see them, but then it looks like I am being rude. I can't seem rude. I will have to pretend to enjoy the interaction to make sure I do not offend anybody.

"Hey there, mind if I sit here?" a man with a southern accent says to me. He sets his food down and walks away before I even have the chance to respond. I see the back of his blue suit as he walks away. On his plate are piles of watery eggs and questionable meat. In a separate bowl is oatmeal with chunks of melon. A weird combination.

"Sure," I say to nobody, annoyed. I didn't think I would have to pretend so soon. I eat another spoonful of my oatmeal with added purpose: to finish my meal and get out of this situation.

The man returns with a glass of milk in one hand and a mug of coffee in the other. After he sets them down he reaches his hand out to me. "Dell. Dell Cooper. Nice to meet you."

"Corvus," I say as I shake his hand and eat another large spoonful.

Dell is heavy set. It doesn't surprise me when I see all the food he has in front of him. He has the round, jovial face of someone who has never learned to deny himself of any pleasure. His beard is well-groomed but I suspect its main purpose is to hide the chubbiness of his cheeks.

"Here for the conference?" he asks me.

"Yes."

"Me too! Who do you work for?"

"Decant."

"The coffee shop! I can't do all those fancy drinks. I like my coffee black," Dell says as he takes a drink from his mug.

"We have black coffee as well," I say after I swallow another spoonful of oatmeal.

"That's cool. I sell crazy straws. Do you know what crazy straws are?" he asks me through a mouthful of eggs.

"Of course I know what crazy straws are. People still buy

those?" Who talks with their mouth full? This guy knows just how to get on my nerves.

"They sure do! Kids love 'em," Dell says. He shovels a spoonful of melon oatmeal into his mouth even though he has clearly not swallowed the eggs. "Hey, do you think Decant would be interested in selling crazy straws?"

I stare at him for a full second, take a mouthful of oatmeal, and shake my head.

"Thought I would ask. You never know!" He shovels another bite of food into his mouth and continues, "You seem tired. Did you get in late last night?"

"I seem tired because I am tired," I reply. I decided to stay up late last night to beat the story mode of Invader Assault. Some exhaustion is worth it to be able to achieve the perfect game. Hardest difficulty, no deaths, record time. It won't be easy for other players to beat the score. I can't wait to rub it in the faces of my team members tonight at practice.

"Night out on the town eh? I plan on getting into some trouble tonight," Dell says with a twinkle in his eye.

"No, I was up playing Invader Assault."

"Invader Assault? The death game?"

I roll my eyes. "It's the biggest game on the cloud. People who signed up to have their consciousness uploaded once they died have their minds kept on the death server. Their minds control the non-playable characters in the city."

"In the city? Which city?" He takes another large scoop of melon oatmeal before he continues to talk with his mouth full. "Sorry, I don't know much about video games."

"The game is based on whichever city you live in. Since my home console is in Bodalís, the city I play in is Bodalís. The game changes depending on whether you live in the city or not. If you live in the city, a lot of the game is spent gathering intel from various people. If you live outside the city, your time is spent gathering resources in order to get into the city."

"Sounds complicated. I play Tetris on my phone whenever I have to sit on the toilet."

"That's really nice," I comment.

"How old are you? Aren't you a little old to be playing video games?" he says with a chuckle.

"I am thirty-two," I say, exasperated. The number of times I have been asked this question amazes me. I didn't know there were age-acceptable ways to spend free time. I take another bite of my oatmeal and decide to throw the last bite away in order to get away from Dell. I stand up and gather my trash. "Enjoy the rest of your meal. I'm off to the conference," I say as I make my way to the lobby to wait for the shuttle.

Dell nods with his mouth full, the first time he has chosen to chew instead of talk.

---

THE SHUTTLE to the convention center pulls up to the front of the hotel and parks against the curb three car lengths from the entrance. I make my way through the automatic double doors and am greeted by oppressive heat as I make my way to the shuttle, squinting my eyes to deal with the brightness of the morning sun. The shuttle is white with large black tinted windows on all sides, including toward the sky. People must like the open feel from inside the shuttle but I couldn't care less. As long as there is air conditioning and the glare from the sun isn't too bright, I am happy.

I step onto the shuttle and see the steering wheel but no driver. Vehicles have been autonomous for so long now I do not know why they even bother to include the steering wheel. I think it must help people feel more secure. Like somehow, in the event of an emergency, a human could take over and control the situation. Even though it has been proven that autonomous drivers are now better than even the best human drivers.

There is only one other passenger onboard sitting near the front. I pick a seat next to the window in the back, thankful to be out of the sun. I open the book on my phone again and start to read as the shuttle begins to move. It should take about fifteen minutes to get to the convention center from here.

Somebody begins to bang on the side of the shuttle and it skids to a stop. I look to the side and see greasy handprints on the windows and the back of a man's head as he shuffles towards the front door in order to be allowed on before it's too late. We were just about to leave the parking lot. The door opens and the man climbs onboard. Dell. I turn my attention back to my phone and reread the sentence that was interrupted by the sudden stop and, the next thing I know, Dell plops his bag in the seat right next to mine as he sits down two seats over. There are over fifteen seats still available on this shuttle but he has to sit near me— again.

"Man, I almost missed it!" he says between gasps for air.

"Maybe if you hadn't eaten so much you wouldn't have such a hard time running down the shuttle."

"Well, if I hadn't eaten so much there wouldn't have been a need to run the shuttle down! I would've been out here when you were." He takes two panting breaths and feels his under-arms for sweat. "Oh well, at least I made it."

"You sure did," I say, turning my attention back to my book, making it the third time I have read the same sentence. The shuttle begins to move again and turns into the street in front of the hotel.

"Your SimScore must be through the roof," Dell says. He stands up, grabs his underwear through his pants in order to rearrange himself, and sits back down. "Mine isn't that great. I don't bother to do any education on the cloud. Is your Sim good enough to do work for you?"

My eyes stay focused on the words in front of me. "I don't let my Sim do anything for me, I prefer to take care of all my own interactions."

"Really?" Dell says, surprised. "I have to do all my communication for work myself. The company found out I let my Sim respond to clients and I nearly lost my job. I let my Sim respond to all my personal messages and phone calls though. Especially the ones with my mom. Haven't talked to her in ages."

"Maybe she lets her Sim talk to you as well," I suggest. I would. I doubt even his own mother can stand him.

"I never thought of that," says Dell. He falls silent beside me and I read in peace for the rest of our trip.

The Phoenix sun greets me as soon as I step onto the concrete in front of the convention center. I look down at the ground with squinted eyes because the sun is so bright. It doesn't help that the building is covered with windows that reflect even more sunlight onto those who approach. Through the windows that cover the building I can see plants inside the large glass atrium that serves as the lobby. Another example of design that takes advantage of natural sunlight, something I will never understand. The glass atrium inside extends at least seven stories up. Such a waste of vertical space.

Construction surrounds the venue this year. The concrete walkways around the building are all blocked off to pedestrians. A bottleneck of people wait in line between chain-link fences in order to get to the revolving doors which will take them inside. Without a word to Dell, I turn left and begin to walk to the Decant I know is close by, less than a block away.

I keep my head down and walk on the black asphalt next to the fence which keeps me off the sidewalk. Cars pass close by, each headed back to the street having dropped off their passengers. My shirt sticks to my lower back and I can feel beads of sweat from my calves absorb into the fabric of my pants. A solitary bead of sweat begins at my hairline and drips down my forehead before it finds my left eye. The sting makes me stop and rub the pain away and I continue with my eyes half closed to enable me to see where I walk.

I open the door at Decant and make my way inside, standing just inside the front door for three long breaths, grateful for the air conditioning. The familiar decor of a Decant store greets me once my eyes adjust. The walls are all white. Light brown wood is everywhere, from the accents on the walls to the tables. Only two of the dozen or so tables are occupied, everyone else stands in a line six people long. They are all dressed for business and must be here for the conference. Some of them have already put their name tags on which shows the company they are here to represent. I take my place at the back of the queue and pull out my phone to continue reading.

As I stand, absorbed in my book, a force pulls my gaze to a table at the back of the store, near the restrooms where an old man is staring straight at me. I look around the room to give the man a chance to divert his gaze, but when I return my sight to where he sits he is still focused on me. Unsettled, I try to go back to my book but it is no use. Thoughts of the old man occupy my mind.

The old man has on khakis and a white shirt with the top three buttons left undone. The shirt has sweat stains around the collar and the armpits. His face is lined with deep wrinkles and his head moves with a constant tic, like he is cursed to shake his head to a demon only he can see. The white paper cup in front of him has brown coffee streaks down the front. If I had to guess, he has used this same cup for days on end. Or he has taken it out of the trash in order to get the cup discount at the register. Whatever the case, he needs to ignore me.

When it is my turn to order I step up and order my usual drink. Medium iced coffee, black which I like because the barista can never mess it up. The iced coffee is prepared each morning and sits in a pitcher as it waits to be poured. They just put it in a cup and add ice. Minimal wait time. To pay for the drink I put my face up to the scanner and see the three green dots of the retinal scan that is linked to my account.

I can feel the old man's eyes on me as wait for my drink. With my morning coffee in hand I make my way out of the store, turning one last time to look at the old man before making my way back out into the Phoenix sun. Part of me hopes to confirm that his eyes are still on me and part of me hopes that I am wrong. The old man continues to stare.

# CHAPTER TWO

I SURVIVE the heat on the way back to the convention center and pass through the revolving doors into the glass atrium. Although I am not a fan of natural light and expansive ceilings, I have to admit the grid from the windows casts spectacular shadows over the floor inside. I wonder if the people who work here realize they could tell what time of day it is based on the angles these shadows create. They cast a checkerboard over the indoor fountain and rows of planters in the middle of the expanse. The shadow grid also covers the crowd of people who wait to get onto the escalator that will take them up to the East Hall where the International Non-Alcoholic Drink Conference is held each year.

I walk towards the elevators beyond the rows of plants. Most people don't know about these so there is no queue of people waiting to use them. I throw away my coffee cup and board the elevator, alone, and the doors are about to close when a hand holds them back at the last moment. The doors open again and I see the hand belongs to a curly-haired woman in her mid-forties. She is at the head of a group of six others. All of their blue tags, the color assigned to exhibitors, read "Uniforms

Plus." I pull my own badge out of my back left pocket and hang it around my neck in order to make it through security. My badge is pink to let others know that I am an attendee and don't have an exhibition booth.

The woman who held the elevator pushes against my left arm in order to make more room for the last of her group to board. I lean away, annoyed that people can be so inconsiderate with personal space. This is why I can't stand elevators. Nobody would stand this close to me under normal circumstances. A whiff of her cheap perfume hits my nostrils. I shouldn't be exposed to the smell of others without my consent. I watch the "2" light above the door blink. Only one more level to go. What if the elevator breaks down? I could be stuck with these people, engaged in small talk to pass the time, for an eternity while it gets fixed. My vision narrows as I inspect the four walls that keep us so close together.

The "3" light blinks to life and the doors open.

The security station is straight ahead. Each security guard wears the same yellow jacket as they scan all badges to make sure people have the proper credentials. There are only a few attendees ahead of me in line. The chance to go through the shorter security line is one of the benefits of using the elevator. I look over the railing to my left and see the mob of people who line up to get through security on the lower level—the same people who took the escalator. There is one final escalator after the security station which will bring them up to the level I am on now. A security guard scans my badge and I can see my face pop up on their screen. Once my identity has been confirmed, they wave me through the doors and into the East Hall.

Each time I attend I am always in awe of the large space. Booths extend off in each direction, each of them on the lookout for the big fish they hope to reel in. With Decant on my name tag, exhibitors usually treat me like one of these big fish, making it a point to pay extra attention to me. Often times their most senior team member will be the one who comes to talk with me.

I look up at the sheet metal pipes, at least two feet in diameter, which cover the ceiling, over forty feet above me. The amount of energy it must take to heat or cool the exhibition hall amazes me. There must be at least a thousand display booths, all arranged in neat rows and columns.

I take a deep breath and exhale. Each year, I begin with a walk through every row in order to gauge the temperature of the conference. The walk costs me a few hours but I believe it is important to see what is hot this year and where I might be able to find the next big thing. Last year nobody would have thought that a drink whose flavor changes based on the temperature would be popular. This year it seems that every booth has a drink that changes flavor. I want to be the one who helps Decant set the trend. I also want to see where all the big companies like Coca-Cola and Pepsi are located and see which smaller booths catch my eye. The walk must be done first in order to give my brain time to digest the information while I continue with the rest of my day. It will give me something to think about in the background while I suffer through the client meetings lined up for this afternoon.

I walk by a booth on my right which sells stainless steel juicers. "Excuse me, sir; do you like juice?" a voice says to me. A young Asian woman holds out a tray of samples in my direction. She is short, less than five feet tall and wears thick-rimmed purple glasses which match the purple streaks in her hair.

"Do you like juice?" she asks again.

"What kind?" I say. The booth is on the smaller side with blue walls. The company appears to sell three different juicer sizes.

"Apple."

"Which machine did this come from?" I ask as I reach for one of the small cups.

"The Deluxe. All of our juicers deliver the same quality of juice they just vary in how much volume they can handle."

I choose one of the samples and try it. Not bad, but it is hard to mess up juice. The problem is always the machine—the blades either don't spin well or the machine gets clogged. It makes more sense to buy the juice already squeezed.

"Our juicers are a wonderful retail opportunity for any size store. Customers come in, they get a fresh squeezed juice. People don't want to do the work themselves, why not have them pay you to do it for them?"

"We already sell juices at our stores," I tell her. She looks at the ID badge around my neck.

"Customers could buy our juicers at your locations! Some of our larger companies prefer to do that. You already sell coffee machines, no? Well now you could sell juicers as well."

I throw my cup in the small trash can by her feet and begin to walk away as her voice fades behind me. Not bad juice but nobody buys juicers.

---

NEAR THE END of my walk through the conference I come across a booth with a crowd of people standing around it. The booth is located in front of an entrance to the East Hall opposite to where I came in. A large booth in prime real estate. From what I can see from my place behind the crowd it looks like a typical juice bar. What is it with juice this year? When will these companies learn? The walls of the booth are gunmetal grey and fresh fruit is piled high on stainless steel counters. There are three large square displays that show different kinds of fruit combinations: strawberry banana, peach mango, and pineapple blueberry. Above the signs the company name is written in bold white block letters: Next Level Automation.

I bet this booth gives out full-sized samples, that is why there are so many people here. The majority of attendees who walk around are smaller operations, each with less than ten stores. They are here to find products they can sell in their locations in order to encourage their customers to spend more money. These are the type of people who take advantage of free samples.

How many disposable cups will be used this weekend? This must be the holy grail for companies that make those small cups.

I am not in the mood for juice again and decide to walk around the crowd. I pass by the side of the booth, close enough to see behind the counter. Three people, two men and one woman, have their hands full as drink orders pile up. They each wear white dress shirts, black pants, and black aprons. I look around to see what it is they sell. Nothing about the booth seems automated. The juicers don't seem to be displayed where they could draw attention and there are no signs of a prepackaged juice they sell. I look for a salesperson to ask for more information but don't see one anywhere.

I continue to walk down the aisle, resigned to the fact that I will not be able to find out more about Next Level Automation, when I realize the other half of the booth is behind the wall and this is where the sales people are. Each of them is dressed in a navy-blue suit with tan shoes. While I wait for one of the salespeople to finish with one of their potential clients, I notice a display that goes into more detail about their main product: Customer Service Androids. A female salesperson near the display exchanges business cards with her client before she turns her attention to me.

She has straight blonde hair and would have been attractive if it wasn't for the piles of makeup. I can't decide if she does it for the conference or if this is how she wears her face on a typical day. We introduce ourselves and I find out her name is Denise. I tell her my name and she checks my badge to find out I work for Decant before she tells me about the androids.

"They can be programmed to make drinks, clean and, most importantly, handle all customer interaction. Pretty much anything a company like Decant could want them to do," Denise tells me.

"So, we wouldn't need any humans to run the store," I say, thinking out loud.

"We don't recommend human-less operations. In trials we have found that some people will test the limits of their programming and push the androids past their capabilities."

"With complicated orders?"

"It isn't the physical tasks that suffer. We can make sure every possible order can be fulfilled; that's just a simple program. Social interactions is where the limits of the androids show up. Conflict is the main problem, they are not given a response to anger. In any situation with an angry customer they are programmed to defer the interaction to a human. We recommend at least one human for every three units."

"Interesting."

This could mean thousands of Decant employees would be out of a job. Might be worth it, I think.

"How long do they last?" I ask Denise.

"Most will last around seven to ten years with standard maintenance before needing to be replaced."

"And each unit costs how much?"

"Eighty thousand dollars. Plus the cost to keep them connected to the cloud."

A large initial investment but it is easy to see how much money would be saved over the life of the android.

"Why do they need to be connected to the cloud?"

"We have to keep their data current. If one of the androids gets disconnected it increases the chance for an undesirable interaction."

"How so?"

"Well, the first interaction is almost guaranteed to generate an appropriate response. Statistically, the next few interactions would be acceptable too. But, if they are unable to confirm the probability of their responses with data on the cloud, they begin to base their next response on their previous responses and, in time, this will lead to malfunction."

"I remember robots were placed in drivers' seat in the beginning of the driverless revolution," I say. "They were only there for show, the car drove itself. Once the auto makers realized that people felt the same way about a robot driver and no driver at all they stopped making them. Even stopped including a driver's seat. They only had the most basic communication skills and they were all pre-programmed, if my memory serves me correctly. How did these learn to interact with humans so well?"

"We use expired Simulations. Have you ever wondered what happens to the Sims of dead people?"

"No, I haven't. How are they different than the uploaded minds on the death server?" I ask.

"So, you know about the death server? Well, this is another part of the same server. Most people associate the death server with replicated minds of the dead. This is a little different. You know how everyone has their own personal Sim based on the data they create? Well, when people die their expired Sim gets transferred to the death server. Normally, the Sim would disintegrate over time without any new data from its creator. We make sure these Sims stay viable using data from social interactions in the cloud."

"You have access to those interactions?"

"We are sold the interactions as anonymous data," Denise

tells me. "Everything from phone conversations to collaborative games are useful for generation."

Collaborative games. Like Invader Assault. I wonder if any of my interactions have been used to teach these androids.

"The biggest hurdle was the robotic technology," Denise says, "in particular the hands. Fine motor control is what has kept our product off the market. Testing showed that people feel uncomfortable interacting with robots who spoke well but moved poorly so we had to wait until the androids were indistinguishable from humans."

"I thought it was illegal to upload a mind to a physical form after Amanda West tried to achieve immortality by replicating hers and putting it into a robot. That is why nobody is allowed to have a replication if they are still alive and, even if they are dead, they can't put their mind into an android."

"These aren't replicated minds, these are Sims."

"Isn't that illegal too?"

"That's why we use expired ones. No laws exist against using them."

"What if the law changes? If we buy them and they become illegal, that would be a lot of money wasted."

"We are confident the laws won't change. Our androids cannot make any decisions that affect their physical actions, they are only useful for social interactions. We could sell you a robot designed to just make drinks but we think there is more value in an android that can handle customer service as well. The ability to interact with customers is the only difference between the robot programmed to make drinks and our androids."

"Got it," I say. "You have given me a lot to think about." We exchange business cards and shake hands before I go back to the side of the booth to get a second look at the androids as they work.

Their movements are indistinguishable from humans. They move slower than the age they appear. The androids look to be no more than in their early twenties and work at the pace of our older baristas. But they don't make a mistake and haven't spilled a drop since I have been here. Each drink comes out as if they are on an assembly line and their only job is to make these three flavors. We would have to downsize the workforce in order to roll them out nationwide. Will Seraph let me get my hands on one to try in our test store? Would the employees be able to tell if one of their members isn't human? I have to consider the team dynamic Decant works hard to cultivate among the employees of each store.

"You aren't seriously thinking about putting those things in your stores, are you?" a voice says behind me.

I turn around and see a man who wears his hair in dread-locks. He has on baggy shorts and a Grateful Dead t-shirt. The blue badge around his neck is for a company called Kappa Hemp.

"Do I know you?"

"No. But these things are going to take jobs from millions. I saw your badge, you work for Decant. Think about all the people who would be out of work."

"What's it to you?"

"You don't feel like you have an ethical responsibility to your employees?"

"This is none of your business." I read the front of his shirt. "You worry about Kappa Hemp. I'll worry about Decant."

"I know it isn't, but I decided that I had to say something. You corporate types, all you care about is the bottom line!"

I turn around and walk away, annoyed at the man and impressed with the androids.

# CHAPTER THREE

Booths on either side of me seem insignificant compared to the new android technology I just witnessed. They will be a game changer. Based on how many people were around the booth it is safe to say other people recognize the importance of this technology also. Androids have been around for a while now but never have they been so available to the general public. As I walk along the carpeted aisles, I hear someone call out my name.

"Corvus! Corvus!" There are people all around me. I turn around to check behind me, but I don't recognize anyone until I look to my right. Brianne makes her way towards me from next to a UV machine down the aisle that sterilizes cups. As I walk forward to meet her, I extend my hand. She goes straight in for the hug.

"It's so good to see you! How have you been?" she asks me after releasing me from her clutches. Her voice isn't normally so high pitched and it won't stay this way for long. She does it every time she sees somebody after a while, I think to make people believe she is excited to see them. I'm not sure if it bothers anyone else, or if they even notice, but I count down the time until she talks like a normal person.

"I've been good," I say to her. "Another year at the show. On the lookout for Decant's next summer launch. How have you been? Are you still doing PR for Java the Hut?"

"Sure am, it's been great!" Brianne says. She has on a square blue dress and red heels. The dress would look good on her if she hadn't gained a few pounds. It doesn't surprise me that she would hold onto her dress size but she doesn't seem to understand that just because you can fit into it doesn't mean you should. Her shoulder length brown hair is cut at a sharper angle than I remember and she has added blonde streaks. Her earrings look like red seashells and match her shoes.

"You look like you've been working out," she says as she squeezes my left bicep through my suit jacket. Her voice is still high. Here comes the flattery, all on script.

"Only my thumbs," I say as I hold up both my hands and mimic the actions I make when I use a controller. "I spend a lot of time gaming. How's Terry doing?"

"He was good the last time I heard from him. We are separated." Her voice drops to her normal pitch.

"Sorry to hear that. Hopefully it wasn't too messy."

"It wasn't. We both knew it was time. We're in the process of getting a divorce." I catch a glimpse of sadness before her eyes fall to the ground.

Do I look like a shoulder to cry on? I need to change the subject before this gets too deep. "How is everything at work?"

Brianne picks her head up as she gathers herself. With a professional air she says, "We are looking at expanding into the Mexican and Canadian markets. There could be a lot more work on my table. If we go through with expanding into Mexico I already told the company I will need to have another person on my team, somebody who speaks Spanish. It seems like forever ago that I was interviewing you for my team. Luckily you turned out alright!" she says. Her left hand rests on my right shoulder as her eyes look me up and down. Still too familiar, even after not seeing each other for almost four years.

"Yes, I did. You were a good teacher." A simple lie to make her feel better about herself. With any luck she has somewhere to be and will leave me alone soon.

"Hey, have you eaten yet? I know this great sushi spot a few blocks away. It would be a quick cab ride." Seems like she can read my thoughts and has decided to fuck with me. A very Brianne thing to do.

"I had planned on going to this sandwich shop I go to every year," I say.

"Are you meeting with a client?"

"No, I just like the place. I guess I could go tomorrow."

"Well why don't we go there then? I like sandwiches too," she says.

I pause for a moment as I try and come up with a reason why this lunch won't work but nothing comes to mind. "Great, it's going to be good catching up with my old mentor," I say. It won't be great but I have to eat lunch anyway. Brianne beams with pride when I call her my mentor. My time at Java the Hut with her was just a job to me, one that I left in order to work for Decant. She could have been a rock and I would have learned the same amount. I want her to feel good about herself though, to feel like she made a difference in my life. She could use the confidence boost as I've heard divorces can be tough. Plus, she has been stuck in the same position since I left.

Brianne fills me in on her life as we leave the convention center, while we wait for the cab, and on the cab ride over. I ask her a few open-ended questions to seem like an active listener and to make sure she continues to talk about herself. We get to the sandwich shop halfway through her account of a Caribbean vacation she and Terry took right before they split, twenty minutes into our trip. I can't believe she hasn't run out of things to say by now.

The sandwich shop is called Platters. It is a hole in the wall shop with no seats inside. The floors might have been white at one point in time but now they are a dull yellow and covered with black stains that can never be removed. A teenage girl stands behind a rusted metal grate, five feet from the front door. A twelve inch square is cut from the metal to exchange payment. Cookies are on display on the counter on each side of the hole in the metal and potato chips hang from clips underneath.

While we stand in line, Brianne finishes her story about a dive off the coast of Aruba on the last morning of their trip. Before they almost miss their flight. I order a Reuben and she orders a BLT, both of us grabbing a bag of chips to go with our sandwiches. After we pay for our food we go through a screen door to the covered outdoor patio. I lead the way to my favorite table, the one in front of the fans, and the screen door slams shut. Brianne puts her purse over the back of her chair before she sits down.

"Sounds like a busy vacation!" I say once we settle into our seats.

"That was the last good time we had together. Everything before that was strained. When we got back we went right back to the way things were. I think we both felt it but I was the first one to vocalize it." Here we are, right back to the feelings.

"Have you taken any time off? Sounds like you could use another vacation, alone. Or maybe a girls' trip. Just to get away from it all."

"I haven't taken another trip yet, other than this conference. My friend and I are supposed to go to Las Vegas in December. We are both looking forward to that! How about you, any trips coming up?"

"Well the trips I take are usually for tournaments. So—"

"Can I just say that I've missed you, Corvus? I enjoyed when you were around. Everything just seemed to work. Know what I mean?"

Everything always works. I don't know what she means. "Those were good times." They weren't. "Hard to believe it was so long ago!" It isn't.

"It does. Sorry to cut you off. You were saying about your tournaments?"

"Oh yeah. Nothing important, just that I use my vacation days when I compete."

"Do you have to travel for those?"

"For some of them. The championships are actually held in Bodalís each year. That is part of the reason why I was happy to get the job with Decant at their Bodalís office. The city built a special venue just for e-sports. Since Invader Assault is the biggest game out right now, our tournament is held the weekend after Thanksgiving."

"Is that a special weekend or something?"

"Kind of. They reserve that weekend for whichever game is most popular so they can be ready for the crowds. Before Invader Assault came out, I would go to Bodalís on the same weekend for the Ronin world championships."

"I think I remember you going to Bodalís over Thanksgiving when we worked together. I never knew why though."

Our sandwiches arrive, brought out by the same girl who took our order. My Reuben looks as good as I remember. Brianne's BLT is piled high with bacon. Too bad I won't ever get the chance to have one since I order the Reuben every single time.

"So, tell me more about this game you play," Brianne says. She opens her bag of chips and pours them onto the tray alongside her sandwich. "Is it on the cloud?"

"Yeah it is."

"And it counts towards your SimScore?"

"It does."

"Your Sim must be able to do everything online just like you would," Brianne comments popping a chip into her mouth. "I have mine set up to do the most basic stuff. It finds articles and recipes for me. But I never feed it any data so it never gets any better."

"I don't really use my Sim at all. I do everything myself," I tell her.

"Could a Sim play the game for you?"

"In theory, yes, but it wouldn't do well at all."

"Interesting. Do you shoot people in your game?"

"Well that's part of it." I pick up my sandwich and take a bite. Brianne waits for me to continue.

With a sigh I put down my food. "In multiplayer, the object of the game is to complete objectives with another team trying to stop you. For example, the objective can be to carry a bomb to a point. Once the bomb is planted you have to stay and protect the bomb so the other team cannot defuse it. Another objective is King of the Hill. An area is designated as the hill and your team has to hold it for a total of sixty seconds while the other team tries to take it from you."

"So, you shoot people who are trying to stop you from completing the objective?" she says moments before she takes a bite of her BLT. She chews with her mouth open just enough to make a slight smack. I had forgotten about this quirk of hers. Her potato chip bag gets caught in the breeze from the fan and tumbles off the table to the ground. I reach over and grab it, storing it under my sandwich tray.

"Thanks," Brianne says.

I get settled back into my chair. "The kills don't count though. Well, they count but they are only a means to an end.

What matters is completing the objective. The other team cannot disarm the bomb if they are all dead."

"Do you wear a headset like the people on TV? They say it's the future of entertainment."

"You mean the holo lenses? Yes, I wear them. They're customized to my eye movement. The more I use them the more they learn the way I play." At the mention of eyes I can see her look into mine, like she wants to see through to what lies behind. If I had ever noticed the hazel color of her eyes I'd forgotten. Uncomfortable with the eye contact I break her gaze and take a bite of my Reuben.

"Sounds like a fun game! Are there a lot of people that play?" I know she doesn't mean to sound condescending. At the end of the day, all sports are games. Mine just happens to be electronic.

"There are a lot of us. Girls too! Can you believe it?"

"Sarcasm doesn't look good on you," she says with a smirk. "Are there girls on your team?"

"Not on my team. There are twelve guys, six of them are alternates." Brianne has a smug look on her face. "But there are plenty of girls on the other championship teams."

"Sure there are," she says. "Six people playing at a time? How do you decide who carries the bomb?"

"Any of us can carry the bomb, it depends on the situation. There are four basic classes: Slayer, Scout, Quartermaster, and Mauler. The difference in characters is based on the type of Exo Suit they wear."

"What kind of player are you?"

"I am a slayer. We have high damage output and average health. My job is to kill as many of the opposing team as possible."

"And what do the other classes do?"

"Well, the scouts are the shifty characters. Their Exo Suits are minimal and provide little health or ability boosts. They are the small, quick characters whose main job is to run around causing mayhem. They never have too much health or inflict too much damage, but their speed is useful in providing distractions."

Brianne is already done with her sandwich and eats her chips one at a time while I talk. I still have half of my sandwich left. My food doesn't normally last this long in front of me but I have slowed my pace to talk about Invader Assault. She watches me come to this realization and rests her chin in her hand. "What do the Quartermasters do?"

I take another bite of my sandwich and swallow. "The quartermaster is responsible for collecting health packs and ammo for the team. They have high health but no real ability to do any damage. Their suits come with a bit of a twist: the ability to manufacture new objects. They can turn large amounts of ammo into extra grenades for their teammates or they can take health packs and create armor. Playing with a smart quartermaster, one who divides the upgrades properly among the team, can make or break a bombing run."

Brianne continues to stare. "Lastly, there are Maulers," I continue. "They are the slowest class of characters. Their gear weighs them down to a crawl but they have high health and high damage capability. Stick one of these guys at the objective and they make sure nobody gets close."

I take another bite of my sandwich and swallow it before it was fully chewed. "I don't even know why I am telling you all of this," I say with food caught just below my throat. "You'll never play."

"I might not play but I like the way your eyes light up when you talk about it." Her chin is still in her hand as she looks at my face. She searches for my eyes again. Not in a discerning, scientific way and not in a romantic way. More maternal than anything else, like she is proud I have found something I can speak about with passion. She is only about ten years older than me so maybe it is more like an older sister. Either way, it interrupts our conversation while I focus on my sandwich.

I finish my sandwich in three large bites as she watches me eat. Her last statement threw me off and I don't have much else to say to her. As I read the label on the ketchup bottle to avoid more conversation, Brianne asks, "So why is the game called Invader Assault?"

I put the ketchup bottle back in the exact place it was on the table, with the label oriented the way I found it. "It is called Invader Assault because of the single player story mode. The Invaders are an alien race who have parked a spaceship over your city. In my case the city is Bodalís but it changes depending on whichever city is closest to the player. Most of the game is spent getting a bomb made on Earth and the final level is when you take the bomb to blow up the spaceship. I finally got a perfect game last night when I blew up the ship without dying once."

"Wow, good job! Did you do this with your team?"

"No, the story and multiplayer modes are different. I completed the story alone. The championships I was talking about will be with my team."

"So, the story mode is basically you in Bodalís? Do you have to shoot any Invaders?"

"No, the Invaders are only in the last level. The characters I have to go up against in the city are humans. They are controlled by the uploaded minds on the death server.

"All the characters in the game are controlled by dead people?"

"By their minds. When people die, they have the ability to replicate their minds and upload onto the death server. From there, the creators of the game use them to live as and control characters in Invader Assault."

"You're lying," Brianne says, her mouth hanging open. "Why would anyone want to play a game with dead people's minds?"

"Because it's more realistic. The makers of the game pay for access to the death server. It's like hiring actors. Except that they are digital. And dead."

"I have definitely never heard of that. Are any of your team-mates controlled by the death servers?"

"No, it doesn't work that way. All of the members of my team were recruited. Each of us had spent time playing the game competitively, individually and with various teams, until our manager convinced us to play together. Last year was our first World Championships, after playing together for almost a year, and we came in fifth. We were pleased with the result but fifth still isn't first. This year we are going to win it all."

"Have you met them before?"

"All of them except the newest member, Wonky. I should be meeting him in person this year at the championships.

"Him? I thought you never met them."

"I can hear his voice."

"That doesn't prove it's a him. Or even that they are alive. What if they are on the death server? Or what if they are an android! You saw the Next Level Automation booth, didn't you?"

"I did. The androids blew my mind. I was thinking about trying to get one for our test store." I grab a sugar packet from the container and fold it in half, then try to fold it into quarters but the packet bursts in my hands. "I told you, Wonky can't be from the death server, they are only used for the characters in the story."

"He could still be an android..."

"If they are as good as Denise says they are I could see how one would be able to fit in on the voice chat. She also said they can be programmed to do anything, that might even include playing Invader Assault."

"Denise?"

"The saleswoman at Next Level Automation."

"See? You never know. Used to be we couldn't assume someone's gender. Now it seems we can't even assume somebody is human!"

The waitress comes to the table to clear our trash.

"Would you care if Wonky was an android?" Brianne says to me after the waitress leaves the table.

"He isn't. But I'd rather not know. He is a good player and works well with the team."

The androids I saw today had to be tested somewhere, why not in multiplayer games? Denise said collaborative game data helps to keep the expired Sims viable, ready for use in their androids. What if they also used video games to test the androids, to see how well the expired Sim can maintain appropriate communication while they play? Gamers aren't known for their eloquence. Any atypical responses would be assumed to be the quirk of another anti-social player.

"This place is good," Brianne says. "I don't know that I would come here every year but they definitely make a quality sandwich." She stands up and slings her purse over her shoulder.

"Once I find something I like I stick with it. I like to know what to expect," I tell her.

She puts her hand on my shoulder as we walk out of the restaurant. "You need to come out of your comfort zone, Corvus. Things will never change unless you do." She smiles and I can feel her eyes regarding me. I focus on her mouth in order to avoid eye contact while I look at her face.

"Why have a comfort zone unless I stay inside it?" I say, turning and walking towards the door.

"One day you will have to come out of it. When you do you will find out that it isn't the end of the world!"

"I can cross that bridge when I get there." We leave the shop and face the Phoenix heat. This sun never lets up. We hail a cab and get inside.

"Want to go to Decant before we go back to the show? There is one a block away from the convention center. My treat," I offer.

"No thanks. I promised a client I would stop by right after lunch. Plus, my bosses wouldn't like me with a competitor's cup in my hand."

"Makes sense," I say.

"Maybe we can meet up later? You have my number."

"Yes, I do."

There is no way we will meet up later. Lunch with Brianne is enough for one day. "Good luck with your client."

The cab drops us off at the convention center. I know Brianne will go in for the hug so I decide to initiate so we can get it over with. "See you later, Corvus, take care of yourself!" She begins the walk back into the convention center as I turn to walk to Decant for my second coffee of the day.

## CHAPTER FOUR

BACK IN DECANT, I stand in line to wait for the chance to order my iced coffee. I put my badge back in my pocket so the baristas here don't know that I also work for Decant. The old man is still here, sitting at the same table near the restrooms. He stares at me as I wait in line, his head shaking as he mutters to his invisible demon. Suddenly, there is a loud scrape of his chair against the floor as the man pushes himself away from his table, stands and walks towards me.

"Goddamn president," the old man growls to nobody in particular. "Can't just leave me alone!"

He turns around and walks back to his table. His face contorts into a grotesque mask as the words he tries to hold inside spill out, louder as he gains momentum. "Their faces don't belong to themselves! Everyone walking around with fake hair and fake faces, afraid to be." He turns around and walks back towards me.

The other people in line stare at their phones in an effort to ignore the frenzied man. From behind the counter a male barista calls out, "Jesse, we can hear you. Please go sit back down." The barista is taller, a little over six feet, and looks to be of mixed race. Caucasian with some African sprinkled in within the last two generations.

The old man exchanges his demonic mask for a cherubic one. "Sorry," he says. "I'll behave." His voice is sweet.

The old man reminds me of a paranoid schizophrenic that used to hang out at my store when I was a barista in college. We would let him stay in the store as long as he behaved. He had to be quiet, that was the rule. We had an agreement: if any customers complained about him he had to leave and couldn't come back for a week. He was a bit of a celebrity among the regulars. If they had been around long enough they would have seen one of his meltdowns. He was never as loud as this guy though, and he never stood up and walked around. He would sit in his chair and rock back and forth as he muttered to himself. He wasn't so much of a distraction; he just made people uncomfortable.

The customers in this store maintain their distance from his table while they wait for their drinks. It's as if they think his condition is contagious. While the person in front of me pays for his medium vanilla latte, I take a good look at the old man. His head continues to shake. When he sees me looking his left eye begins to twitch and his head shake becomes more violent. It reminds me of a bottle of Coke as it gets shaken up and how the pressure builds inside. I hope I can leave the store before his lid comes off.

The tall male barista's name tag says Peter P. I order my medium iced coffee from Peter and go to wait for my drink, close to where the man sits at his table.

"Damn communists with their satellites," the old man mumbles behind me. "Always watching me."

I turn around and look at the man. His grotesque mask is back as he focuses his attention on me.

"And you. YOU!" His words are said the same viscous way poison drips from a rattlesnake's fang when it is harvested.

"Do I know you?" I ask.

"You ruined it! He was finally going to return and you blew up the ship!"

"I have no idea what you are talking about." I turn around and look to see if my drink is ready. The cup with my order is the next one to be made.

"JESUS CHRIST! Heard of him? He was going to come back and you blew up his ship!" I hear his chair scrape on the floor and turn to see his back as he walks away from me towards the front door. He paces along the length of the line again.

"The president. The communists," he says before he whips around to face me. "And you! All conspiring to make my life a living hell!" The eyes in his twisted face are filled with hatred.

Peter P. has come around the counter and places his hand on Jesse's shoulder. "Time to go," he says. "Grab your stuff. You can come back in a few days."

The cherubic mask returns in a flash. "I was doing so well, wasn't I? It had been so long," the old man says.

"Yes, it had been a while. But now you need some time away," the barista says.

"Okay. I understand." The old man grabs his drink and walks out the door. Peter had handled the situation very well.

"Sorry about that," another barista says from behind the counter as she makes drinks. She gives me a free drink coupon along with my iced coffee. I have so many of these coupons already that I choose to never use.

"No problem. Nice of you guys to let him sit here." She doesn't need to know I don't need the free drink because I work for Decant as well.

"I haven't seen him get like that for a while now, a few weeks at least. Sometimes he forgets to take his meds."

"Makes sense," I say. "Thanks again."

I leave the store, drink in hand, and head through the heat towards the convention center. The old man is seated against the building in the alley next to the store. When he sees me walk by he gets to his feet.

"Hey!" he shouts. I don't stop.

"Hey!" he says again, close behind me. I ignore him until a hand grabs my left elbow and twists me around. We both stand on the sidewalk in front of a warehouse door, just before the sidewalk ends and construction work begins.

I pull my arm away in disgust. "Don't fucking touch me," I say as I turn to face the old man.

"I just wanted to say I am sorry," he says in his sweet voice. He continues to shake the contents inside his head.

"Apology accepted." I turn and continue on my way.

As I am about to step onto the asphalt the old man says, "You shouldn't have blown up the ship though," in his poisonous tone.

"You keep talking about this ship!" I yell before I turn around. "I have no clue as to what you're talking about!" I watch his face contort back into the mask he cannot control.

"Last night! You blew up the ship and killed Christ!" His head shakes and saliva froths at the corners of his mouth as he speaks.

I can feel beads of sweat gather on my forehead. "I don't have time for this." I turn to step off the sidewalk. The old man grabs my left arm again and I drop my cup. I turn around and swing my fist, the blow landing on his left cheek.

"What did I tell you about touching me?" I yell. The old man crumples in a heap on the ground, blood trickling out of his mouth as he lies unconscious.

He should never have touched me again. I warned him but he didn't want to listen. I hope he has learned his lesson.

I look around to see if anyone has seen what just happened. There is nobody outside, they must all be inside to escape the midday heat. I can feel my pants sticking to my calves again from the beads of sweat gathered there. I lick my upper lip and taste salt. Time to get back inside; I can't afford to be sweaty when I meet with clients later this afternoon.

I pick up my cup and take one look back at the old man as he lies on the ground while I massage my sore knuckles. He can stay where he is. Maybe now he won't feel the need to explode since his head no longer shakes.

# CHAPTER FIVE

I THROW AWAY my cup once I enter the convention center lobby and sit next to the plants to cool down. People hurry past me as they head towards the East hall. There's a large mass of people waiting to get onto the escalator, looking like sheep as they are herded through a gate.

I look down at my hand and see that my knuckles are still red. Bright red. I must have hit some of the old man's teeth. I hope I didn't knock any of them out, I don't remember any teeth on the ground. A lady in a red dress walks by me. When we make eye contact she smiles, a tight-lipped smile that doesn't show any teeth. I put my left hand over my right to hide my knuckles. There is no way for her to know what I have just done to the old man. He deserved it! Normally I would look past her but today I smile back, my secret knowledge in the back of my mind.

I pull out my phone and look at my calendar. There is a meeting scheduled with our caramel sauce producer at three and, at some point this afternoon, I am supposed to stop by the booth that supplies our convection ovens to see the newest model they have available. The time was left open-ended. I check my watch and see that it is only 1:30. I have some time to go back to the Next Level Automation booth and check out the androids again.

After I put my badge back around my neck and pass through security, I plunge into the East Hall and walk towards the android booth. I wonder if anyone who works the other booths are androids. If they are as good as Denise said they were, the androids would be able to handle the human interactions as people stop by in search of new products. Some of the people who walk around could be androids too. Makes me wonder how long I have before an android makes my job obsolete. They would be able to provide a complete report of the information at the conference and whoever was able to access their data could watch video from their perspective. It would be easy to edit out the parts of the video where the android walks around and focus only on the relevant information. The most complete notes possible.

The aisles between booths are even more packed than they were this morning. I like to take my time as I walk and appreciate the hard work the companies have put into their booths. These booths might not sell anything Decant can use but anything that catches my eye is worth the time it takes to digest. Some of the attendees rush around as they try to pass people who walk too slowly. I try and stick to the edges of the aisle so none of these people brush against me as they rush by.

I stop to look at the booth of a company who makes t-shirts. All of them have something to do with beverages. I recognize the caffeine molecule on a red t-shirt which reminds me of the redness of my hand. I massage my knuckles with my left hand and turn to continue to the android booth. I walk right into a tray of drinks and pull my hips back to dodge the liquid as it falls with partial success.

A woman with a tray of samples was standing next to me.

Now she wears most of these samples on her sleeveless pink dress. "I am so sorry!" she says.

"Why were you standing so close?" I say. She works for a company called Pumpz who makes European sodas. At least that's what the placard on the tray says the samples were before they were scattered on the carpet.

"I was trying to give you a sample. I thought you heard me when I said 'excuse me.'"

"Well, I didn't." I look down at my blazer and the beads of liquid pooled on the fabric. Some have already been absorbed. "I am going to go get some napkins."

I walk to the Pumpz booth situated across the hall from the t-shirts. They have set their booth up like a 1950s diner, complete with black and white tiles and red bar stools with ribbed chrome rings set up beneath the counter. "Can I get some napkins?" I say to one of their employees behind the bar.

"Hold on. I will grab some for you," the man says. He wears a black bowtie and black suspenders. Tattoo sleeves show on both arms left exposed by a short sleeved white button down. He walks the length of the bar as another woman, dressed in a navy-blue suit and white shirt, comes to talk to me on my side of the bar. She rests her hand on the counter as her trained eyes go straight to my name tag. I close my eyes and release a purposeful exhale through my nose, aware of the interaction that is about to occur.

"Mr. Okada. My sincerest apologies! Come, come, let me wipe off your jacket. They can take care of the spill," she says gesturing with her chin towards her other employees.

"I'm fine, I'm fine. I just need some napkins."

"Come with me, there are some paper towels over here." She reaches out her right hand and puts it on my shoulder. I let my shoulder sag and pull it away from her grasp.

"Lead the way," I say, determined to wipe off my jacket and move on to the android booth.

I follow the well-dressed woman along the length of the bar to where a meeting area is set up—four chairs around a coffee table. A large plant between two of the chairs looks out of place. I can see the tumble of wires the plant is supposed to hide from view. She wets a paper towel and goes to wipe off my suit jacket before I can stop her.

"My name is Padma," she says with one hand inside my jacket. The back of her palm brushes against my stomach as her other hand wipes against my jacket as if she needs to work her way through to the other side of the fabric.

"I can take care of it, thank you," I say as I grab the wet paper towel from her with my right hand and take a step back. She takes a moment to look at my hand, at my red knuckles. Does she know?

"It just needs to be absorbed. Not scrubbed away. Give me a dry one," I say holding out the wet paper towel for her to take from me. It is stained red from the spilled soda. Dark red.

Padma hands me a dry paper towel. I blot the rest of the dark red liquid from my suit with my left hand as she watches me work.

Once I wipe the spill from my jacket, Padma says "Please, sit down, Mr. Okada," as she gestures with her hand to the chair on my right. No easy way out of this. I flex my jaw as I sit down and resign myself to hear what she has to say.

"So, you work for Decant?" she says as she takes a seat next to me. "How are you enjoying your time at the conference?"

"It is what it is," I say, annoyed at the small talk. "Some great booths this year." She smiles and looks around her booth.

"Why thank you," she says, as if what I said applies to her booth. "Do you have a lot of clients at the show this year?"

"No, not a lot. There are a few I have to meet with shortly though."

She gets the hint that I don't have much time. "I will get right to the point. Here at Pumpz we make all kinds of syrups but we pride ourselves on flavors not typically seen in stores. Decant could add flavors like cotton candy and bubble gum to their teas."

Those sound terrible. "Kids drinks? Kids don't have any money."

"You could market to parents looking for something for their kids."

"That could work," I say. That will never work. "Could you ship samples to my office in Bodalís?" She might as well throw them away. "I can have my team take a look at them." The boxes will never be opened. "Of course, make sure to send over pricing information along with the samples." This will get thrown away as well.

I reach into my back pocket and pull out a business card. I hand her the card with my right hand. Her eyes linger on my red knuckles for far too long. She knows. She knows! How could she know?

I stand up. "I need to leave," I say.

Padma stands up as well. "More client meetings?"

"Something like that."

She pulls a business card of her own from the inside of her suit jacket and hands it to me. It is white with dark red letters. I grab it from her with my right hand before I realize I should have used my left. I wait for her to grab my right wrist. To accuse me of being the one who punched the old man in the face. "Here he is!" she would say to security. "Here is the one who killed the old man with one punch to the face! Grab him before he punches and kills me!" I would never kill her. I never meant to kill him. I didn't kill him. He had to learn his lesson.

"Of course, we can send those samples over as soon as we get back to the warehouse after the show. There are a few smaller samples here. Did you want to take any with you now?" she asks as if she hadn't noticed the blood on my hand. "I can make sure they are wrapped up tightly so there would be no risk of a spill in your bag."

My chest rises up and down as my breath quickens. She has to have noticed. My guilty heart races. "No. I can't do anything without my research team. Send it to me and I will make sure it gets to them."

She pulls out a small journal from her jacket pocket and scribbles a note. It must say *murderer*. She knows. Does she know that I didn't mean to kill him?

I look around and notice the booth next door sells sports drinks. A large display shows which sample they offer: Blood Orange. I twist my head around and see the booth on the other side sells a herbal drink from the mountains of Peru. An older woman grabs a sample of the drink. "To die for," she says, smacking her lips. I have to get out of here.

The well-dressed woman watches me look around at the other booths. She has to be able to tell my mind is elsewhere. She extends her right hand. "Mr. Okada, it was a pleasure to meet you. Expect to hear from me sometime next week."

I remember to keep my right hand to myself and exchange an awkward shake with my left. "Yes. I will look for your email." There have been worse Hail Mary sales pitches at past conferences. This one was rather quick compared to the gentleman last year who tried to sell me single-use stir sticks that dissolve into whatever drink was stirred. The only thing he didn't do was restrain me to make sure I didn't leave. He seemed to know the extent of the business he would ever conduct with Decant would end as soon as I left his booth.

I rush out of the East Hall and go down the escalator two steps at a time. People still pour in and stand in line for the escalator in the opposite direction. There are still a few hours until the conference ends for the day. I am one of the few who have decided to leave and none of them move with my speed. I jog through the building until I find myself outside, for once grateful for fresh, albeit hot, air. The sun is bright and I have to squint my eyes until they have a chance to adjust. The heat is oppressive. I count backwards from ten and take a deep breath at each number which helps me calm down. Should I go check on the old man? I open my eyes further and look to my right. There are four police cars lined up at the end of the construction zone where I left him unconscious. I turn left and walk to find the hotel shuttle. I exhale backwards from ten again as I wait to return to the hotel.

## CHAPTER SIX

A MAN TAKES a seat on the bench opposite me just before the shuttle doors close. He has on a striped orange and white button-down shirt under a khaki colored suit. He looks to be middle eastern. It is just the two of us on the shuttle.

I look at my phone and watch the time change from 14:29 to 14:30. I open the reading app on my phone once the driverless shuttle follows its programmed schedule and begins to move.

"Going back to your hotel?" the man across from me says as we turn onto the street in front of the convention center.

This is the hotel shuttle. Where else would I be going?

"Sure am," I say.

"Where ya from?" he asks.

"Bodalís. You?"

"Washington D.C." A momentary pause. "Shariq," he says as he leans forward and extends his hand.

I reach out my right hand to shake his, careful to keep my red knuckles pointed down. "Corvus," I say.

At the first stop only one passenger gets on board—they take a seat all the way at the back—but at the second stop enough people are lined up to board that it looks like there will not be any seats available once they all get on. Before the doors open and the first passenger can climb the shuttle's three stairs, Shariq crosses the aisle and sits next to me.

Every seat fills up and two young men are left to stand in the aisle near the shuttle doors. They had to run the last fifty meters to the stop just to make it on time.

Shariq studies my face. "You look familiar," he says as we begin to move again. "Have we met?"

I close my eyes and wonder if I will be left alone at any point today. "I don't think so."

The shuttle merges with the traffic on the highway.

"You must have one of those faces," Shariq says. "So, what do you do?"

"I work for Decant." The small talk needs to be over with so I can get back to my book before the shuttle drops me off.

"The coffee shop? Very interesting. I take my son there after his soccer games for their fruit punch. He loves it."

I get the feeling he wants me to ask what he does and why he is at the conference but, the truth is, I don't care one bit. My eyes stay focused on my phone and the words that fill the screen.

I look out the window to my left as the shuttle slows. I hope to see the familiar front of my hotel and am disappointed to see half a dozen people already formed outside a third hotel. They stand beneath a dynamic billboard, an advertisement for Coca-Cola. Bubbles rise to the top on a molasses-colored background and cluster together to create the familiar logo. The two young men are forced to the back of the shuttle as more passengers embark. Together, they all have to hold on to railings for support.

A larger woman, one of the last to board, stands in front of me, a little too close, as the shuttle doors close and we begin to move. She has a belly but I can't tell if she is pregnant. I would offer my seat to a pregnant woman because it is the right thing to do but not to a woman just because of her gender. We both have legs, what difference does it make if I stand or she stands based on which body parts we have?

What I do have a problem with is the uncertainty. I can't ask if she is pregnant. She should broadcast her pregnancy, maybe with a shirt that says *Expecting*. On the other hand, she can't wear a shirt that says *Not pregnant, just heavy*. If she could just say, "Excuse me, I am pregnant. Could I sit down?" then I would know and wouldn't have to think about it.

I decide to pretend I don't notice anything at all until Shariq leans over and whispers, "You should offer your seat." He has to have the loudest whisper I have ever heard. I am positive the heavy woman has heard him too. Maybe along with half the shuttle.

"No," I tell him as I lean back and cross my right leg over my left. "You should offer yours." I read the same sentence for the second time.

"She's pregnant," Shariq says in what he somehow believes is a whisper. "And she is right in front of you, not me."

"I don't care." I try my hardest to read the words in front of me. If she is pregnant then I would offer my seat, not just because Shariq thinks I should.

By now other passengers have started to look at the two of us as we argue. The woman in front of me turns around. "Even if I am not pregnant, you should still offer your seat to a lady," she says to me.

I look up from my book. If she is pregnant I want to meet the man with a strong enough stomach to give her a child. Her eyebrows run together and several large moles on her face are hard to ignore. Somehow, I am able to look past the moles and find myself focused on the mouth of a horned toad with discolored, uneven teeth.

"*If* you were a lady," I say.

I have to look back down at my book to hide the satisfied smirk on my face. Shariq leans away from me in an effort to put some distance between us.

"Miss, would you like my seat?" Shariq asks in a small, sheepish voice.

"No! I want this jerk to apologize."

I look up at her face, red with anger. "Apologize for what?"

"For insulting me!"

"Grow up. You're not even pregnant, are you?" She closes her eyes and clenches her fists before she opens her eyes again and glowers at me.

"No. I am not." Her voice quivers as she tries to control her temper.

"Alright, we are equal then. If you are not pregnant, what difference does it make if you stand or I stand? Besides, it might be good for you." I stare at her wide mouth and am pleased to see the slight twitch that begins at the corner of her lips.

She turns away from me and makes her way deeper into the shuttle.

More than a little amused, I turn my head and look out the window at a billboard—an advertisement for cologne. *Your best you is within reach* is written above the square blue bottle surrounded by water, as if somehow a smell can make you a better person.

"Holy shit!" Shariq whispers to me. "It's you. I knew you looked familiar!"

I turn back to Shariq. His eyes look past me to the window at my back, where the billboard just passed.

"You saved the world!" he says.

"I don't know what you're talking about," I say.

What is this bullshit about how I saved the world?

"Your face was on the billboard we just passed!" Shariq

says. "Why are you here? Shouldn't you be out doing interviews and stuff?"

"I have no clue what you are talking about. I just want to go home. Okay?" I turn and look back out the window to the other cars on the road. Where do these people who are confused about my identity come from? First the old man and now Shariq. Must be something in the water in Phoenix. It's almost like they have blurred the real world with the story of Invader Assault.

A new thought descends from the sky, through the top of the car, and hits me like a ton of bricks. What if they are both androids? Denise did say game chats helped to develop their androids' ability to speak natural language. What if other data from Invader Assault has leaked into their program? That would explain why they believe the events in the game actually happened.

I realize Shariq said he saw my face on the billboard. Confused, I turn back around and say to him, "Wait, how did you see my face on the billboard? It was an ad for cologne."

"What are you talking about? It was your face looking up with confetti streaming down. I can't believe I am here with you! My son will never believe this."

"You saw my face on that billboard?"

"Yes," Shariq says.

This android's program is screwed up. He sees images that don't exist. "I must have seen a different billboard," I say, perplexed.

"I'm surprised you don't have corporations or billionaires clamoring to drive you in private cars. They owe you, in a way. If you hadn't been successful in saving the world their wealth wouldn't matter. The Invaders would have killed them regardless."

"And yet, here I am."

Silence.

"Before the crisis I used to work all the time," Shariq says out of nowhere. "Non-stop. I would go days without seeing my son. But when the Invaders showed up above Bodalís I stopped going to work. What was the point? I spent two wonderful weeks with him. The world was going to end soon anyways. Once you saved the world I promised myself I wouldn't work as much as I used to. I can always earn more money but these are the years I can't get back with my son." Shariq becomes quiet as his voice chokes up.

"You know it was just a game, right?" I say.

"It was only a game to you? It wasn't just a game to all the lives you saved." His eyes are moist with tears that have welled up and wait for a reason to fall.

The only lives I saved are the characters controlled by the minds on the death server. "I just beat the game, man. I don't know what you want from me."

"I don't know what I want either," Shariq says, a single tear sliding down his cheek. "I appreciate what you have done but I never expected you to be so... cold." He wipes away the tear with the back of his hand. "I'm sorry. It's just that this is my first trip away from my son since you saved the world."

I look outside, uncomfortable to be near a choked-up grown man. We continue the ride in silence. The shuttle stops at yet another hotel and the large, not-pregnant woman bulls her way off. She is the only one to leave at this stop and I am confused why she would get off before we got back around to the convention center. The confusion goes away once I see the 7-11 next to the hotel as we pass.

Through the window I notice billboards for food, gas, and lotteries as they go by. Does Shariq see the same advertisements? I can't believe the androids have been programmed with family connections. Does the ability to show emotion make them seem more human? Is this a typical response to somebody who contradicts their fundamental beliefs about reality? If so, I will have to be sure to agree with them in the future, so I don't have to deal with the tears.

I turn to look at Shariq. For some reason, even though I won't see him again, I don't want him to think of me as cold. "I am glad you and your son are getting so close." The statement seems awkward after so much silence between us.

He closes his eyes. Another tear falls. "I am so proud of him," he says.

I look back outside the window and see my hotel down the street. I watch it get closer until the shuttle stops out front.

"Nice meeting you, Shariq." I grab my bag and stand up.

He grasps my arm and I turn to look at him. My mind flashes back to the old man. Shariq looks me in the eye. "Nice meeting you too, Corvus. Thank you for saving us."

I pull my arm away, say nothing more, and disembark. The shuttle closes its doors behind me and begins to pull away to take Shariq far from me and the painful contradictions of his reality.

## CHAPTER SEVEN

I SIT DOWN on my bed in the hotel room and send off two quick emails from my phone to the clients I was supposed to meet with this afternoon. I explain that I had to leave the conference earlier than expected and hope to stop by their booths tomorrow. Aware of the sunlight that spills in, I curse the maid and stand up to close the shades that have been opened. I can see the roofs of the building across the street from me outside the window over what I believe to be the strip mall across the street, a laundromat and two restaurants, one Mexican and one Vietnamese. Looking down on the street below, the cars file by on a one-way street from right to left. I am struck by their regularity, how they all travel at the exact same speed with the exact same distance between each other. I am rooted to the spot, appreciative of the natural order the cars have fallen into, until a police car comes into view with its siren on. The other cars move to the right to let the car speed by. I shut the blinds and turn on the light in my room. I sit back down on my bed.

I grab my phone and look at my inbox. I could have my Sim organize and respond to any emails but prefer to do it myself.

There are two emails from the office I have been copied in

on. Seraph has a vacation coming up and an intern is organizing a happy hour next Friday. Nothing important. I can respond when I get back to the office. I highlight these and move them to my folder of things to do for work. Some other junk emails get deleted. The last email is a reminder from my team manager about tonight's Invader Assault scrimmage at 19:00.

After the events of today the scrimmage tonight had slipped my mind. We play the alternates tonight in a series of matches. Since we know how the players on our lower team play, the manager will often throw in a guest player to change the dynamic of their team. After the conversation with Brianne this afternoon I can't help but wonder: could it be an android?

Decant is supportive of my competition schedule. They always let me book rooms that have the high-speed internet required to play the game. There is also a loose guarantee that no events will be scheduled in the evenings so I can get online with my team. Thoughts of the old man unconscious on the ground creep into my mind and I realize the last thing I want to do is spend time online this evening.

Tonight will be our third scrimmage against the alternates in the past week. Practice went well two days ago when I was back in Bodalís. Our team moved like one fluid unit and we were able to win the best of ten by a score of 7-3. Each match lasted around ten minutes. I was unofficial MVP. I was able to secure the most checkpoints while we played King of the Hill and spent the second most time on the team as escort and defender of the bomb during Sabotage, when our goal was to blow up the target. When we were on defense, the traps I set up twice enabled my team to rally around a location and stop the enemy team's advancement with the bomb. The momentum from two nights ago would be good to build upon if I am able to collect myself by the time the scrimmage starts.

This last email gets moved to the INVADER ASSAULT

folder and I take a moment to enjoy my clean inbox. There is something special about zero.

Taking a shower, I let the hot water spill over me, a welcome relaxation after an eventful day. I can feel it wash away the soreness in my knuckles. As I wash the sweat from my body I think about the old man and how there was nobody outside to witness my assault on him. That was lucky, but then it was rude for him to ruin my afternoon. As I rinse the soap from my body I hope the clients I had to cancel with today have time to meet with me tomorrow.

Finished with my shower I turn off the water. I grab a white robe from the closet and wrap myself in it before I lie down on the bed, hands behind my head. If nobody saw me punch the old man, what is there to worry about? Sure, there were cops at the end of the construction zone when I left the conference but they could have been there for anything. Even if they are there for the old man there is nothing to worry about. He grabbed me first. Not once, but twice. It was self-defense. Worst case scenario the old man has a broken jaw. Worst.

My phone buzzes—an email from the caramel sauce guys. They tell me it is okay to stop by at any time tomorrow. I watch the time change from 16:02 to 16:03. There is just under three hours until the scrimmage starts. I open my book and begin to read about Amanda West's pivot into uploaded consciousness. I read about how she was met with resistance from her shareholders when she announced her newest project and the steps she took to educate herself about the latest research.

---

I WAKE up and look at my phone, nervous that I have missed practice. 18:34. Good, I haven't missed anything. I fell asleep as I read about the textbooks Amanda read to teach herself about how to map the brain. If I ever get the time I would like to check these books out as well, even though they are now outdated. I like to think of myself as someone who can get things done but I don't think I can find enough time to read textbooks about new technology while I work a full-time job.

Time to fire up Invader Assault. On top of the dresser is the TV with my Janus console attached on top of which sit my holo lenses. I turn on my console through the app on my phone, get out of bed, grab my lenses from the dresser, and turn on the TV. I put the strap around the back of my head and leave the lenses over my forehead. I see the world through my characters' eyes with the lenses. Whichever direction I look is the direction my character faces. I sit back against the headboard and pick up my phone. I tap on the screen as many times as possible. This lets the system know the state of my central nervous system. The more taps I can accumulate the better my CNS is able to fire. The lenses will adjust the sensitivity of the controls if my CNS is fatigued in order to accommodate the change in speed of my eyes. Nothing worse than when an injured enemy player is near the objective and the computer misreads an eye movement.

I get the gloves out of my suitcase and put them on. They are lightweight and only cover my fingers. There is a small pad on each fingertip that controls your character and I tap them against the same hand's thumb multiple times to warm up my fingers—my four main controls. Then I hit the combos on each hand: index and middle against my thumb, middle and ring against my thumb, ring and pinky against my thumb. The old man tries to ruin my day again through the stiffness in my right hand.

My movement controls have been mapped onto my left hand. Thumb to index moves right, thumb to middle moves left. The majority of the time I have my thumb in contact with my index and middle fingers to make my character move forward. A double tap of these fingers will get my character to jump. Thumb to middle and ring fingers moves the character backward.

On my right hand, my primary weapon is fired with my thumb and index finger. Secondary weapon is fired with my thumb and middle finger. My grenades are thrown with my thumb and ring finger. I have two abilities mapped to thumb with index and middle finger and thumb with middle and ring finger. It took me a while to get used to the gloves but once I did I was able to play faster than those who still use classic controllers.

I look at the monitor and see red all over the screen. The death screen. It means I am not connected to the game. I think back to the old man, how the specter of death has followed me back to my hotel. There is no way I killed him. Not with one punch! Did I kill him?

I turn off my console and turn it back on. Still red. This is for the best, my stiff right hand will slow me down tonight. I pull out my phone and send an email to the team manager telling him I can't connect to the server. Won't be online tonight. I take the lenses off my head and pull the gloves off my hands and set them on the bed next to me.

Within two minutes my phone rings. It is the manager, Seth.

"What the fuck man. We need you," he says, getting straight to the point.

"I can't connect. What do you expect me to do?"

"Did you try restarting it?"

"Of course."

"What did the hotel staff say?"

"They said they don't know why it won't connect," I lie. "I am on the hotel wi-fi now and it's working, that's how I sent the email."

"Go to global."

"Global wi-fi? It isn't fast enough to play. You know that."

"Phoenix is a major city. It might work."

"Alright let me try." I set the phone down and stay seated. I wait until enough time passes to be believable and pick the phone back up. "Still red."

"Fuck. Alright. You come home tomorrow? I don't want this happening again."

"Relax," I say. "Yes, I will be home tomorrow."

"Don't tell me to relax. If we don't win our funding gets pulled. Or did you forget?"

"I didn't forget, Seth."

"Okay, good. I expect you to be practicing tomorrow night when you get home. We have another scrimmage Tuesday night."

"I'll be there."

Seth hangs up the phone. "Asshole," I say as I turn off my phone screen and throw it on my bed. I never know if it is actually Seth or if he has his Sim talk to me. If I had to guess he is somewhere else in the cloud, busy with yet another hand of online poker.

I look around the room for something to do, as if this tiny space is enough to do anything. It is 19:00. I should eat but I don't have an appetite. There are at least four hours for me to kill before I could even think about bed. I put my gear back on and try another game on the cloud—Ronin. It works fine on the hotel wireless and, if Ronin works, Invader Assault should too. I try Invader Assault again but still encounter the red screen. "So weird," I say out loud. Unless the problem is with the game and not with the internet. If there was a problem with the game the other players would be affected as well and Seth would have told me. It hasn't happened before but it is the only explanation I can come up with.

I already beat Ronin. I had to save the seven towns from the seven corrupt samurai masters. There are so many side missions that I ignored while I beat the game. Tonight, I work on a side mission where I have to save the farmer's daughter from bandits and rescue her pet chicken. I play the game until 22:00 and decide to read my book until I fall asleep. I unplug the old LED alarm clock to make sure nothing wakes me up before the alarm on my phone.

I pull my phone out and see that I have an email from my teammate Marvle, telling me how the team beat the alternates but it wasn't pretty. He says that I will have to make sure I am there for the next scrimmage.

I open my book and begin to read. Not even a paragraph into the story about the acquisition of a company in 2025 that had figured out how to measure individual synapses in the brain, I start to think, yet again, about the old man. I double my focus and try to reread the same paragraph two more times before I give up. This is the third time the old man has ruined my day. It is only 22:30 as I turn out the lights and the last time I see when I check my phone is 23:41 before I manage to drift off to sleep.

# CHAPTER EIGHT

LIGHT PEEKS THROUGH THE CURTAINS. I can't stand when light peeks through the curtains. I made sure the curtains were drawn shut but thin rays of morning light shine through the edges of the window to my right. There should be signs for light that say "Keep out" or maybe "Beware of Dog" if I could ever find a dog that could scare photons away. I roll onto my left side and reach for the lamp that sits on my nightstand. I turn it on and roll to sit on the left edge of my bed.

My console, with the outline of holo lenses on top, is visible in the rays of light on the dresser. I grab my phone from the nightstand and can feel the stiffness in my right hand. It is 6:32. I disable the alarm for 6:45 I no longer need.

There are two missed calls, both from the same number. Whoever it was has left a voicemail. I read the transcript my phone provides: "This is Sarah from the Daily Donna show! Hope you are having a great day. I sent a few messages and wanted to follow up with you to talk about getting an interview set up on our show. Please call me back when you get the chance!"

Who the hell is she? No way I take the time to call her back. I delete the voicemail.

Seven new emails wait for me in my inbox.

Four of the emails are from Sarah. I have no idea who she is or how she got my address. The first message serves as another introduction. Sarah explains again, in writing, that she works for the Daily Donna show and would love to book me for an interview.

Why would anyone want to interview me?

The second message asks about what I think about saving the world. Then she asks me which time works best for me to appear on the show. The third talks about blowing up the ship—asks if I was nervous when it happened.

The emails leave me confused. Shariq talked about how I saved the world, the old man talked about how I blew up the ship, and now she comes out of the woodwork to join the two of them? Is she another android?

My phone rings. I recognize the number. Sarah again. She is persistent! I push ignore.

The fourth and final message asks about the people who believed the ship was the second coming of Christ. Sarah wants to know my thoughts about the people who are calling for me to be killed because they believed I was Satan.

Does Sarah believe the events from Invader Assault occurred in real life, or is it only her Sim that has been corrupted? The story mode of the game involved a religious group known as The Society of the Stars that tried to stop me as I made the bomb that blew up the ship. They believed the ship was the second coming of Christ. Are these the people she thinks call for me to be killed?

"Have they affected your day-to-day life?" she asks in her email. They have. The old man talked about how I ruined the return of Christ. I look at my right hand as it holds my phone in front of my face. Does she know that I am the one who hit him? Is this an attempt at blackmail, to get me to do the interview? I look at the time this message was sent. 6:24.

I highlight the four messages and press delete.

There are three messages about the scrimmage last night. In the first one, my team manager has replied to the email I sent last night. He tells me that the game was closer than it should have been because I chose to not play. How many times do I have to explain myself? It wasn't a choice, I couldn't connect. I delete the message.

Two other team members have messaged me to ask if I will be at the scrimmage on Tuesday night. I reply to each that I will be home by then and will be there.

I get up and flip the light switch between the closet and the door to flood the room with light.

There is an arm's length of space on each side of the bed. Just enough room for the closet doors to open and just enough room in front of the window to access the blinds. At the foot of the bed is a dresser whose drawers open towards the bed without an inch of room to spare.

This is the smallest room I have ever stayed in. Decant can afford a much better place than this but Seraph, my boss, decided to be cheap. This is the third year in a row I have traveled to Phoenix for work. Each year, the company decides it is best for me to go to the conference since I am single with no pets. Seraph knows I hate the breakup of my routine but sends me anyways. He makes it his mission to "teach me how to get out of my comfort zone."

The tiny bathroom is past the front door. I go inside and take a shower. There is just enough room in the shower to stand and my elbow bumps into the side wall twice as I wash my face. I let the water run over my head in the shower which helps wake me but I still don't feel well rested at all.

Finished with my shower, I get my blue suit from the closet. "Looking good," I say to myself in the bathroom mirror as I button up my shirt.

My appetite has returned but I just can't muster enthusiasm for the breakfast buffet downstairs.

I go down the elevator to the buffet in the front lobby and make the same meal as yesterday—oatmeal and orange juice. As I go to sit down someone calls my name.

"Corvus! Over here, buddy!" Dell.

He sits at a table at the front of the room by himself. Two plates, a bowl, a glass of orange juice, and a glass of chocolate milk are all lined up in front of him. He slides down in his seat and kicks the chair opposite him out from under the table. "Take a seat," he says to me from across the room.

I sigh and begin to navigate between the tables that separate us. With each step the dread I feel towards another meal with Dell increases. I sit down. "Morning, Dell," I say.

"Morning C," he says. "Sleep well?"

C? When did this happen?

"I slept alright," I say with a shrug.

"Me too. I am always so tired after a day at the conference," Dell tells me.

I don't care how he slept, that's why I didn't ask. I pull out my phone and begin to read about Amanda West as I eat my oatmeal.

A few minutes go by in silence. I can feel Dell's eyes on me. He wants to say something, I know it. I keep my eyes focused on my phone and continue to read about Amanda's decision to upload her consciousness.

"So..." Dell says. The word hangs in the air.

I close my eyes and exhale through my nose, slow enough to give me patience. Here it comes.

"What exactly do you do at Decant?" he somehow manages to ask through a mouth full of food.

There it is. He just couldn't sit in silence and let me read my book.

I put my phone down on the table, facedown, and turn my attention to Dell. "I find new products."

Dell sits up a little straighter and adjusts his suit jacket. "Are you in research and development?"

"In a way. I went to school for business."

"How long have you worked for them?" asks Dell

"Almost four years."

"I don't know how anyone can afford to go there regularly. Everything is so expensive!" Dell says.

"We aren't for everybody. Decant prides itself on quality; some people can't appreciate that."

"What kind of products have you found?"

"In my first year at this conference I was able to find the point-of-service software that rolled out to all our locations earlier this year. It took some time to implement but it will make managing the inventory of each store much more efficient. Last year, I found the micro water heater currently in use by our city locations. It heats up the water on demand through a series of heat exchangers and microwaves, dispensing at the same rate as the cold water."

Dell tries his best to be an active listener by nodding along while I talk but I can tell his thoughts are elsewhere. If I had to guess, he wants an opportunity to bring up his crazy straws again. I decide to throw him a bone. "This year I also need to find a product or two we can roll out next summer. The company is running out of time to get the next summer launch ready."

"Just so you know, we have all the promotional materials

ready to help Decant launch crazy straws nationwide, if you are interested," Dell says. I knew it.

I pretend to be interested. "Oh really? Do you have a business card?"

Dell fumbles in the right breast pocket of his suit coat before he pulls out a handful of paper scraps. He looks through them and when he realizes one of his cards is not in the pile he stuffs the papers back into his jacket before he leans over into me to gain access to his right back pocket. The bag that had rested against his chair topples over onto the ground.

"Sorry about that," he says as he pulls a stack of business cards out of his wallet. I have no idea how he manages to carry so many in his pocket at once. He has to have back issues from the crooked way his thick wallet makes him sit. "Here you go," he says as he hands me a business card. To my surprise, the card is very high quality, stark white and thick stock. His name is underlined with a knot and his contact information is listed underneath. The company name, Loop to Loop, is on the back in block letters.

I reach into my left breast pocket, put his card at the back of the stack, pull one of my cards from the front of the stack, and hand it to him.

"Corvus Okada," he says as he reads my card. "Hope we can do business together!" He pulls out his phone and scans my card.

"Holy shit!" Dell exclaims. "You have a perfect SimScore. You said it was high, but perfect? Wow." He looks at me with reverent eyes. "How did you get it so high?"

"It just kind of happened. I played a ton of Ronin, and I play Invader Assault all the time now. The game is an opportunity for my Sim to measure my reaction time and analyze the different decisions I make in the game. Split second decisions provide a lot of insight that gets reflected by my SimScore.

Plus, when I play with my team it records my speaking patterns."

"So, to increase my SimScore, I need to find a game I like to play."

"That's not all I do, I also read a lot on my phone. My phone scans my eye movement and is able to tell the pieces of information I find most interesting. The more I read, the more my Sim is able to develop a database of my working knowledge. Combine that with the data from the game and it has led to that SimScore."

"And you don't let it do any of your work for you?"

"I don't let it do anything for me. Every time I communicate with somebody myself it provides more data for my Sim. If I stopped the flood of data I probably wouldn't have a perfect SimScore anymore."

"You feed in so much data! It makes my head hurt to think about," Dell says.

I take another bite of oatmeal and estimate there can't be more than half a dozen bites left.

"Hey, did you hear about the old man that was attacked yesterday?" he says as he forces his wallet into his back pocket. "There were cops at the convention center when I got back from lunch."

I pull my right hand from the table, put it on my lap and reach across my bowl to grab my spoon with the left. "No, I never heard about it. What happened?"

"Some old guy had to go to the hospital. The police are looking for a guy in a suit. Good luck with that, right? Everyone wears suits at the conference."

"Yeah, that's like finding a needle in a haystack," I say. I take a bite of my oatmeal and wash it down with orange juice. "Did they say anything else about whoever did it?"

"Not that I know of. I hope they find the guy. Who would

be fucked up enough to hit an old man? They got old bones, ya know? Easily broken." Dell forks a large bite of ham and watery eggs into his mouth.

"Maybe he pissed the wrong guy off," I suggest.

"Maybe." Dell forces another bite of food into his mouth. "Did you have any luck at the conference yesterday?" he says through a mouthful of food.

"Some. How about you?"

"Not as much as I'd have liked. But there's always today! Have you thought about selling crazy straws in Decant?"

"Haven't had the chance to. I have your card though." I take a sip of orange juice. Dell makes me nauseous. It's not just the way he eats, it's also what he said. If the old man had to go to the hospital, I could be charged with assault. Numbers are on my side, there must have been thousands of men in blue suits at the conference yesterday. The cops will have a tough time narrowing down which man in a blue suit it was.

"Did you see the booth with the robots?" Dell says to break the silence. "I forget the company name but their robots were making drinks for everyone. Amazing!"

"Next Level Automation. Yes, I saw their booth. Very impressive." I take a spoonful of oatmeal, turn the spoon over my bowl, and watch my food fall.

"Do you think Decant will hire robots in the future?"

"I'm not sure. I wanted to swing by there today to talk to one of their salespeople again."

"I couldn't even tell they were robots! One of the younger women was looking good. She made my drink. If I didn't know she was a robot I would have flirted with her!"

"It's hard to tell the difference, I think that's the point," I say.

"Would you ever sleep with a robot?"

I put my spoon back in the bowl. "I don't know, Dell, I haven't really thought about it."

"I would. I mean, as long as the parts are all the same down there. I bet that's the future too!"

"Do you think you have run into androids in any other places?" I ask. "They had to be tested somewhere right?"

"Hmm, I never thought about that," he says before he shovels more food into his mouth. "I don't think I would be able to tell."

"Neither do I. Now that I know they exist, I don't think I will be able to look at people the same way again. Even if they are acting weird, it could just be something in their programming."

"That's crazy to think about!" Dell says. "I think it would be obvious. Like if there is no way a human could be so perfect." I am sure his thoughts are on the android at the booth, the one who made his drink.

"Or so repulsive," I say. Prime example is the man in front of me.

"I bet if you uploaded your Sim to a robot, nobody would be able to tell since your SimScore is so high."

"Maybe. But that's too similar to uploading a replicated mind into a robot. It's illegal."

"Just because it's illegal doesn't mean it doesn't happen. Besides, it is just a Sim upload, not a replication. The company already uploads Sims to their androids. I'm saying that with how powerful your Sim is you could have an android that would be almost identical to you."

"Next Level Automation can do it because they use expired Sims. It's illegal to upload a personal Sim to a physical form."

Dell takes a drink of his chocolate milk. He sets the glass on the table and sports a brand new—brown—milk mustache.

"You don't think a robot could hurt a human, do you?"

"What do you mean?" I say.

"Just thinking that whoever punched the old man has to be a human."

"You never know. There could be androids all around us, either uploaded Sims or replicated minds from the death server. Like you said, just because it is illegal doesn't mean it doesn't happen. Who knows what their response to a trigger would be."

What if the old man talks about when we were in Decant together? My stomach drops all the way to my feet. All the police would have to do is check the time we were both inside and they would be able to find me. I could lose my job. Or worse, I could be thrown in jail. I feel like throwing up. I can't go back to the conference today. Should I go back to Bodalís?

"I have to go," I say to Dell as I stand up.

"You aren't even done with your food!" he says.

"I lost my appetite. Good luck today."

"Um, okay. Guess I'll see you around." I leave Dell alone to finish his massive breakfast. I don't mention that he just spilled oatmeal on his shirt.

I throw my food away and put my bowl and my cup in with the dirty dishes. I need my usual coffee, not the brown water they serve here. I pull out my phone and use it to look for the nearest Decant. There is one, three blocks away. I decide not to wait for a car to take me there but leave the hotel and begin to march through the miserable sun.

## CHAPTER NINE

THE SMELL of roasted coffee mixed with cooked sugar hits my nostrils as I walk through Decant's front door. Sweat has dripped into my eyes twice on the way here. My pants stick to my calves and beads of sweat causes my shirt to stay pressed against my lower back.

This store is smaller than most. Bar-style seats line the walls and a single long table is situated in the middle of the floor. Three out of the eight available seats at the table are occupied by people with their computers in front of them. There are only three people in line to order their drinks from the young woman behind the register. I take my phone and check the time: 8:01. Monday through Friday, at this time of day, Decant stores are always busy with people on their way to work. Either this store just doesn't get busy or right now these guys are in the eye of the storm. Whatever the case, I am glad there isn't a long line. I can order my coffee and sit down to figure out whether or not it is best to go back to Bodalís.

How will I be able to write my report about the conference for Seraph if I decide to go back to Bodalís? He likes when new launches add value to our core products: iced tea and iced coffee. The tricky part is the presentation. Last year, in the middle of my presentation, I mentioned the micro water heaters then glossed over them on purpose and continued to talk about the dissolving stir sticks, a product I knew he would have no interest in. Once he asked me to elaborate on the water heaters I made it seem like I hadn't considered them for our city locations. In reality, I had planned to all of a sudden realize the opportunity of using the micro water heaters in the city at the end of my presentation. Seraph believed he was the one who found the diamond in the rough and was able to take credit for the idea. I got the reputation as his sidekick.

Really, all I need to do is to find one quality product and make sure I get other, smaller ideas that I know will be thrown away. Even though they have nothing to do with iced tea or iced coffee, Next Level Automation's androids would work well as the centerpiece of my report. Maybe Dell's crazy straws can be used as noise to help me direct Seraph's focus where I want it to go.

Two teenage boys in front of me in line talk about their plans for the day while they wait to order. From what I overhear of their conversation, they've decided to skip school together. Each of them still has their backpacks on and plan to spend the day in an internet cafe to level up their Ronin characters. I wish I could skip work to play Ronin just because I felt like it. Instead, I am worried I will get arrested and lose my job. I could tell them about the time I went to the Ronin World Championships three years ago, the year before Invader Assault came out. Or I couldn't. I look at the pastries on display and realize I still feel sick to my stomach and don't have an appetite.

A drawing on one of their backpacks catches my eye. My former clan's logo, gunmetal daggers in the golden spiral on a black background, sits above my gamertag in light blue letters:

_Raven_. It glows like it is drawn with some sort of florescent marker.

Why my gamertag? I'm not that good. Competitive, yes, but middle of the road at best. By no means worthy of display on a backpack. Confused, I tap the shoulder of the boy who wears the drawing. "Excuse me," I say. "Why do you have that drawing on your backpack?"

He turns around with a scowl before he sees my face. He could be anywhere from fourteen to eighteen years old and sports a buzz cut. It has been so long since I have had any inter-action with teenagers I have no clue how to tell their age. His eyes widen and his jaw drops. He clenches his hand into a fist and hits his friend on the side.

"Ow! What'd you do that for?" his friend says.

The first boy stays silent but uses his chin to nod in my direction. The second boy is mixed. Tanned but hard to tell which culture gave him the color. He is long and lanky, like his limbs grew and he still hasn't gotten used to them. They both stand still in front of me, mouths wide open. Neither of them says a word.

"Next in line," the girl at the register says. When they don't move she repeats herself, louder. "Next in line!"

"How about we talk after you two order," I say. "I want to know about that drawing."

"Sure thing. Yeah, okay. Order. Talk. Got it," says the long-limbed boy. He turns around to order. Once he realizes his friend hasn't moved he turns back and grabs his friend's arm to pull him to the register. The two of them order and move to the side to wait for their drinks.

I step up once the boys are finished and order my usual iced coffee. My retina is scanned to pay for the drink. The machine beeps once the transaction has been completed and I go to the side to wait for the barista to make my drink. "So guys, why is my old clan logo on your backpack?" I say.

"Tons of people have it, man. I'm getting it on my backpack tonight. Gamers gotta stick together!" says the lanky one.

"And rep one of their own," says the one with a buzzcut. These are the first words he has spoken and his voice is deeper than I expected it to be.

"I hear you. It's cool to meet some fellow gamers. But why that clan? I don't even play with them anymore. Why not draw my new clan?"

"When did you switch? I was just watching you play Ronin with them the other day," says the boy with a buzzcut.

"I haven't played with them since I started playing Invader Assault," I say.

"Never heard of it," the lanky boy says. His friend shakes his head.

"Really?" How have they not heard of Invader Assault? It has a larger audience than Ronin ever did.

"Nope. I wanted your gamertag on there because you saved the world! That's like the coolest thing ever," says the boy with a buzzcut.

"The way you defeated the Invaders was so awesome! What is it like wearing the Exo Suit?" the lanky boy asks.

"So, you guys have heard of the game," I say. "The Exo Suit is cool I guess. Did you guys watch when I beat the story?"

"Two large, extra fizz fruit punches on the plane!" says the barista. The two boys punch straws through the lids of their drinks before they pick them up from the counter.

The boy with the buzzcut takes the straw wrapper from the lanky boy and throws both pieces in the trash. He turns back to me. "Yeah, we watched. Everyone watched! Everyone knows how you saved the world from the Invaders! I drew this on my backpack yesterday. I am going to do draw it on his backpack tonight," he says using his head to point to his lanky friend.

"It's really awesome that one of us took it upon himself to blow up the Invader's ship," the lanky boy says. "You made it cool to be a gamer!"

"Thanks," I say. It is easy to get confused talking to these two. Every gamer that has beat the game had to blow up the ship. There have to be millions of people who beat the game before I did. All I did was beat the game with a perfect score.

"No man, thank you. Can you believe those religious nuts? Acting like it was the second coming of Christ," the lanky boy says.

The old man talked about the second coming of Christ.

"Medium iced coffee!" says the barista. I grab my coffee, open the lid and take a long sip, the familiar taste helping me find my center.

"Ricky's never going to believe we got to meet him," the boy with the buzzcut says to his friend. There is a momentary pause before he turns back to me. "Ricky is your number one fan."

"He is? Tell him I say hi." My mind is stuck on the old man and the blood that trickled from his mouth as he lay unconscious on the concrete.

"Alright, man, it was good meeting you. We'll watch your stream if you are online later!" says the lanky one as the two of them head towards the door.

"Bye! And thanks again for saving the world!" says the friend with a buzzcut.

"Bye," I say. They both leave and I watch them through the window as they pass by the front of the store.

I put the lid back on my coffee and stab a straw through the lid. I am flattered that these kids somehow know who I am and are proud to display my gamertag although it is weird that it is my old clan logo. I can't believe neither of them have heard of

Invader Assault. It isn't even a new game, it's been out for two years now.

Why did they mention the Invaders if they haven't heard of the game? And if they never played the game how did they know about the return of Christ? Has data from the game mixed into their reality? If so, why are their androids designed to look so young?

I try to remember exactly what the old man said to me about the second coming of Jesus. The picture of him as he lies on the ground, unconscious, pops crystal clear into my head. I focus on the blood. How bad was he hurt? It was only one punch. Is he still in the hospital? I get anxious at the thought of him in the hospital bed, interrogated by the police.

I take another sip of coffee to calm down. I can't go back to the convention center. I don't want to be in the same city as the old man any longer. Not just because I could get caught but because I don't want to meet anyone else who thinks I saved the world. My flight home is supposed to be tonight but the airline should be able to find a seat for me if I show up at the airport. Either way I have to try.

## CHAPTER TEN

THE SUN HAS GOTTEN STRONGER and its heat buries through to my core as I walk from Decant to the convention center. It feels like God has a magnifying glass between the sun and me, the same way a curious kid would experiment with ants.

The decision to leave the conference early has given me anxiety. I feel guilty, like I have ignored my responsibilities. Sometimes, to navigate through any negative feelings I experience, I pretend I am a stranger who has somehow slipped into my own skin but this trick doesn't work today. The old man has affected me too much. I look down at my swollen knuckles. Each time I use my right hand I think somebody will see the evidence of the attack and expose my secret to the world.

A horn honks and I look up. A car swerves into the other lane so it doesn't hit me. Distracted, I somehow ended up in the middle of the left lane. I must have stepped off the sidewalk. One more step and I would have been hit. Thankful for the quick reactions of the driverless car, I step back onto the sidewalk and wait for the signal change. The light turns, the walk signal lights up, and I step into the street again.

Invader Assault should've worked last night. Based on how

sore my hand was when I woke up though, I can tell it was too fucked up to play last night anyways. The old man almost took my game from me as well. With any luck my hand will feel better this afternoon. I need to log on and blow off some steam when I get back to Bodalís. I look down at my hand and flex. The heat has already helped to limber it up.

My clothes begin to stick to my skin again. My navy-blue suit traps the heat and I feel like the ant when the kids are through with their magnification game. This feeling could have more in common with the frog who is boiled alive in water. The temperature creeps up slow enough that he never realizes the change in temperature until it is too late. The difference is that I realize.

I almost walk right by my hotel before I escape my thoughts and realize. If the heat hadn't been so unbearable, who knows how far I would have continued to walk as I sorted the questions in my head. I walk through the parking lot and go inside.

My phone buzzes as I walk through the hotel lobby so I pull out my phone and realize there are two messages that need to be answered. The caramel sauce team have messaged me fifteen minutes ago and ask what time I will show up at their booth today. I don't have an excuse ready to send to them so I file the message away. I can repair the damage I created once I get back to the office. The message that just caused my phone to vibrate is from Brianne asking if I would be interested in lunch again today. She says that she has something she wants to talk to me about. I delete the message.

I ride the elevator up to my floor and make my way to my room. I should have asked Brianne what she wants to talk to me about. I think back to the conversation we had while we were together at lunch. All that comes to mind is the question she asked about Wonky. How do I know that he isn't an android?

It's a very real possibility. Part of me wants to meet him in person but even if I do, would I be able to tell?

Back in my room, I grab my suitcase from the closet and throw it, open, onto my bed.

Wonky could have been planted by Seth to test how our team responds to different situations. None of us have any reason to suspect that he is an android. Why would anybody go through all the trouble to plant one?

I grab my underwear and socks out of the top drawer of the dresser and throw them into my suitcase.

An android designed to optimize teamwork would be helpful to get us to work together. We *have* been more cohesive as a team since Wonky has arrived. Teamwork has carried us through the last four matches. Wonky's placement on the team could be an experiment to optimize a group of humans, a team-mate without emotions or ego who could work with the group to accomplish the goal. Military, business, and sports could all benefit from the technology if it could be developed well enough. What better place to test the technology than a group of people who only ever interact with each other online?

I take my suit off and put on a pair of athletic shorts and a white t-shirt. I grab my sneakers from the closet and put them on. My suit gets stuffed into my suitcase on top of my shoes. No need to fold it when I need to get it dry cleaned anyway.

What if all of my teammates were androids? They could be programmed to move as a more cohesive unit with me as the focal point. The more we play together, the more they would learn about and adapt to how I play the game. Practice would be program optimization. A swarm centered around my character. Especially if all the androids run a copy of my Sim. Would it be possible to get more than one Sim on the cloud? Not with only one Sim allowed per person. I would need a separate cloud account.

Better yet, what if they used a full replication of my mind? Too bad it is illegal to have full replication of my mind on the death server while I am still alive. How many people have illegally replicated their minds? Have any of them then uploaded their mind into an android?

My toiletries are all thrown into my travel bag which I throw into my suitcase. I force the lid closed and zip my suitcase shut.

The old man had to be an android. Shariq probably is too. The teenagers could be androids but it's hard to tell, all teenagers are weird in their own way. There could be androids hidden in plain sight all around me. At the front desk in the hotel lobby. Dell. They could be planted in an effort to see my reactions. Androids had to be introduced into the world somewhere, why not here? Next Level Automation, or any other company with a similar product, could have placed them in positions with the most basic social interaction and let them engage in small talk.

I survey the room and double check that I have everything before grabbing my suitcase. In the elevator down to the lobby I pull my phone out of my pocket and request a car to take me to the airport. I don't want Decant to know I left the conference early so I use my own account. To save some money, I check the box marking that I am willing to share a ride. Then I decide that I would rather pay more to be alone and uncheck the box.

I have been in Phoenix long enough. There isn't anything I miss at home other than my couch where I can play Invader assault on my monitor, the one it took me a year to save for because I only allowed myself to use money I had earned from gaming.

If anybody around me is an android I will have to be deliberate with the data I provide so they can react in a way that benefits me. Everything matters. I will have to control what I say and how I say it in all forms of communication, digital and face to face.

The young woman at the front desk, a short brunette with her septum pierced, smiles at me as we make eye contact. "Have a good day!" she says.

I nod. She could be an android too. Was that the proper way to react? Should I have smiled back? Engaged in small talk?

I sit down in the lobby to wait. After five minutes my phone buzzes with the notification that the car has arrived. A purple sedan rolls by outside the front door, the rear of the car visible from where I sit. I walk through the automatic double doors and the car door pops open when I am three feet away. I set my luggage down inside before I get in. Two grey bench seats and three strips of blue lights on the ceiling run the length of the car. A touch screen is situated in front of the driverless car, below a tinted windshield, next to the steering wheel. The door closes on its own as soon as I sit down.

# CHAPTER ELEVEN

THE AUTOMATIC DOORS of the airport part as I approach and I walk into the cavernous lobby. The white floors are polished and reflect the light from above. Airline employees stand behind bright white counters. There is no queue to check in with the airline but the line to get through security is long, snaking and turning through nylon straps, filled with people who wait to enter the terminal. I walk across the bright floors and approach the desk.

"How can I help you?" the male employee asks. His name tag says Phil. Phil's eyes are puffy from lack of sleep and there is no warmth in his voice.

"I need a flight to Bodalís. I have a flight already booked for later this evening but I need to get back as soon as possible." A pang of guilt hits my chest when I think about how I didn't attend the second day of the conference.

"What is your ticket number?"

I look up the number on my phone and recite it out loud as he types into his computer. He punches the keyboard for a few minutes before he looks back up at me. "I can get you on a flight in two hours, at noon. Does that sound good?"

"Perfect, let me get that one. How much is it going to cost?" I ask.

"I can switch your flight for free," he says.

"Perfect."

Phil types on his computer again. After another few moments a ticket slides out of the printer next to him. He tears it off and hands it to me. "Here you go," he says. "Any bags to check?"

"No, only my carry-on."

"Then you are good to go. Enjoy your flight."

"Thanks," I say as I grab my ticket. I walk over to security and stand in line, at the tail end of the snake. I grab my phone out of my pocket and begin to read my book.

I am able to read a good amount while I wait in line for the next half hour, at least thirty pages. These pages cover the struggles Amanda faced before and after she acquired a company that could measure and control an individual synapse. Once she acquired the company, Amanda discovered how to acquire the rough outline of an individual's brain. She found that the conductivity of synapses is a function of a person's DNA. From there, she was able to calculate how much noise could be expected from the surrounding synapses. Once the noise was accounted for, experiments showed that there were far fewer synapses involved in any given task and a lot of the brain activity was just noise.

I reach the front of the line and put my phone back in my pocket. Passing through security I collect my carry-on bag from the conveyor belt on the other side and walk straight to my gate. I want to get there so I can grab a seat and continue to read. I look at my phone. There is still over an hour until my flight takes off.

While I walk through the airport I am fascinated by how people choose to dress for their flights. Some of them look like they are dressed to impress. They look professional in their suits and dresses, like they might have a business meeting as soon as they get off the plane. Other passengers might as well wear their pajamas while they walk around. In their sweatpants and sweatshirts they look like they should carry a pillow and a blanket under their arms so they can make a bed and catch a quick snooze. I wonder about one of these people dressed in pajamas, a college aged girl, as I walk to my gate. Where is she from? What does she do? I don't care to talk to her but I am still curious.

I get to my gate and find a seat, alone, next to the wall. I pull out my phone once more and read about how once Amanda was able to figure out which synapses were fired during a given task's performance she decided to work backwards to provide an outline for how her own brain performed. She would fire those particular synapses, this time with the noise included, and measure the results, both physical and experiential.

"Excuse me, sorry," a woman voice says as she sits down beside me. "Is anybody sitting here?"

"I guess you are now," I say with my eyes still on my phone. I check the time: 11:23. What was the point her question if she already had sat down?

"Guess so," she says. She pulls out her phone and begins to type. She holds her phone above mine so I can't see my screen. On her phone she has typed *I know who you are.*

Why do people love to interrupt me? "How do you know who I am?" I ask, annoyed. I move my phone to the side so I can continue to read.

"You don't care if they figure it out?" she whispers as she gestures with her hand to the few people scattered around us. "Everyone knows who you are after you saved the world. If not, you look just like him." She says this so only I can hear.

Saved the world? Ridiculous. Is this another android? I put

my phone face down on my right thigh and look at her. "Doesn't look like they know who I am," I say as I look around. Two middle aged men in dark suits and a grey-haired couple sit near us.

"You are Corvus Okada right?"

"Yes," I say.

"I knew it! They must be pretending," she says as she looks around. "Are they so disconnected from their surroundings that they don't even recognize Corvus Okada when he is right in front of them?" she asks.

Will she begin to cry like Shariq if I don't agree with her that I saved the world from the Invaders? Or will she get irritated like the old man? I don't want to deal with such strange reactions from an android again.

"Guess they are," I say. I pick up my phone and go back to the words of my book.

"My name is Paige," she says. "You think it's because you don't have the Exo Suit on?"

"That must be it," I say. The Exo Suit only exists in the game and nobody around me looks like they have played video games within the last decade. While Paige is preoccupied I take a look at her face. Nice eyes, smoky blue with flecks of hazel. Pretty face. She looks like she could be of middle eastern descent but I could be wrong.

She turns back to look at me and catches me as I study her face. "What was it like getting ready to blow up the Invader's ship? Were you nervous?" she asks.

The information comes from the game. "It was cool. Luckily, I did it without dying. That was tricky."

Paige laughs and displays a full set of straight, white teeth. "I'm glad you didn't die! I figured as much because, well, here you are." For some reason she reminds me of a librarian. Like she is the type of woman who always has a pen in her purse. "You weren't nervous at all?" she says.

"I guess I was a little nervous," I reply. "I had to be extra careful." Truth is, I was nervous as I got closer to the end of the game. It took a lot of work to get to the end without a single death.

Once I accept the fact that I won't be able to read with her next to me, I shut off my phone's screen and put it back in my pocket.

"So you *were* nervous. I knew it! Don't worry, I won't tell anyone. It can be our little secret," Paige says to me with a wink. Her tone becomes serious. "You talk about it like it wasn't a big deal. So much rested on your shoulders. All of us depended on you to save us. The whole planet. And you did. We owe you our lives!"

Of course I act like it wasn't a big deal, it's just game.

"I don't know, I guess I'm still not used to the attention," I say. I would rather read.

"Well, you had better get used to it. It's only been two days but your face is everywhere. I'm surprised you are able to leave the house without being swarmed by reporters."

The airline attendant comes on over the loudspeaker. "Noon flight to Bodalís is now boarding."

I grab my stuff and stand up, Paige following close behind. The airline lets us pick our own seats and I have a feeling she will sit beside me for the flight. Part of me wants to turn around, to tell her to leave me alone, to find her own seat, away from me, so I can read. But another part wants to continue our conversation, to figure out how she came to believe I saved the world. To find out what I can about androids and determine how deep the corruption of her program goes.

We get on the plane and my curiosity gets the best of me. I keep my mouth shut as she puts her luggage next to mine in the overhead bin. I sit down next to the window and she takes the middle seat next to me.

An old white veteran sits on the other side of Paige in the aisle seat of our row. His faded leather jacket is covered with patches from the Army. He wears his long hair in a ponytail. He puts his backpack on the ground instead of the overhead compartment and takes a full minute to force it underneath his seat. Some of his backpack still pokes out even after he decides he is finished and settles down.

I lean my head back against the chair as soon as the flight attendants begin their pre-flight routine and soon the sound of the plane's engine takes over the cabin. My head gets pushed deeper into the headrest of my chair and I close my eyes as the plane gathers speed. The takeoff is the worst part of the flight. All I can focus on is the disorientation. The cabin is quiet while the plane ascends to cruising altitude. The seatbelt sign turns off.

"Are you from Bodalís?" I hear the veteran ask Paige. He has a high-pitched voice. I keep my eyes closed.

"I am," she says. "What about you?"

"Nope, I am only going for a procedure. My dentist is in Bodalís and I don't trust anyone else to make my dentures," he says. "My teeth rotted when I was homeless there and he took care of me."

Way too much information. He must be lonely.

"That was nice of him," Paige says. "Do you live in Phoenix now?"

"No, I was just in Phoenix for a layover. I live in Rhode Island with my mom. She didn't have anyone to take care of her and I didn't have anywhere to live. Part of the deal is that I had to quit drinking. I can still smoke though!" he says with a wheezy laugh which turns into a cough.

"Maybe you should give up smoking too," I say with my eyes still closed.

"You're right about that one! What do you do?" the veteran says. I open my eyes and look at him. His eyes are on Paige as he waits for the answer to his question. His lips sag into his mouth. If I knocked out the teeth of the old man in Phoenix would his mouth look the same?

"I am a doctoral student, working to get my Ph.D. in psychology," Paige says. "I am having a hard time coming up with a topic for my dissertation."

"You must be really smart! I never went past high school. I enlisted in the Army just after I graduated. I was an airplane mechanic."

"How long were you in the service?" Paige asks.

"I got medically discharged after seven years because I shattered my foot. I still walk slowly. Sometimes, if it really bothers me, I have to use my cane."

"Sorry to hear that," Paige says.

They continue to talk about his time in the Army. He was stationed in the Philippines and Alaska at different points in his career. Paige also talks about herself, how she went to school in Rochester before she got into the doctoral program at the University of Bodalís. I wait for sleep so I don't have to hear their conversation, but it doesn't come.

After five minutes of silence Paige nudges my left arm with her elbow. "Take a look at this," she whispers.

I open my eyes and look down at her phone. She is on a news app. There is a headline about a mysterious plague outbreak in Central America and another about how a rogue mind on the death server tried to convince American Sims, and by extension Americans, that dietary cholesterol was bad for humans even though decades have passed since the government came out and said the real danger was sugar.

"What am I looking at?" I ask her. She holds a finger up to her mouth and motions with her eyes to the old man on her other side. I lean forward to get a better view and see that he is asleep.

"The top headline. Your broadcast of when you blew up the ship, now has the most views of all time."

"I don't see anything about a broadcast."

"Right there," she says and points to the top story. The one about the plague. "The broadcast you made on the way to plant the bomb has the most views of all time."

"That is a story about a Central American plague. Plagues happen all the time."

"What are you talking about? It says it right there." She uses her finger to point again, as if this time her magic finger will show me what she sees.

There is nothing about a broadcast on her screen. Details from the game must have altered her version of reality. Not only what she believes but also what she sees.

Time to pretend.

"Most views? I never expected that," I say. "What did you think of it?"

"It was inspiring. My favorite part is when you looked at the camera and said 'cut off the head and the body dies.' I didn't see the video until after the ship was already destroyed. I wish I had watched it live," she says. Her voice drifts off as she thinks about the missed opportunity.

I remember that line in the game. It was just before the last mission. I had to fly the plane through the ships defenses and land it in the hanger before I jumped out and planted the bomb on the power core.

"I didn't realize so many people saw the live video," I say.

"It seems like everybody did but me," Paige says. "Now the

broadcast has the most views all time. It's crazy that nobody recognizes you," she says looking around the plane.

"I know but I prefer it that way," I tell her. It's not crazy Paige, you are an android with corrupted data. They are all humans.

"I can't believe they considered arresting you before the official Presidential pardon. Some thanks for saving the world."

"I didn't know that was public knowledge," I say. I never thought about what would happen to my character once the game ended. It makes sense why he would have been arrested in the game world. To beat a few of the missions I had to work with terrorists to get the parts I needed to make the bomb. Then I had to steal an American fighter jet to fly up to the ship.

"Well, the President made the speech on live TV. That's pretty public," she says.

The game ended as the ship blew up. How could she know something that would've happened after the credits? Maybe the sequel?

Paige turns off her phone and puts it back in her pocket. "Bodalís is going to be busy with repairs for a long time," she says.

"What makes you say that?"

"The bomb ripped the tops off all the buildings downtown. Not to mention all the pieces of the ship that scattered on the ground. A lot of the people who lived downtown are still homeless."

"I didn't know about the damage to the buildings," I say. The end of the game didn't show this either. These facts have to come from the sequel that is rumored to be in development.

The old veteran stays asleep for the rest of our three-hour flight. As the plane descends, Paige reaches across me, opens the window shade, and looks out the window at the Bodalís skyline. "See downtown? The buildings all look so short. Hard to believe the ship hovered above the city for almost two weeks..." Her voice trails off.

I look out the window as she leans back. I don't say a word when I see Bodalís the way I remember her, tall buildings intact.

Our plane lands and we each retrieve our bags from the overhead storage area. The rows ahead of us empty and we follow each other off the plane. The smell of the river hits me as I step into the portable walkway that leads into the airport. It feels good to be back in my city.

Paige and I walk towards the airport exit behind other passengers from our flight. We pass the old veteran as he limps along. He looks at Paige and nods his farewell. "Nice talking to you!" she says as we pass.

We approach the luggage claim. People are already lined up as they wait for their suitcases to slide along the conveyor belt back into their lives. Paige turns to me. "Are you hungry?" she asks.

"I could eat," I say.

"Let's get lunch," she says. "I just need to grab my bag."

"Okay," I say. I have enjoyed my time with her and, by some miracle, don't want it to end. I am not too pleased that I have to wait for her luggage though.

She walks to the luggage claim to take her spot and I check the time on my phone too often as we wait. Time drags by. After twenty minutes, luggage begins to pour in from the conveyor belt and it is another three minutes until her luggage arrives. She grabs it from the belt and together we wheel it out into the humid air of Bodalís.

The line to get a car has over a dozen people in it already. We take our spot at the end.

"I know a great spot downtown with the best rice bowls in the city. Sound good?" she asks me.

"Sounds good," I say. I haven't had a rice bowl I didn't like. I make a mental note to compliment her decision later regardless of how good it is.

Two cars take away three of the people in the line. Paige looks around. "There are so many people here. I can't believe none of them have even taken a second look at you!" she says while she is turned away from me.

Of course they haven't taken a second look at me. "Maybe they don't recognize me out of context. Hiding in plain sight."

"Maybe. But still. Your face is all over the place! You would think at least someone would recognize you."

"You recognized me, didn't you?" I ask.

"Yes, I did. I meant someone other than me."

"Maybe they are being respectful. They see us walking together and don't want to interrupt." Paige smiles, an innocent smile that I am surprised an android can create.

We move forward six in line after two more cars pick up three people each.

"I'm sure they appreciate their lives being saved," I say. "I don't want to be stared at anyway."

Paige looks at me long enough for me to notice the color of her eyes again. Does she do this to fuck with me after what I just said?

The last of the people get in their cars and we step up, first in line. Our car rolls up, an old yellow cab. We both get into the backseat of the driverless car. Paige puts the restaurant into the touch screen that sits atop the center console and a low hum accompanies our movement as we begin our trip downtown.

# CHAPTER TWELVE

THIS PART of downtown is new to me. I know about the main strip on Orchid Avenue and am surprised the two areas are in the same part of the city. This area is much more residential. The cab drops us off in front of a strip of row-houses. They would have been new fifty years ago. Each of them has been covered in black solar panels, some of which are covered in yellow pollen, leftover from the summer. However, the house we are in front of keeps their panels clean. The windows of this house are solar panels as well, each of them a shade of grey above clear with thin lines of green circuitry running through them. For a moment I think that we have been dropped off at Paige's house until, through one of the solar windows, I see a server carrying a tray of food.

The restaurant is small but cozy. There is not enough space for more than ten people. The only other people inside, besides the server, are an elderly couple that sit by the window next to the front door. Paige and I put our bags against the wall behind a table two away from the couple and sit down.

"The owner does everything here," Paige says. "He takes the orders, makes the food, and serves it. He should be out soon." As soon as these words leave her lips the owner comes out from the kitchen—an Asian man, no more than thirty years old. Under his white apron he wears jeans and a t-shirt. His long hair is tied back into a ponytail.

"I recognize you," he says to Paige with a smile. He sets a piece of paper that serves as the menu in front of each of us. "How have you been?"

"I've been good," Paige says. "We just flew in from Phoenix. Ben, meet Corvus."

He nods at me. "Good to meet you, Corvus. First time here?"

"Yes, it is," I say.

"Glad to have you. Funny you just came from Phoenix, our bowl of the week is a southwest dish. Chicken with black beans, peppers, and onions. Topped with a fried egg. I'll give you two some time to look at the menu and decide what you want. Anything to drink?"

We each order a water. Paige also orders a kombucha. Ben walks back to the kitchen. We are ready to order when he comes back out with our drinks. Paige orders the southwest bowl without chicken and I order spicy chicken.

"Are you vegetarian?" I say to Paige when Ben walks away.

"No, I am just not in the mood for chicken," she tells me.

I look at the elderly couple while we wait for our food. They each have stark white hair. Their outfits match. The man has on light colored khakis and a short-sleeved canary yellow button-down. She wears a canary yellow dress, the exact shade of yellow as her companion's shirt. They are slow when they bring food to their mouths, slow when they chew, slow when they pick up their glasses to drink. Their lives are untethered from clocks. They have to be retired. Neither of them talks but it doesn't seem to bother them. They are comfortable in silence, a testament to how long they have been together.

Less than ten minutes later Ben drops off our food before he checks on the elderly couple. The smell makes me realize how hungry I am and I dig in. It is the best rice bowl I have ever had. Uncomplicated and delicious. The heat of the spice doesn't overwhelm. It builds in each bite with a subtle smokiness that gets caught in my nostrils. "This is amazing," I say.

"Told you they are the best," Paige says with a smile.

"How did you find this place?"

"Ben's mom is one of the professors in my program. She told us all to check out her son's new restaurant. Needless to say, it didn't disappoint!"

"Agreed," I say before I take another bite. "I am glad you brought me here." I am also glad she is with me, we get along well. Too bad she is an android.

We finish our food and ask for the check. Ben informs us that the elderly couple has already taken care of our bill.

Paige leans in their direction on her left. "Thank you," she says to them. "We really appreciate it."

"Our pleasure," the elderly woman says. "You two remind us of when we were young."

I see Paige blush. I am surprised androids have this level of nuanced emotional output. "That's very kind of you to say," she says.

"My world changed once I had her by my side," says the old man as he reaches out his hand and places it on top of hers where it lays already on the table. "We have been together fifty-two years last July. The time has flown by."

"Well, thanks for the meal," I say to the elderly couple. I push back against the table and get up from my chair. "Let's get out of here," I say to Paige.

"Okay," she says, startled by the abrupt shift in conversation. She stands up from her chair and we both grab our bags. "Bye Ben!" she yells to the kitchen. Ben sticks his head out from the back and says goodbye. "Thanks again," she says to the elderly couple as we leave.

On the sidewalk outside the row-house, Paige turns to me and says "What a cute couple! That was nice of them to cover our check."

"I can't believe we reminded them of when they were young. That must have been so long ago! Did you see how white their hair was?"

"I did. They have been together a very long time." I have no idea why she sounds sad.

Together we roll our bags to the underground train station three blocks away. The leaves on the trees that line the street have already changed color but none have begun to fall.

The two of us need to take the train in opposite directions and split up inside the underground station. We exchange numbers and make tentative plans to see each other again before we part ways. I have made this type of hollow plan before and know that we won't see each other again any time soon. It often comes down to the fact that I enjoy my time alone more than I enjoy my time with other people.

I descend the stairs to my platform. While I wait for my train I can see Paige across from me, absorbed in her phone. She doesn't notice me. It makes me uncomfortable how much I have enjoyed my day with her. How can it be so easy to get along with an android?

The train pulls up and I get on with my bag. I take a seat and think about work tomorrow. I will need to do my research on androids in order to suggest to my bosses at Decant that we do business with Next Level Automation. I decide to make time to see Paige again. For work purposes, of course.

# CHAPTER THIRTEEN

I DISEMBARK at the station for Monocots Avenue where the escalator carries me up to street level. The Bodalís Music Academy is across the street, a square building with a six-by-six grid of square windows at the front. A bright metallic sculpture of a G-clef sits on their manicured lawn, the only indication that this is a music school. I turn to my right and begin the walk to my apartment a block away.

A high-rise apartment building takes up the block between the station and my home. A bodega, connected to the high-rise, is on the corner across the street from my apartment. Do I need anything? I think about what food I have—there should be some leftover Chinese, noodles I got the night before I left for Phoenix. It should still be good. If I get hungry tonight that's what I will eat. Worst case scenario I have to walk back down to the bodega to grab a Reuben for dinner.

My building is short compared to the high rise, only four stories tall. The walk symbol to cross the street isn't lit but, since no cars come from either direction, I walk across anyway. At the front door I stand in front of the terminal to have my retina scanned. The screen below the scanner says "Welcome Corvus" as the door clicks open.

The elevator takes me up to the fourth floor and I walk to my apartment, #407. I put my hand on the lever-style door handle with my left thumb over the spot where keyholes used to be. It takes a fraction of a second for the system to recognize my thumbprint. I push the handle down as soon as I hear the beep and go inside.

"Finally," I say to my home. It feels like I have held my breath for my entire trip to Phoenix and am just now able to exhale. I turn the lights on and set my keys, phone, and wallet on the small gunmetal table next to the door, underneath the mirror I use to double check my appearance each day before I leave the apartment.

The place still smells like lemon from when I cleaned. The kitchen is on my right, separated from the living room by a black marble counter that runs all the way to the far wall. I wheel my bag past the kitchen, turn right, and walk along the length of the counter towards my bedroom.

The first thing I do is put everything back where it belongs. My dirty clothes go in the hamper to be washed next Sunday when I do laundry. I put my shoes back in the space between my other brown dress shoes. My suit goes in a white cloth bag and is placed on the floor by the bedroom door to be taken to the dry cleaner when I get the chance. I set my laptop, charger, and toiletry bag on my bed and take my console, gloves, and lenses into the living room and set them on the couch. Back in my bedroom I put my suitcase in the closet and my toiletries back in the bathroom. The labels all of my deodorant and cologne face forward and the toiletry bag goes under the bathroom sink. There is a smudge on my mirror and I take a moment to grab a paper towel, wet it with cleaner, and wipe it off.

I go back to my bedroom and take off the shoes I wore for

the flight. They get placed into the empty space among the rest of my sneakers. When I realize the laces are still in a knot, I retrieve them, untie the laces so they are ready to be put on whenever I decide to wear them next, and put them back where they belong. With my bag unpacked I walk out to the living room with my laptop and charger in hand.

My phone vibrates as soon as I sit down on the couch in the living room. There are dozens of messages I haven't seen. Seventeen new emails, three from Sarah and seven from unknown senders upset that I blew up the ship. I delete the four emails with advertisements and file the remaining three of them in the folder that I use to save emails to look at later.

The message that caused my phone to vibrate was from Marvle. YOU BETTER BE ONLINE TONIGHT. He is upset that I wasn't able to practice with the team. We message each other all the time but when I see the last message I received from him I realize we haven't talked since before I left for Phoenix.

THE SERVER WAS DOWN IN PHOENIX. BE ON IN AN HOUR, I text back.

I close my messages and see that I have missed a call from my dad. I should call him back, we haven't talked in a few weeks now.

I also need to log on and warm up for tonight's practice at eight. I have two hours. My accuracy must be terrible as I haven't played for a few days. I don't even think I should play against any of the Dead Server players, I should stick to the standard, robotic AI until I get back into the swing of things. If I have time I can switch over and play against some players from the DS. I get up from the couch and reconnect my console to my monitor. It takes all of five minutes before I turn it on and sit down to take the tap test with my gloves and lenses next to me.

My phone rings, a call from my dad. I pick the phone up and tap to answer.

"Hey, Dad."

"Too busy to call your old man?" he says. It is a joke the two of us have. He knows I am always caught up with my own life and don't think of anybody else.

"Yes," I say with a laugh. "You know how I get."

"You're right, I do know. How was Phoenix?"

"It was good. Hot. I can't believe you remembered I was there."

"Of course I remembered. I know how you hate the weather down there. Anything interesting happen?"

I tell him about the old man. About how I had to leave the conference early. About how I met Paige in the airport and spent the day with her. It is a relief to share what happened to me with someone who has my back, no matter what.

"Do you think they will be able to find out you were the one who hit the old man?" he asks.

I tell him about Decant, about how easy it would be to look at the cameras.

"Have you talked to a lawyer yet?" he says.

"No, I just got back."

"What have you been doing all afternoon?"

"I told you, I was with Paige." I leave out the part where she is an android.

"Enjoy your freedom while it lasts. First thing tomorrow you need to find a lawyer," Dad says.

"I will, Dad, I will," I say. I hesitate for a moment. "The old man said the weirdest thing. He accused me of ruining the second coming of Christ. There are other people who seem to believe I blew up a ship and saved the world."

"Really? Sounds like someone is playing a joke on you."

"Doesn't it? But the people I have talked to really seemed to believe it. One guy even cried he was so thankful. It was so strange. To be honest with you, I think they are all androids." The words sound strange the moment they leave my lips.

"Androids? What the hell are you talking about?" Dad says. "They probably have you confused with someone else."

"They have me confused with a character in the game I play. That's why I think they are androids. It's like the video game leaked into their daily lives." My theory about why people have recognized me as the one who blew up the ship is lost on him.

"I don't know about all that. You know what I think? I think you should report the old man to the police. Tell them the truth, that he grabbed you first and you struck him out of self-defense. Keep all this talk about video games leaking into humans or androids or whatever to yourself. Last thing you need is to have the police think you are crazy."

I look at my monitor. The death screen is back up. I lean my head back against the back of the couch.

"Not again," I say.

"What's wrong?"

"My game isn't working."

"And you should spend less time on that game. It sounds like it is rotting your brain. Maybe if you weren't spending so much time playing your games you wouldn't be having these thoughts. Go spend time with your new girlfriend."

"Paige believes I saved the world. She's an android too."

"Stop saying that!" Dad yells into the phone. "Don't tell anyone else about your *idea*. You need to think about your future. About how you are going to get off the hook from the assault of an old man. Please, I'm begging you. As your father. Can you do me a favor and keep these thoughts to yourself?"

"I can. Right now, I need to go though. I need to figure out why I can't connect to my game. I have practice in little over an hour and this needs to be sorted out. I *do* make money from these games, remember?"

"I remember," my dad says. "I just want you to be careful. Good luck at your practice tonight. I will give you a call tomorrow to make sure you got a lawyer."

"I will. Talk to you later."

I hang up the phone, annoyed. Annoyed with my dad for the lecture. Annoyed with my console that won't connect *again*. I disconnect the power to the console and reconnect. I turn it on and still the death screen shows up. I try other games which work. Invader Assault is the only one that doesn't.

I type an email on my phone and send it to Seth telling him my console still can't connect to the server. I ask for forgiveness and promise I will get a new console tomorrow, that maybe mine is broken and won't let me connect.

I order a new console from my phone and pay the extra cost to have it delivered tomorrow.

One positive, at least there will be some time to read tonight. I get my leftover Chinese from the fridge and sit down on my couch with my food on the coffee table in front of me. As soon as I open the book messages begin to pop up from my team. I am in the middle of a group thread of people upset that I have missed practice again. When the messages continue for the next ten minutes I abandon any hope of reading tonight. I turn on my monitor and watch a series of documentaries about US presidents until I fall asleep on the couch. At 2:00 I get up, turn everything off, and go to bed.

## CHAPTER FOURTEEN

I WAKE UP REFRESHED from a night in my own bed. My room is pitch black, if it wasn't for the alarm I would have no idea what time it is. I missed the darkness. I begin my morning routine: shower, get dressed, eat breakfast (three eggs with cheese and bacon) at the kitchen counter, then clean the dishes. It's good to be home.

I pack my bag for work and begin to dread my first day back. I missed the conference. What will I include in the report? Are there any products I could present among the dozens of emails I receive from various salespersons? I already know Seraph won't go for Dell's crazy straws but I will include them in the report. My report depends on the reception of the androids by Seraph. If he doesn't go for them things could go south in a hurry.

I walk the block to the underground station and take the train to my office building. The train is packed today. Standing room only. A young hispanic man's backpack hits me every time the train car shifts. I hate it when the train is packed like this. People right on top of each other, no respect for personal space. All I can focus on is how suffocated I am with so many people around me.

I ride the train to the Decant station and get off. My office building sits right on top of the station that bears its name. The escalator takes me up to the building lobby. The lobby is busy with people headed in every direction. Some, who work for Decant, enter the building and head to the elevators. There are some who were on the train with me that leave the building to go to their own offices close by. I get on the elevator alone, relieved to have the space to myself, until five people all manage to squeeze into the car before the doors close. They push me to the back corner of the elevator. I close my eyes, checking which floor we are on every time the elevator beeps, and wait for the doors to open on the 12$^{th}$ floor.

I get off the elevator and walk past our secretary, Patrick. He is fresh out of college and always too eager to engage in small talk. I am grateful to see that he is on the phone. He smiles and waves as I pass. There are two rows of four cubicles in the main room past Patrick. I am the fourth person to come in this morning, Linda, Ron, and Andy are already here. I nod to each of them as I walk to my desk, the same nod we exchange every morning. It feels good to be back in my routine.

My desk is just how I left it. I open my drawer to double check that nobody has moved any of my stuff. My three pens are all still oriented in the same direction. I leave my belongings in a particular order so that I can see if anyone has touched anything.

The door to Seraph's office is closed, his blinds drawn shut. If he is in he must not want to be disturbed. I set my bag down and sit at my desk with my back to his office. I pull out my laptop and get to work on the report I will be expected to give tomorrow about my trip to the conference. Not five minutes goes by before I hear Seraph's door open.

"Welcome back, Okada. Find some good stuff for us?" Seraph says behind me.

I spin around in my chair and come face to face with my boss. His fat hand rests on the corner of my cubicle wall for support. His fingers are thick as sausages and he sports a gaudy gold ring on his pinky finger. I always forget how fat he is until I get back and see him in person. Until I met him I never knew clothes could be made so large. His suspenders strain from exertion as they struggle to keep his pants up while his pants struggle to make sure his gut doesn't spill out. His chest rises and falls from the exertion of leaving the chair in his office, or from the exertion of standing, or from existing with so much mass on his frame. It is all the same.

"Yes, sir," I say. "I was able to come up with a potential retail item for summer launch next year. Plus a big development that we could use in our stores. I am writing the report now—it will all be in there."

His face is blank and lacks any recognition of what I just told him. When he doesn't respond I turn back around in my chair to get back to work. I'm not sure what else he could want from me.

"Good. I want to have the meeting today. Right after lunch. You think you can be ready by one?"

Is he crazy? I close my eyes and take a moment before I turn to look at him again. Beads of sweat gather on his face. They match the sweat already present in the armpits of his shirt.

"We always do the briefing the day after I get back," I say. "There isn't enough time to prepare a report worthy of sharing. Can we do it tomorrow?"

"No, we can't. I am leaving for vacation early tomorrow morning. I want to have this wrapped up before I go. Get to work and make it worthy. Meeting's at one. Might have to skip lunch today." He looks at his watch. "That gives you five hours to put something together." He walks into my cubicle and places his think palm on my shoulder. "I believe in you," he says, his best attempt at encouragement. I shudder and drop my shoulder, already damp from where he placed his clammy palm.

Seraph walks back into his office and closes the door. Linda looks at me from her cubicle. She has heard the whole exchange. She raises her eyebrows and gives me a nod. She understands, she has been in my situation before. Everyone in the office has. Two Thursdays ago, she had to stay late because Seraph wanted to take Friday off. He can be inconsiderate in that way.

As soon as he leaves I lean my head back and stare at the ceiling. Less than an hour and he has already found a way to get under my skin. I lean forward on my desk and begin to compile the report. I work for the next three hours, from 8:30 to 11:30. The morning flies by while I am absorbed in my work. The ability to lose track of time is the closest humans will get to time travel. I include Dell's crazy straws and the new convection oven I was supposed to see at the conference. It was easy to research their new product online and find out what has changed. There isn't enough improvement for Decant to be interested but I want to make sure Seraph sees the option. I also include some products from companies I know were at the conference that I never planned to see. There is a company that makes reusable cup sleeves; their salesman has sent me weekly emails for months now. There are also cups with a new outside chemical lining that slows the dissipation of heat from hot drinks. Each cup is triple our current cup cost. A quality concept but not worth the price.

The androids are the future. My job is to make sure Seraph understands it too. The trick is to make him think he came to this conclusion on his own. I already know the line I will use. "There was an interesting option, it might be too far in the future to consider now though. Made by a company called Next Level Automation. They have made androids that can make drinks and serve customers. From what I am told, a few chains have already approached them about placing them in their stores. They are indistinguishable from human workers." Sure, some of it is a lie but how will he find out? I imagine Seraph will look through my report and see a small section about Next Level. He will say "Is this all the information you got?" Then, after I tell him there is more information at my desk, he will demand to see it. Once I come back with the information I will make my suggestion that we get one to place in our test location.

My phone buzzes and interrupts me from my work. A message from Paige. WHAT ARE WE DOING FOR LUNCH? I wasn't aware that we are supposed to have lunch today. Rather presumptuous of her.

I look down at my laptop. If I stay focused I can finish in about half an hour. I would have liked the whole day to work so I could have added in more product options for Seraph to consider, but without the afternoon I don't see how much more I could include.

I type out my reply. I'M AT WORK NOW, I'LL PROBABLY GET FOOD AROUND HERE. YOU CAN MEET ME AT DECANT OFFICE IN HALF HOUR IF YOU WANT. I push send.

She replies right away: OK, I'LL BE THERE.

Over the next half hour I put the final touches on the report. After a message from Paige telling me that she is downstairs in the lobby, I shut my laptop and stand up from my chair. I've done the best I could. After lunch I will find out whether I sink or swim.

It makes me happy to see the incredulous look on Seraph's face as I poke my head into his office and mention that I will be back after lunch. As I pass Patrick, Seraph yells out behind me "you better be ready at one!" I get on the elevator and push the button for the lobby. I smile to myself as the elevator doors close and seal me inside, alone.

# CHAPTER FIFTEEN

PAIGE SITS on a bench near the front door of the lobby with her bag next to her. Her legs are crossed and she is on her phone while she waits. She looks up when I approach, smiles and stands up. I stand still, with my arms at my side, as she lunges forward to give me a hug. I feel the need to reciprocate in some way so I pat her on the back twice with my right hand before she lets go.

"Hi! How's work?" she says.

"Busy," I say. I tell her about the report, about how Seraph expects the presentation after lunch.

"That's annoying," she says. "But at least it will be done with!"

"Yeah, I guess so." I hadn't thought of it that way.

She grabs her bag and slings it over her shoulder. "Where should we eat? Can we get pizza?" she says, eyes wide. She looks at me and nods yes over and over, as if she will convince my head to match the movement of hers and therefore agree to get pizza with her.

"I get sushi on Tuesdays. Is that cool with you?"

"I like sushi too," she says, less passionate than before. "Maybe we can get pizza next time."

We walk out of the building. It is hotter outside than when I walked to the station this morning. I check my phone to see the weather for the day. It is 82 degrees and the high for the day, which will be at 16:00, is 86.

I lead the way to my sushi spot. Each of the four blocks between my office and the restaurant has a skyscraper on them. After my weekend in Phoenix this heat doesn't bother me. Paige turns to me while we walk and says, "What if you don't feel like sushi on a Tuesday?"

"Why wouldn't I feel like sushi?"

"I don't know. Because you want pizza!" she says.

I laugh. "It's never happened. If it does I'll let you know." We come up to an intersection just as the light tells us we can walk. "There is a pizza place close by the sushi restaurant you can go to if you want. I can get my sushi to go and meet you over there," I say.

"No, that's okay, I like sushi too. It's just so peculiar that you always get the same thing on a Tuesday. Is every day of the week like that?"

"Monday and Wednesday is a salad, Tuesday and Thursday is sushi. Friday is the day where I get whatever I feel like but it is always either sushi or salad. I like to keep things simple," I say.

"I could never do that," she comments.

"This lifestyle isn't for everyone," I say with a laugh.

When we get to the sushi restaurant I grab the door and hold it open for Paige. The moment before I turn to follow her in, I hear someone close by me say, "It's you, isn't it?" Two men are in front of me, fingers interlaced as they stare. One of them, a heavy-set man with a beard, lets go of his partner's hand and reaches out for a handshake.

I stare at his outstretched hand until he takes it back to his side. "Are you talking to me?" I say. Of course I'm me, who else would I be?

"Sure am! You are the one who saved the world!" the bearded man says. His eyes are wide as he stares at me.

His partner stands off to the side with an awkward smile. He is tall and thin. His hair is spiked with gel, not a strand out of place. He seems to want to continue to their destination. They both wear green track pants and white v-neck t-shirts. Their faces are still red from what I assume is their time in the gym next door.

Another android who has mixed up the events of the video game with reality. I can't believe so many are able to walk around among people. How many more are there? Will all of their programs get corrupted? This could get out of hand.

I look at Paige as she comes out from the restaurant smiling like a proud mother. I don't know what to say. "Nice to meet you," is all I can manage. I want to yell "it was only a game!" at the top of my lungs.

"I guess we should thank you," his partner says, as detached as I feel.

"We never took our health seriously before, or at least I didn't," the bearded man says. "Now we plan on going to the gym every day!"

"He still isn't used to the salads," the thin man says.

"It's a whole lifestyle shift," Paige says. "Give it time."

The bearded man flashes a smile at Paige. "It is," he says. "Now we both want to stay healthy not just for ourselves, but for each other." They enjoy a moment locked in the eyes of the other until the thin man looks down.

"I am glad the two of you decided to get healthy," I say from a world away. "I'm going to go eat lunch now." I am aware of how awkward it is to end a conversation this way but I don't know what else to say.

This is the first relationship between two androids I have seen. They seem so human. More human than I feel. Was this type of connection programmed or was it developed by the androids on their own?

I squeeze past Paige into the restaurant and she follows me in.

"Thank you again!" the bearded man says to my back as the door closes behind me.

# CHAPTER SIXTEEN

THE RESTAURANT IS BUSY, typical for this time of day. The place started to become busy when the Bodalís Monthly ran a review three months ago claiming that it had some of the best sushi in the city. The space is small, intimate. A plaque on the wall from the Fire Marshall, above the register across from the front door, says that no more than forty people can occupy this space at any one time. Next to the plaque is a large poster of an orange dragon, the same height as the small Asian hostess that stands underneath. A visual menu hangs over the door between the waiting area and the dining room to the right of the register.

Paige and I sit down on a bench just inside the front door to wait for two seats on the wooden bar in the dining room to open up. Years of neglect have turned the light brown trim in the waiting area into a dingy chestnut. The whole place feels like it belongs in a strip mall and could use a deep clean. The register beeps almost every minute as customers walk in to pick up their carry-out orders.

There is one seat available at the end of the sushi bar. Two seats away from the open chair a diner sets his cash down and leaves. Paige walks up to the two people who eat lunch between the two open seats and gets them to move one seat to their left. She waves me over and we take the two seats on the end of the bar.

There are at least seven chefs at work behind the bar, all of them busy pulling fresh fish from refrigerated display cases and building roll after roll. We pull paper menus off a stand that holds dozens of copies.

"What are you in the mood for?" Paige says as she looks over the menu.

"He is in the mood for his spicy yellowtail roll," a voice says behind me. I turn and come face-to-face with Katsuro, the owner of the restaurant. An Asian man in his mid-forties and almost bald, he has deep-set eyes that make him look sleep deprived every time I see him.

"I get the same thing every time," I explain to Paige.

"Why am I not surprised?" she says shaking her head.

Katsuro places his hands on the back of our two chairs. "Every. Single. Time." His voice delivers each word like a punch. "My name is Katsuro," he says to Paige.

"The owner," I say.

Paige introduces herself and the two of them shake hands.

"I can't believe you get the same roll every time! Where's the fun in that?" Paige asks me.

"I don't like to make decisions," I say. "I try and put as many tasks on autopilot as possible. Once I find something I like I stick with it."

"I'm sure it makes sense to you," Katsuro says with a laugh.

"I don't know how you do it," says Paige.

"What are you in the mood for?" I ask Paige once the two of us have ordered our drinks and Katsuro has returned to the kitchen.

"I think I am going to get the Eel Avocado roll."

"I had it once, before I found the spicy yellowtail. It's good," I say.

"Why don't you try something different today?" Paige says.

"Why would I do that? What if I don't like it as much as my usual roll?"

"What if you like it more?" she counters.

"Think of it like this. If I like it *less* than my usual roll then I will be upset that I have to eat whatever roll I get instead of the roll I already know I like. If I like it *more* than my usual roll, then I will be upset that I have wasted so much time getting a roll that is second best to another roll. Either way, I am upset. Might as well stick to my usual."

"Trust me, Corvus, it won't be that bad. Just try something new!"

Paige wears me down over the next five minutes. By the time Katsuro comes back with our waters and asks us if we have decided what we would like, I have given in and let her order for me. Paige orders the eel avocado roll for herself and orders the rainbow roll for me. Katsuro stands still for a moment and waits to hear an order for my spicy yellowtail roll.

When it doesn't come he looks at Paige, impressed, and says, "You got him to try a new roll?! Not an easy task."

"She's persistent," I say.

The chef brings our food to us ten minutes later. "Rainbow roll," he says. I raise a finger to indicate that it is mine. He sets it down then takes a long look at my face. We exchange a nod every time I am in here but have never spoken a word to each other. For some reason he looks surprised to see me today. He fumbles as he sets down Paige's plate and almost knocks over her water.

"My mistake," he says. He looks at me again. "What are you doing here?" His English has a Spanish accent. I am surprised to hear his voice.

"It's Tuesday," I say. "I'm always here on Tuesday."

"I just thought after what happened Saturday night you wouldn't come back. You aren't worried about being out in public?" he asks.

Saturday night? That was my first night in Phoenix. The night I beat the video game. Does he think I blew up the ship in real life too? Another android? We have seen each other so many times and I had no idea. A seamless blend with the other chefs, unless they are all androids too.

"Nobody ever recognizes him," Paige whispers. "I think it is because he isn't wearing the Exo Suit. Plus, nobody expects him to be out in public."

"You aren't worried about the people who are upset with you for blowing up the ship?" he says so only the three of us can hear. "I saw online that a group called the Society of the Stars wants revenge."

"Revenge?" I say.

Another chef walks up and hands the chef a handwritten order on a piece of paper. "Carlos, I need these rolls prepared."

"Yes, sir," Chef Carlos says to his coworker. "Enjoy," he says to us with a nod to the rolls before he walks away.

We eat our rolls in silence. Revenge? Society of the Stars? I try to look them up online and nothing but articles about Invader Assault come up. If there are androids who got corrupted with data from the members of the Society in the game, then the old man in Phoenix could be the first of many who won't be so grateful that I saved the world.

I am halfway through my rainbow roll when I stop to think about how I feel about my different order. I decide it is not as good as my spicy yellowtail roll. This is why I don't try new things. I already knew which roll I like. Not that I hate this one but it just isn't as good. Annoyed with Paige, I turn to her and am about to bring it up when I realize she has only eaten two of her eight pieces.

"What's wrong?" I ask.

"We shouldn't be out in public," Paige says. "I looked up the Society of Stars. They say that you deserve to be killed since you ruined the second coming of Christ. We just walked over here in broad daylight. Now we are sitting in a crowded restaurant. No security or cops anywhere. If anyone wanted to attack you they would have no problem getting to you."

Cops surrounded the old man in Phoenix. I shudder at the thought. Have they figured out that I was the one who assaulted him? I think about what my dad said, how I should get a lawyer and turn myself into the police.

"We'll be fine," I say. After all, it was just a game.

A car screeches to a halt outside. Everyone on the bar turns to look. A police SUV is parked at the front door of the restaurant. An officer jumps out, runs towards the restaurant, rips the door open and rushes inside. My breath gets caught in my throat and my pulse skyrockets. They are here for me, they found out I am the one who punched the old man! I look down at my right hand. At first glance it looks normal but the longer I look the more red it becomes.

He heads straight for the host who hands him a brown paper bag.

"Picking up lunch," Paige says. "The way they whipped in here I thought something was wrong."

"So did I," I say. She has no idea.

"Now my stomach is in knots," she says. "Before I saw it was the police I was scared it was the Society, here for their revenge."

I look down at the rest of my rainbow roll. I am not in the mood to eat another bite but I know that I will be hungry if I don't. I begin to shovel down the rest of my food.

Paige waves down a server as they pass behind us. "Could I get a box?" she says.

"Certainly," the young woman says.

By the time Paige's box gets to her, I have forced down the rest of my roll. Each bite reminded me how annoyed I am that I listened to her and tried something new.

"What'd you think?" she says when she sees my empty plate.

"Spicy yellowtail's better." I grab my napkin and wipe my mouth before I put the napkin on my plate beside my used chopsticks.

"Well, now you know!" she says.

"I already knew." I push my plate forward with more force than I intended.

"Are you mad at me?" she says. "Because I made you try something different?"

"No, I am upset with myself for listening to you."

She puts her hand on my shoulder. "I'm sorry," she says. "I thought you might like it."

I shift my shoulders so she has to remove her hand. "I'll get over it," I say. "We should get the check. I need to get back to work."

Paige offers to pay for my roll since I didn't like it but I insist that we split. Chef Carlos looks like he wants to say something else to us before we leave but he doesn't pull himself away from his work.

Paige turns to me once we are out of the restaurant. "Are you still mad at yourself for listening to me?" she says.

"No," I say. "I know that I am weird." Most people don't understand my need to keep things standardized.

"Promise?" she says.

"Promise," I say. Funny that an android cares so much about how a human feels towards them.

# CHAPTER SEVENTEEN

The walk back to work is tense. After the restaurant my head is on a swivel as I look out for cops and android members of the Society of the Stars. Twice a car stops to let its passengers off at a building as we walk past and each time I am worried that they are here for me.

My phone rings and I pull it out of my pocket. "Hi, Seraph," I say.

"Hey, Corvus, how have you been?" His words are quick and he talks as if we are old friends. Not at all what I expect. He must want something from me. I can hear each of his heavy breaths distinct on the receiver. Most people sound this way after exercise, he sounds this way whenever he walks around.

"I've been good?" I say, nervous that I am about to have more work put onto my plate for this afternoon. "I should be back in the office soon. Did you need anything?"

He chuckles. I can imagine his hand over his belly as it shakes, like Santa Claus. The office is his North Pole. "Do I need anything? What would I need? Wait until I tell the crew that you are stopping by! Everyone would love to see you. Did

THE HYSTERIA OF BODALIS

you know that your bag is still here in the office? And you left your laptop on the desk."

"Yes, I know," I say. Why wouldn't they be there?

"We all brag about knowing the man who saved the world!" he says. The words flow out of his mouth a mile a minute.

"About knowing me? Why wouldn't you know me?" Did he just say what I think he said? Not him too. There is no way he is an android. He can't be.

"After you saved the world I didn't think I would see you around here again. I guess today is our lucky day!"

"Must be," I say. "I will be back in the office soon." I hang up the phone, convinced he is an android.

The data from the video game has leaked into Seraph's program too. This is the first person I have interacted with before they switched. There are more androids around me than I ever could have imagined.

"That was Seraph," I say to Paige, confused. "Before lunch he was the same lousy boss he always was and now he is being way too nice. He thinks I saved the world."

"Corvus, you did save the world! Maybe he was having a bad morning."

"Maybe."

"I wasn't going to say anything but I can't believe you went back to work at Decant. There is no way you need the money. Don't you get put on government scholarship or something once you save the world?"

"If so then I haven't heard anything about it yet. What am I supposed to do all day if I don't go to work?"

"Whatever you like! You did enough work for every man, woman, and child on planet Earth. You can relax, take it easy, I don't know."

"But why would Seraph switch on me during lunch?" I say,

more to myself than her. She won't understand. Our physical bodies are together but our minds occupy separate realities.

"Maybe the change isn't as big as you think," Paige says.

"Maybe," I admit. He must be an android whose data got corrupted while I was at lunch. I have worked at Decant for over three years now and I just find out my boss has been an android because my video game data has leaked into his program. Do the developers use management structure to test the best way to keep androids in positions of power?

I struggle to control my thoughts as they spiral out of control. I am on the lookout for an attack from the Society that Carlos says exists and on the lookout for cops. Now I need to figure out what has happened to Seraph and how he switched. Before I know it, we are back in the Decant building. I didn't even realize how hot I was outside until I find myself in the air-conditioned lobby with my clothes stuck to my skin

I turn around when I realize I am alone. Paige has stopped just inside the front door.

"Aren't you coming up?" I say, walking back to her.

"I don't know. Do you want me to?"

"Yes. I want you to see this."

"Corvus! I can't believe you found the time to stop by!" Seraph says as we meet at the entrance to the main office.

"I just told you on the phone I would be here," I say.

"I know but I still can't believe it! We haven't seen you since you stopped coming to work a week ago. I didn't know it then but you were busy getting the bomb made to blow up the ship. Can I get either of you anything? Coffee? Espresso? Water?"

"No thank you, we just came from lunch." I introduce them to each other and they shake hands, Seraph's sausage fingers engulfing Paige's delicate hand.

Seraph looks at me with his mouth open. Must be my turn

to talk. I look around the room for inspiration and find none. "Um... have you had lunch already?" I say.

"Who, me? Yes, yes, I already ate. In my office. Burger and a diet coke. Only got the small fries though!" he says. His hands tap his large belly like he is proud of his meal choice. "What do the two of you have planned for today?"

"Well, I was going to give the presentation. After that, whatever you would like me to do. Once I get back to work she is going to take off, I just wanted to show her the office." In the entire time I have been here I don't think he has ever asked me about my work. He assumes he already knows all that I do.

I walk past Seraph into the main office. Rather, I walk *around* Seraph in order to get to the main office. Paige follows behind me. Linda is at her desk. Our eyes meet as I walk to my desk and I shrug my shoulders. She tilts her head, confused to see Seraph act this way and confused to see me playing along. Ron and Andy are in the office as well. They both keep their eyes on their work and ignore the situation as it unfolds around them.

Seraph laughs behind me, loud enough for the entire office to hear twice. "You almost had me going there!" he roars as he slaps me on the back.

I jump forward from the force. I thought Paige was behind me, I don't know how Seraph managed to get there. Why was his laugh so delayed? He is slow to process.

"Guy saves the world and acts like he is going back to his boring day job!"

Boring day job? I don't know what to think. I *should* be offended. I spent a lot of time here and I am proud of what I have accomplished. Ron and Andy pick their heads up and, along with Linda, glare at Seraph.

"I meant what are you doing after your visit!" he says. "Any interviews? Meeting any celebrities? Photo shoot maybe?"

I won't be able to work here now that I know Seraph is an android. He needs to be treated just like the others who believe I saved the world. Time to pretend.

"Paige and I are going to go over the schedule for the day once we leave here," I lie. "She has been my manager since I came back down the earth. We were in the area when you called and I decided to stop by and show her where I used to work until I saved the world! And of course visit my old friends in the office." Linda, Ron, and Andy all look at me like I am crazy. Seraph beams with pride. Paige seems surprised to see the sudden shift in my tone.

Once I reach my desk, I put my laptop in my bag and sling the bag over my shoulder. No other personal items at my desk need to be packed.

My time at Decant is over. Before I leave the main room for the final time, I turn to my former coworkers. "Well, it was great seeing everyone! Paige and I need to get out of here. Lots to do!" I hear myself fake a laugh.

"Don't be a stranger!" Seraph says as we shake hands. I leave the office with Paige behind me.

# CHAPTER EIGHTEEN

"That was weird," I say as soon as the elevator doors shut.

Paige nods in agreement. "He's a strange one. Everyone looked so confused."

"That's because they were. I don't think any of us have seen Seraph act like that."

As the elevator doors open, I begin to walk towards the escalator that goes down to the train and almost get there before I realize that I am alone.

I turn and walk back to Paige as she stands in the middle of the lobby. "Did you expect me to go with you?" she says.

"Kind of," I say. I hadn't thought about it, I just assumed she would spend the afternoon with me.

"Did you mean it when you said I was your manager?"

"There is nothing to manage..." I say.

"So, is that a no?" She folds her hands across her chest.

"Why do you even want to be my manager? Like I said, there is nothing to manage."

"Then why did you say it?" she asks.

"You know what? Sure. You want to be my manager, you got

it. Welcome to the team. You know I can't pay you right? I just lost my job."

She smiles and her hands fall to her side. "That's fine, the money is on its way. Would you like me to come with you?"

"If you want," I say.

"Is that a yes?"

"Yes."

We ride the escalator down and wait seven minutes for a train. The train car is clean and, from the lack of graffiti on the walls, appears to be new. Paige watches the darkness pass as we race through the underground tunnels to my stop.

It still doesn't feel like I've lost my job. All because my boss turned out to be an android. My last paycheck better be in my account on Friday so I won't have to ask my dad for money. How many more androids will turn up that believe I saved the world? What happens if the leak between the virtual world and the real one gets discovered? If I can talk to the developers and get them to plug the leak maybe I could save my job. But will I be able to work for an android?

How could I find out who is in control of the androids? I make a note in my phone to email Denise when I get back to the apartment. Maybe she knows of other companies or organizations that would have access to this technology.

"I could tell you were faking," Paige says. Her words cut the silence between us.

"What are you talking about?"

"In the office. With your boss. I could tell you were faking, at the end, when you decided to play along with him. You aren't a very good actor you know."

I remember my dad's advice: keep the thoughts about androids to yourself. Paige thinks I saved the world. I want to tell her it was all a game. That there was no threat, there was no ship. That I didn't save the world.

"I was thrown off by the way he was acting, that's all. It caught me off guard."

"You are faking right now. Again. I can tell," Paige says.

"How can you tell?"

"Trust me, I can tell."

"Let's just say the two of us have different versions of how things happened," I say.

"Enlighten me."

I turn my head away from Paige in frustration and look at the rest of the train. Only half of the seats are occupied. I wonder if any of them are androids. I turn back to face her.

Fuck it.

"I didn't save the world," I say. "It was just a video game. Ever since I beat the game people have turned up who think I actually did it in real life. Including you."

"You really think it was all a game?" I see a flash of pity in her eyes before I turn away again. "This was our planet's first contact with aliens. Because of you the world never had to find out what they wanted from us."

"Paige. I don't think it was a game. I know it was a game." I look at her mouth so I don't have to look into her eyes. "The Invaders aren't real. They were never real. There was no ship. And I didn't save the world."

"There are others who prefer to pretend that the whole thing didn't happen too. They are more comfortable with blocking out the whole experience than facing the fact that we are not alone in the universe. Articles have been streaming out from psychology websites about the people who deliberately forget. I can't believe you, the one who actually blew up the ship, are one of the people who refuse to believe ever happened."

I remember she told the army veteran that she is in Bodalis to study psychology. "Is that why you are so interested in me?

Because I am one of your cases? Are you going to write an article about me?" I can't help but be upset when I think that she has been analyzing me this entire time.

She turns her back to me. I can see the reflection of her face in the window. She has tears in her eyes. "Maybe you are pretending it was just a game to protect yourself because your life was on the line. Well, your life is on the line again and I feel like you aren't taking it seriously. I feel bad trying to make you remember that this really happened, in real life, but I am worried about you."

She is worried about what will happen if she contradicts my worldview just like I am worried about what will happen if I contradict hers. We could go in this circle all afternoon. I have to give in and pretend. "I will do my best to remember," I say.

She turns to face me. "You should. There are very real consequences now. If the Society is out for revenge I don't think they will care if you believe it happened in a video game or not. They aren't even the only ones upset with you. I saw an article earlier about how scientists across the world are upset that you ruined the chance for humanity to learn about alien technology. If I need to keep reminding you how your actions saved the entire planet I will, so you take these threats seriously."

She can think whatever she likes. I know I haven't saved the world outside of the video game. I stay quiet until the train slows for Monocots Ave.

Before I begin to walk to my apartment I turn to Paige and say, "I want to be alone tonight. I will call you a car to take you home."

Surprise mixed with sadness fills her eyes. Her voice quivers as she asks, "Did I say something wrong?"

"Nothing wrong," I tell her. "I just need some time alone. Let's talk tomorrow."

"Don't worry about getting a car for me, I will call it myself. Have a good night." Paige turns and walks away from me. She is bent over her phone as she turns the corner.

I begin the walk back to my apartment, alone.

# CHAPTER NINETEEN

A MAN LEANS against the outside wall of the bodega across from my apartment. He stands out because of his outfit: a slim black suit, black shirt, and black tie. He must get hot outside in the sun. He has dark, close cropped hair and sunglasses cover his eyes. His complexion and face are hard to place. He could be Hispanic, Mediterranean, or Asian. I keep my eyes forward and focus on my building, but feel his eyes on me as I pass.

I reach my building and put my face in front of the retinal scanner. The door clicks unlocked. As I pull the door open, a hand reaches out and pushes it closed. I hear the click of the door as it locks again.

"Come on," I say, frustrated. It has already been a crazy day. I turn. The man in the black suit is right behind me.

"What's your problem?" I ask. I can see my reflection in his sunglasses.

"Corvus Okada. It is an honor to meet you in person."

I take a step back and size the man up. He is my height but much thicker than I am. He has at least twenty pounds on me. "Who the hell are you?" I say.

His lips curl up in a smirk. "My name is not important. I am here to pass along a message." He crosses his hands behind his back.

"Get to the point, I don't have time for this. What is the message?"

"I work for The Preacher. She simply wants a guarantee." He paces to the sidewalk, hands still behind his back, before he turns back to the building. "If the Invaders return to avenge the loss of their ship, you will do nothing. No more interventions on behalf of the planet."

"I never did the first time," I tell him.

"So, the ship just blew itself up? Is that it?" he says.

Another android convinced the facts from the video game world happened in real life.

"Done," I say. It was just a game. The Invaders can't come back because they were never here in the first place. I turn away from the man in sunglasses, annoyed, and move my head towards the retinal scan to unlock the door for a second time.

He grabs my left arm and spins me back around to face him. I swing with my right hand and, for an instant, am taken back to the sidewalk in Phoenix. The messenger leans back and watches my fist pass by as if he knew the punch was on its way before I did. He returns to his full height, hands relaxed at his side, and has a large grin on his face.

"To make sure you don't change your mind," he says. He holds out a phone so I can see the screen and presses play. It takes me a moment to recognize the surveillance footage from the Decant in Phoenix. It shows me as I pay for my coffee, before the incident with the old man. The blood drains from my face.

"Where did you get this?" The formation of words is difficult.

"Don't worry about where we got it. Rest assured that we have the only copy. We intend to keep it that way, as long as you are willing to work with us." He puts his phone back into his pocket.

"Work with you?" I close my eyes and pinch the bridge of my nose with my right hand. I look at my reflection in his sunglasses again. "Doing what exactly? You only mentioned that I had to do nothing when the Invaders returned. I can do nothing." The two of us have to take a step back as another tenant from my building walks up and proceeds to use the retinal scanner to enter the building.

"You are under the control of the congregation whether you like it or not. The Preacher would like to meet with you tomorrow," he says.

Under control of the congregation? "Who is the preacher?" I ask.

The messenger crosses his arms and leans against my building. "The Preacher is the leader of the congregation. We believe the ship was the end of times referred to in the bible." He turns to follow a black SUV as it passes before he turns back to me. "We also provide protection for anyone willing to pay. We wanted the Invaders to take over in order scare the heretics. The heretics would be willing to pay for protection. Protection we could've provided. In short, Mr. Okada, when you destroyed the Invader's ship you lost us more money than you can fathom."

Paige was right to be worried about me. "Are you part of the Society of the Stars?"

"You've heard of them? No, that's not us. They are much more impulsive than we are. They want you dead. We prefer you alive and we intend to keep you that way."

"Why do you want me alive?" I cross my arms as well.

"We don't pretend to know what the Invaders want. We want to keep you alive so they can decide for themselves what to do with you."

"It sounds like you are keeping me alive so I can be sacrificed."

"Think of it however you like. As a sign of our good will, and in order to make the most of your remaining time on Earth, we have transferred a considerable sum to your account. In return, you just need to work with us until the Invaders show up again. Can you see how this is a good situation for you?"

"It sounds like I don't have much of an option if I don't want that video to be released," I say.

"See it through whichever lens you choose, Mr. Okada. I will be here tomorrow morning at 9:00 to pick you up."

My phones buzzes and I reach into my pocket to pull it out. A message from Marvle: ARE YOU GOING TO BE ONLINE TONIGHT?

His message reminds me that the new console I ordered last night should be here. "This has been fun but I have to go," I say to the messenger.

He puts his hand in his pocket, pulls out a business card, and hands it to me. All black and blank except for a letter pressed phone number.

"If you need anything before 9:00 tomorrow call this number. Otherwise, I will see you then." The messenger turns and I watch him walk down the block. He makes a right and I lose sight of him behind my building.

# CHAPTER TWENTY

I PUT my face in front of the retinal scanner, unlock the door, and enter my building. Picking up my new console in stark white packaging with JANUS written in bold black letters, I ride the elevator up to my floor.

I set my new console on the couch on my way into my bedroom and text Marvle.

ABOUT TO SET UP NEW CONSOLE, BE ONLINE SOON.

I go back into the living room to set up the console. It is matte black, about the size of my two hands placed together side by side and just as thick. On one side of the console is the power cord and the video cable that attaches to my monitor. I twist my monitor to access the back and disconnect my old console. This console is less than a year old and shouldn't have any problems but I need to do whatever I can to get back online. I attach the new cables to the monitor and connect them to the new console. Once it is hooked up, I turn the console on and log into my account.

My online data needs an hour or two to download. Plenty of time before I need to get online for team practice in four hours. I should take a shower and get ready for the evening while my data downloads.

As the water washes away the day I begin to think about the androids. How many will there be who believe I saved the world? How many are there in general? Paige seems so certain that the events of the game happened in real life. The black and white of the two realities have been mixed for her and are now a dull gray. I can't disagree with her version of reality again the way I did today. Although, to her credit, she took it much better than the man in the car on the way to the airport did. What was his name again? I am annoyed that I forget.

I wash my hair and rinse. While I put soap on my body I begin to analyze the way Paige accused me of not remembering. "I am able to remember just fine," I say to the empty bathroom. I remember I was on the bed in the hotel room when I beat the game.

I wonder if androids ever get caught in their own thoughts. Do they look back at the interactions that occurred that day and try to decide how they feel about them? If so, I hope she is stuck in her head right now, just like me.

I finish my shower and turn off the water. After I dry off I get dressed in sweatpants and a sweatshirt. I look at my phone and see that my dad has called me while I was in the shower. For a second, I debate whether or not to call him back but decide that I am not in the mood to talk to him.

My stomach grumbles. In the kitchen, I look in the refrigerator and see that all I have is ketchup, eggs, and two beers. I use my phone to order tacos from my favorite Mexican spot eight blocks away. The phone tells me my food should be here in forty minutes.

I lean on the kitchen counter and watch the progress meter of the download on my monitor reach 100%. It only took an hour and a few minutes. I go to the couch and plop down, eager to practice against the bots. I take the tap test, put on my holo lenses, and use the gloves to open Invader Assault. I am excited to play again after so much time away.

The death screen covers my monitor as I watch with astonishment. Fuck. I just wasted all that money to get a new console and it doesn't even work. I don't know what to do. The team won't believe me. They have all been able to get online each night and it makes no sense that I can't connect.

I call Invader Assault customer service. We spend an hour together on the phone only to find out the servers still work. They are able to detect my console from their end. They suggest I restart my console. I realize there is nothing they can do and will grasp at straws until the call is over. I hang up.

There is an hour and a half until practice begins. I should tell Seth that I am out tonight so he has time to get a replacement. I get my laptop from the bedroom and sit back down on my couch to write a message to the team manager.

SETH-

I can't connect again. Even with the new console. IA support doesn't know why, they say that everything should work. I think it would be best if I took a leave of absence until this is figured out. I don't want the team to depend on me when I can't even connect.

-Corvus

I MAKE sure the rest of the team is cc'ed on the email and push send. I stand up and pace behind my couch. Today has been a hell of a day. First, I lose my job. Then I lose tomorrow morning to the messenger. Now, I lose my game. This day needs to be over.

I sit back down on the couch and open a new email and address it to Marvle. I have known him from when we played Ronin together. He is the quartermaster of the team. He is also part of an amateur hacking collective called the Onslaught Agency. The OA for short. The other members of the team don't know about this side of Marvle. The reason I know is because he let it slip in one of the messages he sent me.

I rush to type the message so that he can read both of them before he reacts to the first one.

Marvle-

Can you do me a favor and look into why I can't connect? IA support says they can detect my system but all I ever get is the death screen. Help me figure this out I can come back to practice.

-Corvus

I LOOK AROUND MY APARTMENT. What am I supposed to do until it is time to go to bed? I don't even have to be in bed anymore now that I don't have to go to work tomorrow. What will I do for money? I remember what the messenger said about the "considerable sum". I grab my phone from next to me on the couch and look at my bank account. My jaw drops when I see that my bank account has eight digits in it. The part about the money wasn't a lie. How did an android ever get this type of coin?

I call Paige.

"Paige. You are never going to believe what happened." The words rush out of me.

"Hello, Corvus." Her words are crisp, clipped.

"What's wrong?"

"Nothing. I just didn't expect you to call this evening. What's up? Do you need something?"

"No, I don't need anything. For starters, I can afford to pay you now," I say.

I get up from the couch and begin to pace behind it while I tell Paige about the experience with the messenger. She is speechless when she finds out that there is not one but *two* religious groups who are interested in me. Neither of us have heard of the Preacher.

"Are you going to go with him tomorrow?" she says.

"I don't really have a choice. Plus, they deposited so much money in my account I feel like I have to go see what they want."

"You already know what they want. They want to keep you alive until the Invaders return!"

"They aren't going to return," I say.

"You would say that, you don't even believe they came here in the first place," Paige says. I imagine her rolling her eyes. "As your manager I think I should go with you."

"Really? Why?" I say.

"I am interested in hearing what they have to say too."

"He said I would be picked up at 9:00. Be here before then and I guess you can come with."

My phone buzzes and a notification pops up to let me know my food has arrived.

"Hey I have to go get my food from downstairs."

"I'll see you tomorrow," Paige says.

"See you tomorrow."

When I return to my apartment, food in hand, I can't help but to kick myself. All this money in my account and I got tacos? I could've had anything I wanted and I got... tacos. To be fair, though, it's not like I knew how much money I had in my account before I ordered.

I turn on music to listen to while I eat my food. After I scroll through a few playlists and realize I am not in the mood for any of them, I settle on a radio station dedicated to instrumental metal that I listen to when I play Invader Assault. I have a taco in hand and about to take a bite when my dad tries to call me again. I let it go to voicemail. The tacos got jostled in transit and, after I eat what I can with my hands, I get up and grab a fork to finish my meal.

One good thing about my disconnected evening is that I have more time to read. I open the reading app on my phone and pick up where I left off.

Once Amanda had the ability to measure which synapses fire while she performs a particular activity she realized it would take too long to find the full map of the brain by the measurement of individual tasks. She hooked up her brain to a virtual avatar and had the researchers fire the synapses she had already mapped. The first test was to fire the synapses associated with the performance of a song on the piano she knew from childhood. Nobody was ready for what happened next. Her virtual avatar played the piece to perfection, the first time an avatar was controlled by the mind without any other inputs. Even more significant was the way Amanda remembered the time she had fallen from a swing and broken her arm, as if she were back in her childhood at this specific moment of time. Her team had discovered that memories are stored in the synaptic noise. This was the breakthrough that led to the development of the death servers.

Tired, I check the time: 22:31. Team practice ended an hour ago and nobody has responded to my messages. I turn the lights off in the living room and go to bed while I think about the memories Paige thinks I have erased.

# CHAPTER TWENTY-ONE

THERE IS a knock at my door. At least I think I hear a knock. I check the time on my phone: 7:30. I dread that I have to get ready for another day at work until I remember I no longer have a job. It will take a while to get over how conditioned I am to follow the clock from the moment I wake up. I wait a second to see if what I heard was in or out of my dream. After thirty seconds of silence I double check the alarm on my phone to make sure it is set to wake me up in a half hour and lay my head back down to sleep until it goes off. There is an unmistakable knock on the door as soon as I close my eyes. Who would be here at this hour? Paige.

I push the covers off myself and get out of bed. I slip on a pair of shorts and go to the front door to let her in. I didn't take her as an early riser. I assumed she would be here closer to nine, when the messenger is supposed to come pick me up to take me to the Preacher. I open the door for her and she rushes in.

"Good morning," she says as she passes me. She wears a black dress with a red scarf. In her ears are black stud earrings. I don't remember if she wore earrings yesterday. She carries a black leather messenger bag on her shoulder and a ring binder in her hand.

"Morning," I say, wiping the sleep from my eyes. "Why are you here so early?"

"I had to get some stuff printed and it didn't take as long as I expected," she says. "So I just came over. Did I wake you up?" She sets her bag on the ground next to the front door.

"Yeah, but I was going to get up soon anyway."

Paige goes into the kitchen and sets her binder down on the counter between the kitchen and the living room. "Okay, good. Why don't you get ready and I will make breakfast. Do you have eggs?"

I walk around to the living room and set my hands on the counter between us. "Yes," I say.

"Any bacon? Sausage? Ham?"

"No."

"Hm. I knew I should've stopped by the store. Oh well." She opens the refrigerator and pulls out the carton of eggs. "How many do you want?"

"Four," I say.

"Okay. I am going to make myself some too. Go get ready." She bends over and opens the lower cabinet next to the refrigerator.

"Looking for the frying pan? It's underneath the stove."

Paige closes the cabinet and pulls open the drawer beneath the stove. "Got it. Go get ready, I can find what I need on my own."

I leave her in the kitchen and get ready for the day. It feels weird to wear jeans and a t-shirt on a Wednesday morning. I have dressed business casual Monday through Friday for years. As I return to the kitchen, I am greeted by the smell of cooked eggs and fresh coffee.

Paige sits at the counter on one of the three barstools I have, coffee in hand. I pull another barstool out from beneath the counter and sit down. She has a plate with four fried eggs ready for me on the counter. A fork sits on a napkin next to the plate. Steam rises from a mug of coffee.

"How did you sleep?" she asks, as I begin to eat.

"Slept well. Pretty annoyed though, my game wouldn't load last night. I had the same problem in Phoenix. I thought a new console would fix the issue but it turned out to be a waste of money. I had to tell my manager I won't be able to play for a while, at least until I can figure out what is going on."

"Manager?"

"The team manager. I missed practice again last night."

"You have practice?"

"I play Invader Assault on a team. I didn't tell you?" Strange coincidence that the game that doesn't work is the one that has leaked into her reality.

"The game is called Invader Assault? Interesting," she says.

I take another bite of my eggs. She cooked them longer than I would have made them myself. I prefer to have my eggs over medium, with the half the yolk firm and the other half runny.

"Thanks for breakfast," I say.

"You're welcome."

"What's in the binder?" I ask. "Is that what you had to get printed this morning?"

"Yes, it is. After we talked last night I decided to do some research. This is all the information I could find about the Society of the Stars and the Preacher."

"Who prints on paper anymore?"

"I do," she says.

"What did you find out?"

"Well, for starters, the Society is definitely not pleased with you. To be honest, I am surprised nobody has bothered to track you down. It isn't like you are hiding or have any security in place. They have called their followers into action and proclaim that whoever takes your life will be considered a hero. It is probably a good thing the Preacher has decided to keep you alive. They will take care of your protection, at least until we can figure out what to do."

How can there be that many androids who want me dead? And if there are that many, could there be some sort of preventative block that won't allow an android to kill me? That would explain how I am still alive when there is an entire Society of androids who want me dead.

"Does it say how many members the society has?" I say between bites.

"No it doesn't. But there has to be a good number of people who belong because there is an office in most major cities. It seems like a fluke that you haven't been killed."

"What did you find out about the Preacher?" I take a sip of coffee.

She puts her hand on the binder. "So, most of these pages are about the Society. They are much more public about themselves and make no effort to hide their intentions. On the other hand, it was hard to find any information about the Preacher. I found one passing reference to a Preacher on a Bodalís security forum. It said 'if you can find her, hire her.' Sounds like finding her is the hard part."

I finish the rest of my eggs. "Well she found me. That has to count for something."

"I guess. I did some more digging into security firms based in Bodalís with female leaders. There is an agency, Bodalís Blackwatch, who has a female leader. They are known for protecting celebrities. From what I have gathered about them, they are the best money can buy. Assuming this might have been the group who approached you last night, I found out more information about their leader."

"Okay, tell me about her." I take another sip of strong coffee. She makes her coffee the same way I do.

Paige opens the binder and uses a green tab to open to the correct section. "Her name is Eliana Landry. Every review I found mentioned how callous she can be but that it is worth putting up with because of how effective her firm is."

She shows me a page from the binder. "This is from the Blackwatch website." She begins to summarize the page. "As founder of Bodalís Blackwatch... she was the lone defender of her clients' safety for the first four years... Eventually, she was able to hire agents to help her... She has trained each of them herself in order to ensure the quality of her company's service."

"Sounds like just the person we should talk with to help keep me alive." I stand up, walk around the counter into the kitchen, grab my plate and put it in the sink with the dirty frying pan and spatula. I finish my coffee in three long swallows and put the dishes into the dishwasher.

I check the time on my phone. "The guy should be here in fifteen minutes."

"Okay, let me run to the bathroom." Paige gets up, puts her dirty mug into the sink, and goes to the bathroom.

I can't believe she just left her mug in the sink. Even after she saw me rinse the dishes and put them in the dishwasher. I remind myself that she just made me breakfast, the least I can do is rinse out her mug for her. I rinse the mug and put it in the dishwasher.

I notice ground coffee on the counters. I grab a paper towel and wet it before I wipe up the spill. I open the cabinet where the coffee is kept. She didn't fold the coffee bag the way I like so I pull it out and refold it. I make sure to get all the air out of the bag. On a hunch I open the door to the refrigerator. The eggs aren't on the shelf where I keep them. Why would she put the eggs back in a place different than where she found it? It makes no sense to me. I put the eggs back where they belong.

Paige comes back from the bathroom and sits down on the barstool. She pulls out her phone and begins to kill the time until the messenger arrives to pick us up. I sit on the couch. I have two emails, one from Marvle and one from Seth. Seth is upset that I had to miss practice again and manages to yell at me through the letters on the screen to "get my shit together." Marvle's reply is short: "I'll look into it."

My phone buzzes, a call from an unknown number. "Hello?"

"Come downstairs," are the only words I hear before the call ends.

# CHAPTER TWENTY-TWO

A BLACK SUV is parked in front of my building. The hazard lights flash while the car waits for me to arrive. As soon as I walk through the front door of my building, the rear door of the SUV opens up. I can see the messenger inside.

The messenger stays in the door of the car to block my entrance. He has on black tactical pants, a grey t-shirt, and a bulletproof vest. "Who is she?" he says when he sees Paige.

"She is my manager. She will be joining us today," I say.

"Stay here." He sits down in the back seat of the car, puts his hand up to his ear, and begins to speak. I can't make out the words.

"Get in," he tells the two of us eventually.

The car has its seats in the same setup as the old SUVs did before the driverless revolution. It even has a driver. I haven't been in a car with a driver for so long I forgot what it felt like. The driver is up front and sits on the left. I am mesmerized as I watch his hands flow like water over the steering wheel while he weaves through the city streets. The messenger sits with Paige and me in the back seat, three across. Our shoulders span from door to door. The twenty-minute trip is passed in silence.

We end up in an industrial part of Bodalís I have never been to before. We roll past three blocks of warehouses devoid of life. Stop signs separate each block. The asphalt of the street connects to the cement of the sidewalk which connects to the brick of the warehouses and not a speck of green is anywhere. Until we get to the fence.

Behind the fence is an expansive, well-manicured lawn with enough green for the entire block. The lawn angles up and at the top sits a building. I look for a sign to find out what type of institution belongs in a place like this. We begin to slow down as we approach the gate in the middle of the block.

The driver drops us off in front of the building on top of the hill. Two men in suits, each with an Uzi slung over their shoulder, escort us from the doors of the SUV inside. The messenger follows behind the four of us. Inside, the floors are dark brown marble. A handsome reception desk, made of dark brown wood, is across the floor between two staircases that bow out and meet again in the space above the desk. Another man, also in a suit and with an Uzi slung over his shoulder, stands behind the desk. He nods to our group as we are led past by the two armed guards, escorted up the staircase on his left.

We are led to an office that has a large window with a view of the expansive lawn. "Sit down," says one of the guards as he pulls out the brown leather chairs from underneath the desk. "She will be here shortly." The messenger stands behind us. The two guards stand outside the office on each side of the door.

The office matches the rest of the building. Brown marble floors and dark brown wooden furniture. There is a high backed, brown leather chair behind the desk across from where we sit. I stand up to get a better view of the lawn outside the window. I try to find a landmark in the horizon to figure out which direction I face. A woman's voice says behind me, "Enjoying the view?"

I turn around to see a tall Italian woman. She is built like an athlete with the long proportions of a high jumper and clears the distance between the door and the desk in three long strides. I return to my chair as she pulls the leather chair out from underneath the desk and sits down. This must be the Preacher.

"Do you like the view?" she asks me again.

"Yes, I do. I didn't expect this type of lawn next to all the warehouses around here."

"My name is Eliana Landry. We are in the headquarters of my company, Bodalís Blackwatch." She looks at me. "I know you are Corvus Okada," she says before she turns to Paige, "but I don't know who you are. I wasn't aware we were having company." Her voice is melodious, with a natural sweetness to it, but her eyes have a frigid quality that doesn't change as she speaks. The combination produces an unsettling discomfort deep inside my stomach.

"This is Paige." I realize I don't know her last name. I should find that out. "She is my manager."

"Welcome, Paige. And welcome, Corvus. Thank you for coming today."

"I didn't have much of a choice," I say.

"There is always a choice. Let me tell you what would've happened if you decided not to come today. I would have made sure the authorities got a copy of the surveillance footage of you in the Phoenix Decant. Then I would have made sure you were thrown in prison for manslaughter. The old man died. Did you know that?" Her eyes sparkle with enjoyment. "Then I would have made you wait until the day the Invaders came back. Either they would kill you, for blowing up their ship, or the authorities would turn you over to them. I can convince them it is the only way to save the planet."

I killed him? I look down at my right hand. A bright red emanates from the veins in the back of my hand and pools on my knuckles. Her voice is sweet, even when she talks about how she could ruin my life.

"But, since I knew you would cooperate, I made sure you were appropriately compensated. Did the money arrive in your account?"

"Yes, it did."

"Good."

Paige turns to me. "What is she talking about, Corvus?"

"Oh, he didn't tell you?" Eliana asks.

"I punched an old man in Phoenix. It was self-defense," I say to Paige before Eliana can continue.

"There are no witnesses and the old man didn't live. All you have is your word," Eliana says.

Paige doesn't appear to care. "You mentioned that Corvus has to cooperate," Paige says to Eliana. "What does he have to do?"

"All he has to do is let Maximus spend the day with him." She uses her chin to point to the messenger. So that is his name. She turns to me. "Every day. Maximus mentioned that you have heard of the Society of the Stars. They want to kill you. They think they missed their chance at salvation and want to make you pay. I am more optimistic. I think the Invaders will come back and that the choice of what to do with you is best left to them. I intend to keep you alive until they return. So, long story short, think of Maximus as your security against the Society."

I swivel my chair and look at the messenger. Two other men have joined him behind us. Maximus stands still, with his hands behind his back, and gives me a nod when we look at each other. The driver from earlier is next to him. He is tall, much taller than I expected. Somewhere around six feet five inches and has blond, shoulder length hair. The other man is short and thin, with a rat's face. He wears black rimmed glasses and has a tribal tattoo on his neck.

"Call me Max," Maximus says.

"He is the head of Alpha team," Eliana explains. "Along with the driver, Ludwig," the blond man nods to me, "and the tech specialist, Alcide."

"We call Ludwig 'Driver' and Alcide 'Drone'," Max says to me.

The three of them together remind me of an Invader Assault team. Max would be the Mauler, he is built like a tank. Driver must be able to run fast with his long legs and would make an excellent scout. Drone, the tech specialist, is the support character. Just like the quartermaster in the game. They need one more on their team to fill the Slayer role.

I turn back around to face Eliana. "So, you expect me to spend all day with these guys? For how long?" I say.

"Until the Invaders show up again."

"What if they never come?"

"They will."

And now I have lost my freedom. I am torn. Half of me wants to scream "fuck you!" and storm out of here while the other half knows I don't have a choice. At least this way I don't have to see the inside of a cell.

Eliana stands up and extends her hand to Paige. She shakes Paige's hand before she shakes mine. "I look forward to working together."

"One more thing," Paige says before Eliana can walk around the side of her desk.

"Yes?"

"Why do they call you the Preacher?"

"I am the leader of a non-denominational Christian congregation. Our members include some of the most influential people in Bodalís. They worship with me because they appreciate the secrecy and security Blackwatch can provide. We all believe it is important to keep Corvus alive until the Invaders return."

Both Paige and I are speechless.

"I have to go. Max will take care of you." Eliana taps her desk twice and walks out of the room.

## CHAPTER TWENTY-THREE

"LET'S GO," Max says, walking to the office door.

"That's it? We had to come all this way for that?" I say to Paige. "What a waste of time." Paige nods. No response from the members of Alpha Team.

Paige and I follow Max back down the stairs, Drone and Driver following behind us.

"Be right back," Driver says when we are near the front door. Together with Drone, Driver walks down a hall to our right. Each of his strides equal two of mine.

A few minutes later a black SUV pulls up. "This is us," Max says. The three of us walk outside and get into the car.

"Where's the other guy?" I ask Driver as the door shuts.

"Drone? He is in the basement, in front of his computer," Max says.

"He lives down there," says Driver. I can't tell if he is serious or not.

When we pull up to my apartment building twenty minutes later, I put my hand on the back of the passenger seat and lean forward. "There's a parking garage under my building where you can park," I tell Driver. "Turn right at the next street, the entrance is on the back side of the building."

Max asks me about the cable truck parked across the street on the corner opposite my building. "It was there yesterday too," he says.

"I didn't notice," I say.

"You should try to pay attention to these things. What about the homeless man over there?" he says, pointing to the man who sometimes sits next to the bodega and peddles for change.

"Some days he is there, some days he isn't. I don't keep track." The homeless man is a toothless old man with dirty, stringy hair and a beard to match. I think about his mouth, how his lips collapse into the space where teeth should be. It reminds me of the old man in Phoenix. Turns out he never did recover from that one punch. I wish that all I had done is knock out his teeth. Why did I get myself into this mess?

Max leans forward and puts his hand on Driver's shoulder. "Keep tabs on him," he says. "And tell Drone to check the cable company's repair schedule and confirm that the van is theirs."

We turn onto Monocots Avenue. "Pull in here," I say as we pull up to the entrance of the parking garage.

The car descends at a sharp angle below my building. "Visitors spots are in the back," I say when the ground has leveled out. I point to the far side of the parking lot.

"I'll drop you off here," Driver says when we are in front of the elevators.

Max turns to me. "Lead the way."

I get out of the car and scan my eye to unlock the door to get into the glass room where we can access the elevators. Max, Paige, and I wait inside the room for Driver to park the car and join us.

"There's a lot of cars here," Paige says. "I would have thought everyone would be at work."

"I think a lot of people who live here take the train since the station is so close," I say.

Max looks around at the parked cars but says nothing.

A man in khaki shorts and a blue Hawaiian shirt emerges from behind a row of ten parked cars, turns and walks towards the elevators. Each step is deliberate, taken with purpose. Ten feet from the glass wall between us, he stops. We make eye contact and I see a flash of recognition in his eyes. He reaches behind his back and, in slow motion, pulls out a gun. I watch, frozen in place, as he lifts his arm and takes aim at me.

An arm shoves me to the left. I stumble, fall down, and knock Paige over in the process. A gunshot rings out and glass shatters. I use my arms to protect my head from the shards of glass as they rain down around me. I look up and see Max. He stands tall, feet wide, gun drawn. I prop myself up on my elbow and can see the man in the Hawaiian shirt as he lies on his back on the ground. Blood stains the shirt over his chest. The whole thing is over before it could even begin.

"Are you okay?" Max says while he keeps his eyes on the man he has just shot.

"Yeah," Paige and I reply.

"Stay down," he says. He kicks more glass out of the window and climbs through the hole he created. He runs up to the man and kicks the gun on the ground out of reach.

I get up, careful not to cut my hand on the glass that covers the floor. I brush myself off before I help Paige up as well. Driver runs up, gun drawn, to where Max stands over the man in the Hawaiian shirt. He bends over, picks up the gun Max had kicked away, and tucks it into his pants.

Max bends down on one knee, grabs the man beneath the chin, and forces the man to look at him. "Are you with the Society?"

The man stays silent as Max begins to search through his pockets.

I walk through the elevator room door and stand next to Driver. I can't help feel that this man has gotten what he deserves. Bet he didn't expect me to have security. Part of me is thankful Eliana forced me into this situation. It just saved my life.

The man coughs and spits up blood. Dark red streams trickle down his face. The man's breath continues to bubble through the liquid in his chest as he lays on the ground, each breath shorter than the last.

Max pulls a business card from the man's back pocket and hands it to Driver.

"Jason Hart. IT at an accounting firm," Driver read aloud.

"Are you Jason Hart?" Max asks. The man tries to turn his head away but hasn't the strength to break Max's vice grip on his chin.

"Are you Jason Hart?" Max roars. The man's eyes flash a look of contempt before he shakes his head no.

"Maybe it's the next guy he has to hit," Driver suggests.

"Is that it?" Max asks.

The man stares at Max before he closes his eyes and nods. He coughs again and more blood spills from his mouth. His head goes slack in Max's hand.

Max lets go of his chin and turns to Driver. "Get the scrubbers to come get him and clean up this mess. Stay down here until they get here." He turns to Paige and me. "Let's get upstairs," he says. He stands up and wipes the blood from his hands onto his black pants.

# CHAPTER TWENTY-FOUR

THE THREE OF us stand in silence. Paige and I have our backs against the wall of the elevator, opposite the doors, and Max stands in front of us, gun still drawn. He has both hands on it and has it angled down to where the elevator doors meet the floor. The elevator beeps on the fourth floor and the doors slide open. Max raises his arms until they are parallel with the floor and walks out of the elevator behind his weapon.

"What is your apartment number?" he asks. He turns left and right. Satisfied with the emptiness of the hallway, he motions for us to follow him.

"407" I say. "Make a right."

A door opens in front of us before we make it to my apartment. My neighbor, Frank, walks out of his room and comes faces to face with the barrel of Max's gun. He is pale, and skinny, but when he sees the gun he turns two shades whiter.

Frank contorts his body to the right in an attempt to get away from the path of the gun, cowering against the wall. "Whoa man, what's this all about?" He scrambles to get back into his room.

"Sorry, Frank. Close the door and forget you saw us," I tell him.

"Corvus? That you? I didn't know you still lived here." His hair is matted against his head. He told me last week that he doesn't wash his hair so he can grow dreadlocks. It's not a good look.

"I still live here," I say.

"Not for long," Max says.

"What do you mean?"

"I mean we are going to pack a bag for you and get out of here. They know where you live. It isn't safe here," Max says.

"I thought you already got your stuff and moved after what happened Saturday," Frank stammers. "I haven't seen you around in a few days, I figured you were gone." He turns to Max. "Will you get that damned thing out of my face!"

Max stares at Frank as he slinks back into his apartment. "No," he says.

Frank twists one more time, grabs the door, and slams it shut.

"Weird guy," Max says. We continue down the hall to my room.

I just got home from one trip, the last thing I want to do is take another one. "How long am I packing for?" I say to Max.

"For good," he says. "You are moving."

I glare at the back of his head. "Moving? What about all my stuff? I have everything set up just the way I like it." Does he understand how long that took? I can't just pack up and move on a whim.

Max stays silent.

Back inside my apartment, Max keeps his gun drawn and leaves Paige and myself in the kitchen to check each room. Paige hasn't said a word since the parking garage. "Are you okay?" I ask her.

"I'm fine," she whispers. "Just thinking about what happened." She drums her fingers on the counter, over and over again.

Max comes back into the living room from the back. "There's a light flickering in your bedroom," he says. He holsters his weapon.

"So? It's probably just a loose light bulb."

"Probably is. Just thought you would want to know. The suit looks good," Max says.

"The suit? What suit?" I say.

"The Exo Suit, in the display case. I didn't realize you kept the gear once you were finished."

"I still don't know what you are talking about," I say, walking past Max into my bedroom.

"See the light flickering?" Max says to me. His eyes are locked on an empty corner of the room.

There is no display case and no Exo Suit. The program has caused him to hallucinate. What if he hallucinates a threat and kills a human? Would that violate his program? Who would I even contact to figure this kind of thing out?

"This is the suit you used to save the world. I can't believe I actually get to see it. I would have thought it was in a museum," Paige says. She stands in the doorway to my bedroom and stares at the corner too.

Max walks over to the corner and bends forward to get a closer look at nothing but empty air. "Lots of scratches," he says. He points to the empty space about chest height. "This is a big dent," he says. "From a bullet? Did you feel the impact?"

I'm not in the mood to overthink his question. Just another example of two androids who have had their data corrupted.

"No," I say. "I didn't feel it." It gets easier to agree with their version of reality the more I practice.

Max's phone rings. He looks at the screen and turns to us. "I'll be right back." He answers the call in the living room.

This is the first time Paige has seen my bedroom. The fact that I recognize this bothers me. Feels like a worm wiggles behind my belly button. I watch her eyes as she scans the room, her eyes lingering a moment too long on my dresser, on my desk, on the nightstand. Does she imagine what it would be like to wake up here in the morning? Are androids programmed with a desire for sex? I would assume she has the parts for it if whoever made her wanted to convince the world she is real.

Max pokes his head past Paige into the room "We leave in one hour," he says. He still has the phone held to his ear.

One hour? I have to condense my life into a bag and run out of here like a hunted animal in one hour? I don't know what to say. About the move. About the assassination attempt. About all that I have already lost and how I am about to lose my home.

Paige and I look at each other. "We better get started," she says to me. "I'll grab the stuff from the bathroom."

"There's a toiletry bag under the bathroom sink," I say.

"Okay."

I close my eyes and tilt my head to the ceiling. This is too much for me to grasp. I need to be alone. To take a moment to let all of this sink in. To climb up from the hole my thoughts have fallen into.

"Let's get moving, Okada," Max says. He is back in the bedroom and off the phone. "What do you need?"

"Not much I guess. Grab a pair of pants from the third drawer down and one pair of shorts from the fourth."

I grab my suitcase and a light jacket, black and without a hood, from the closet. I put the suitcase on my bed and, together with Max, grab all the clothes I think I will need.

In my suitcase on my bed there are two pairs of shoes, an

athletic outfit, a casual outfit, a pair of pants, my light jacket, and a sweater. Paige places the toiletry bag on top and I zip it shut.

"Do we need anything from the kitchen?" Paige asks Max.

"No," he says. "The new place is fully furnished. Has everything we need." He looks at me. "Ready to go?"

"No. But I am packed and I have a feeling that's what you meant."

# CHAPTER TWENTY-FIVE

DRIVER TURNS the car into a u-shaped driveway, covered by an overhang, in front of a nameless high rise building in the heart of downtown two blocks away from the river walk. I have passed by this building before but have never bothered to go inside.

"We're here," Driver says as he puts the car in park.

I never imagined people could live here.

The valet driver wears white gloves as he approaches the car and opens the passenger side door for Max to get out. As I get out of the car, my reflection in the mirrors that line the overhang above catches my eye. Rows of yellow lights, parallel to the driveway, run the length of the overhang. The air this close to the river smells damp. I begin to go around to the trunk and grab my suitcase before Max taps my shoulder and nods towards the front door. "Our guys will bring your stuff upstairs. Let's get inside," he says.

Everything about the place screams money. The front doors are glass with polished golden handles. It wouldn't surprise me if I found out that a golden skeleton key was used for the locks. "Good afternoon, Mr. Okada," the doorman says with a smile.

Like the valet driver, he also has on spotless white gloves. He turns around, grabs the golden door handle, and opens the door.

"Forget you saw him," Max says to the doorman.

"Yes, sir," the doorman says without a change of expression. He must be used to certain measures of privacy at a place like this.

"How did he know my name?" I ask.

"Everyone knows your name, Corvus," Paige says. I look at her and she rolls her eyes. "You saved the world, remember?"

We walk further into the lobby of the building. A receptionist stands behind a desk to the left and smiles when she sees us. She has on a navy-blue suit jacket and a white button-down. An android would be a perfect candidate for her job, all they have to do is provide information to guests. In front of her, a sign on the desk says "Welcome to the Elenroc Hotel." So that's the name of this place. Max leads us past her, over the wine-red carpet floors, to the elevators in the middle of the lobby.

"So, this is the new place?" I ask Max. He presses the button for the elevator to take us up.

"Yes," he replies.

I never imagined I would live here.

"What about my mail? Will you guys make sure it reaches me here?" I say to Max.

"You still get physical mail?" Paige asks, surprised.

"Not really," I say. "Just wanted to make sure." That was a stupid question. So much of the Postal Service has been automated that they had to cut almost all of its employees within the last ten years. Most of the people who still work for them these days are the ones who make sure the automatic processes stay on schedule.

"Yes," Max says. "We will make sure any physical mail that would have gone to your old place gets sent here, including any packages. After they are all thoroughly screened."

"Makes sense." The 'L' light above the elevator stays lit and there is a loud chime as the elevator doors open. We get inside and Max pushes '19'. The numbers go as high as forty.

Before the doors can close, a young black man with a white toy poodle gets on the elevator and pushes '21'. The silence is tangible. Even the dog seems frozen in time as we wait together in this tiny room to be transported to another level.

On the nineteenth floor Max leads us to room 1901. He places his hand on a scanner. A green light passes the length of his hand twice, from the ends of his fingers to the base of his palm and back again and part of the wall slides up to expose a camera. He maneuvers his face in front of the camera and a moment later the door clicks unlocked.

The front door of the apartment is on the right corner of a large square room. The lights turn on by themselves. The kitchen to the left of the door has white tile floors. Beige carpet begins four feet past an island counter. In the corner opposite the front door is a stairway with an open door underneath. I can see the toilet inside.

In front of us, a black leather couch faces a monitor on the right wall. Perpendicular to the couch is a love seat that faces us and has its back to white shades that cover a large glass door. The railings of a balcony show through the cracks between the individual shades. A coffee table is situated between the couch and the monitor.

The apartment feels brand new yet old, like nobody has been here since it was made and the space has longed for company.

"How long has this place been empty?" I ask. The door clicks shut behind us and I can hear multiple locks engage.

"I don't have access to that information," Max says. "Blackwatch invests in a unit when a new building is built and keeps them as safe houses. Eliana is the only one who would be able to tell you how many times it has been used since then."

"If my memory serves me right this building has been here for almost four years," I say, rolling my bag next to the couch and sitting down.

Max walks around the room while Paige leans against the island counter in the kitchen.

"Okay. So what now?" I ask them.

"Would you like anything to drink?" a synthetic voice asks from nowhere and everywhere.

I look around to try and find the source of the voice. "Who said that?" I say to Max.

"My name is Arcana. But you can reprogram me to whichever name you prefer. I am the intelligence assigned to this space. I am able to do everything from controlling the temperature in the room to preparing you a drink. I can order groceries and make sure they are delivered at the appropriate time or find a recipe online and walk you through it while I use my sensors to help you successfully make your meal. Anything you would like me to do, just ask. If I can't perform the task directly I can find a human who can."

"Who was the last person to live here?" I ask the open air.

"I'm sorry, I can't tell you that."

"How long ago were they here?"

"I'm sorry, I can't tell you that."

"Then what good are you?" I say. So much noise. It is 2049, I should be able to think about what I want and have it done. Other people shouldn't have to hear me.

"Can you disable yourself?" I say.

"If that's what you want," Arcana says.

"Disable yourself."

Paige stares at me. "You don't think she could be useful?" she says.

"I think she is more annoying than anything. Without a body the voice is unsettling," I tell her.

"It's your place, do what you want," Max says. He pulls a stool out from beneath the island and sits down.

The doorbell rings.

"That should be Driver," Max says. "Double check that it is."

There is a screen the size of my hand at eye level to the right of the front door. It shows Driver as he stands outside. I can see him look down the hallway in each direction as he waits.

A message flashes on top of the screen. 'Identity confirmed: Corvus Okada.' There is a small hole for a camera above the screen. It must have scanned my face. The locks disengage and I turn the door handle.

"Thanks," says Driver as he walks inside. He stops to look around. "I like the new place."

"Am I the only one who can open the front door?" I ask Max as I walk back to the couch.

"Alpha Team and you are the only people who can open the door once you are in here. If you are here the door can only be opened from the inside," Max says. "This design lets us turn this place into a panic room in case of an emergency. On the other hand, if you are not here, we can grant access to anyone and they can open the door and come in, even Paige."

I look at Paige then turn back to Max. "Let's set that up later," I say.

# CHAPTER TWENTY-SIX

PAIGE TAKES my credit card to go and get lunch for the four of us. She brings back two Peruvian chickens, white rice, black beans, and corn. Paige and I eat lunch together at the island counter while Max and Driver eat their lunch on the couch. The doorbell rings right after we throw the trash away from the meal.

"Should be the crew," Driver says.

Driver goes to the door, gets scanned, and opens the door for the crew. Five men stream in, all of them wearing the same black tactical outfits as Max and Driver. The first four each have a box in hand. The fifth one carries my monitor.

Max stands next to me. "We were lucky to get a crew today. They will bring up your stuff from the old apartment."

Great. Not only did I have to leave my home but now I have boxes of stuff to deal with. Boxes that I didn't even pack. How will I know which box contains what?

After their third trip, one of the crewmen says, "That's everything. We left the furniture."

"Obviously," says Driver. "What would we do with it here?"

"Just saying," the man says.

The boxes are left unorganized in the middle of the room. I can't just leave them here. I begin to move the boxes from the middle of the room to against the wall between the bathroom door and the stairs. I have no plans to unpack them because if I have to move again I don't want to have to pack up. Maybe the day will come where I am able to live on my own again, in a place that I choose.

Driver begins to help me move the boxes once he realizes where I want them. He places a larger box on top of a smaller one. Wrong. "Leave it alone. I'll do it," I say to him. "It has to be organized."

I have the boxes organized in no time. My monitor sits on top of one of the four stacks. I found my console, holo lenses, and gloves and made sure they are in one of the top boxes in case Marvle is able to reconnect me to Invader Assault.

I grab the bag I brought with me and go up the stairs. I poke my head through a door at the top of the stairs. A small bedroom, with one mattress and a stainless steel dresser. I look into another door to the left and find the master bedroom. It is much larger than the first bedroom. The floor is black carpet and there is a queen-sized bed, without a headboard, in the middle of the room. The stainless steel dresser matches the one in the other bedroom. The rest of the room is empty. So much open space. I roll my bag inside and set it next to the bed.

On the left side of the room is a walk-in closet. On the right side is the door to the bathroom. The bathroom has a porcelain bathtub with golden claw feet and a separate shower with two shower heads. I laugh to myself when I see the bathtub because I know I will never use it. Baths gross me out. The last thing I want to do is sit, surrounded by germs, in stale water. Dual sinks are underneath a large rectangular mirror. I turn the cold water on with one of the golden faucet handles. Laminar flow. I turn the water off, go back to my bed, and sit down. I decide I like the open space. It looks clean. I lie down to let the food settle in my stomach.

I check the time on my phone when I wake up. It is half past seven. I go downstairs. Max sits on the couch with his feet on the coffee table. The news is on TV. He turns around when he hears me come down the steps.

"Feel better?" he asks.

"Yeah. Where is Paige?"

"She went home. So did Driver. Just you and me," Max says.

I go to the kitchen and pour myself a glass of water from the tap. I hold it up to make sure it is clear before I take a long sip.

"Where is your stuff?" I say.

"My stuff?"

"Your stuff. Aren't you staying in the other bedroom?"

"No, I have my own room next door. This place is all yours."

"I thought Eliana said you would be with me 24/7," I say.

"Not exactly. You will be monitored 24/7. This place has sensors everywhere. We can lock the door remotely to make sure you don't leave without a member of Alpha Team."

"So, I'm your prisoner?" I take a drink of water. Max still faces me but doesn't say a word. To fill the silence, I try to change the conversation. "How did you get into this line of work?" I say.

"I was in the Israeli army for ten years. I did similar work for them."

"And how did you get here?"

"Eliana hired me."

"Simple enough," I say. "You don't have any family?"

"They were all killed in a terrorist attack five years ago in Israel."

This is the kind of conversation I try to avoid. "That sucks. I'm sorry to hear that."

162

"Don't be. I found a new family: the congregation."

An android who has been brainwashed? It's not enough that his data has been corrupted, he is also part of a cult.

I finish my glass of water. "Why don't you go to your own room?" I say to Max. "I'm not going anywhere tonight."

Max uses the remote to turn off the TV and sets it down on the coffee table. He places two hands on his knees and gets up. "Okay, goodnight. Call me if you need anything."

It feels good to be alone after a such a long day in the company of people. I sit down on the couch and pull out my phone. Sarah from the Daily Donna show has sent four new emails. I could start a folder with the ones just from her. There are dozens of other emails from people I have never had contact with before.

Marvle has gotten back to me. He says that he hasn't been able to figure out why I can't connect. Last night, he logged into the game lobby early to trace his connection. Wonky was already there. When he scanned his own connection, there didn't seem to be anything wrong. The scan also showed Wonky's connection. He was logged in from the death server. He plugged in his headset and talked to Wonky. Everything seemed to be fine. Marvle thinks Wonky must be a replicated mind. If so, he won't be able to compete with us at the championships. Unless Wonky has an illegal replication and will show up in person on the day of competition. He wants to dig deeper before he says anything to Seth.

I think back to my lunch with Brianne. Could Wonky be an android, placed on the team by Seth to train our team? Worse, what if he was placed there by one of our rivals to gather information about us? My head spins as I try and keep track of the possibilities. I wish everything would go back to the way it was when I could still connect. I respond to Marvle and tell him to keep me posted.

There is also a message from Seth. He has no clue what my message was about. He is grateful that I blew up the ship and he asks if I want to join his team for the Ronin Championships. He thinks we could win. He says it would be good publicity and offers to pay me.

Grateful that I blew up the ship? Seth is an android too? That, or his Sim has been corrupted and responded for him. His program must have switched since his last message. I put my phone on the couch, put my head in my hands, and rub my eyes with the heels of my palms. This is out of control. How can I figure out if the people who believe I saved the world are androids or only corrupted Sims unless I see them in person? I get up, pour myself another glass of water and drink it down in four large gulps.

I look through the boxes and find the one that has Denise's business card. I open a new email and address it to her but I don't know what to write. There is no easy way to say that my world has been turned upside down by corrupted data that could affect her company's androids. I stare at the screen for a full five minutes before begin to type.

Denise-

This is Corvus Okada from Decant, we met at the convention. Random question: Do you know any other companies that make androids? I can't shake the thought that I have come into contact with others after the convention.

Let me know,

-Corvus

EVEN IF SHE says that there are corporations or governments who also use the technology where would that get me?

Around 23:00 I get tired enough to go to bed. I stare at the ceiling for what seems like an eternity, checking the time on my phone every hour. Sometime after 2:07 I am able to fall asleep. I dream about a normal day in my old life, where I go to work and know how my day will go before it unfolds.

# CHAPTER TWENTY-SEVEN

I wake up to a ring from the doorbell. "Good morning," I hear Paige say from downstairs.

"Morning," I hear Max say. The door closes. He must have let himself in earlier.

My phone shows me the time: 8:17. Might as well get up and get the day started. The floor is cold when I step out of bed and my legs are covered in goosebumps as I go into the bathroom, brush my teeth, and get into the shower for a quick rinse. When I get out of the shower the mirror is covered with fog except for a small, clear circle in the center which provides the perfect outline for my face. I left for the conference one week ago. Thoughts about how different my life has become begin to crawl up from my stomach. They claw at my throat as they try and escape.

Everyone knew it was just a matter of time until the technology to replicate human minds would exist. The impact this technology would have on day to day life has been studied and discussed for decades now. Some believed that the androids would try to take over the world while some believed they would have no reason to care about the existence of physical humans. As far as I know nobody ever worried about what would happen if the data got corrupted. Now it has happened and it feels like I am the only one who knows. If I could find the developers of this technology I could get them to help me plug the leak of data that has begun to trickle from the game into their creations. Hopefully Denise can provide some direction on how to find them.

I put my head under the faucet and take a long drink of water. I stand up and look at my face, outlined by the foggy mirror. I have to pretend to be the hero from Invader Assault until I can figure all of this out.

I go into my room and get dressed before I go downstairs. Paige sits on a stool at the island, immersed in her phone, and Max is on the couch with the TV on.

"Good morning," I say, standing across from Paige.

"Morning," she says. Her eyes stay glued on her phone.

"What are you reading about?"

"Articles about how you saved the world. These are pretty negative, they make you out to be a bloodthirsty killer."

"So?" I say. "What does it matter what they think?"

"We need to control the narrative," Paige says. "During the interview."

"What interview?"

"I scheduled an interview with the Daily Donna show. Their producer, Sarah, contacted me last night. I don't know how she got my email address but she was very insistent. Said she had already been in contact with you."

"Bullshit. She has sent me a bunch of emails but I never agreed to an interview."

"Really?" Paige says. She rests her chin in her hand. "Well, one of their people is supposed to be here at ten. They said to be prepared to answer questions specifically about the article that says you are—" she looks down at her phone, "the first of a new breed of American terrorist."

"You have got to be kidding me. Who writes this stuff? The last thing I want to do is an interview..." I look at the time on the stove, "... in forty minutes."

"We can cancel it if you want," Paige says.

Max stands up from the couch. He places both hands on the counter. "Somebody is coming here? Why did you tell them where we are?"

Paige grows smaller as Max leans over the counter, her, and the entire room. "I only told her which building, not which room."

"That hardly makes it any better!" Max roars, pulling out his phone. "Don't do anything else, you've done enough." He walks towards the balcony. I hear him say "Drone" before he goes onto the balcony and closes the door behind him.

"Sounds like Max is going to cancel it," Paige says with timidity. "I thought that as long as they didn't know which room we are in it would be okay." She looks down at her phone to try and hide her red face and swollen eyes.

Max is still on the phone five minutes later when the doorbell rings. I see Driver on the screen and let him in.

"You told them where Corvus lives?" Driver says to Paige. He seems amused. "What made you think that was a good idea?"

Paige blushes. "I don't know," she says. From the quiver in her voice I can tell she is upset.

"Max has his hands full. Drone told me Eliana doesn't care if you do the interview. She has a problem with the crew member who is on their way," Driver says. "Max got Drone to scrub the digital trail so nobody can use the crew member to find out where you live."

"Couldn't they just tell someone where they have been?" I ask.

"Drone already found out that the woman who is on her way over here is cheating on her husband. Unless she wants her husband to find out about the affair she will keep her mouth shut," Driver says.

I put my forehead into my hands as they rest on the counter. "God, I really don't want to do this interview."

"I'm sorry," says Paige. "I thought if we could give everyone a face to go along with the name, they wouldn't hate you."

I tilt my head and look at Paige.

"From what I hear, Eliana thinks the same thing," says Driver. "If the interview can humanize you in the eyes of enough members of the Society the whole organization might be forced to change their stance on killing you. It might make them more open to our idea about what to do with you. She just wishes you had set it up without a crew member coming here."

Paige perks up until she sees my face and realizes I am still upset.

I walk around the island and stand behind her. "Let me see some of these articles you were talking about."

"Here," she says, thankful for the change of topic. She pulls an article up as I lean over her shoulder. Her screen is blank.

Driver places a round disk the size of a plastic lid on the counter. The disk is all black. "Throw it up so I can see too."

"Throw it up?" Paige says. She looks at the disk. "What is that?"

Driver looks at me. He is surprised that she doesn't know what the disk is and even more surprised to see that I don't give him any sign that I know what the disk is either.

"It's a holo generator. Here," he says, holding his hand out for Paige's phone. Seconds later the article is projected into the space above the disk. He hands the phone back to Paige.

CANNOT CONNECT TO SERVER. The black letters are in the middle of a white space the size of a standard sheet of paper.

My jaw drops. I pass my hand through the words and they disappear above my hand, the same way they would if the disk was a projector.

This is the same type of message I get on my console when I try to connect to Invader Assault. Ever since I beat the game my console hasn't been able to connect and androids have started to turn up who think I saved the world. The article Paige sees that I can't is just another way I can't connect to their version of reality. Marvle needs to hurry up and figure out why I can't connect to the game. Maybe then I will be able to figure out why I can't connect to the reality of the androids.

"This article is by a futurist who said that the Invaders could have ushered in a new age of technology if you hadn't blown them up," Paige says.

I realize my mouth is still open and close it.

Paige swipes her phone to the left and begins to summarize another article. "And this article is about the Society. About how they believe the Invaders were the rapture alluded to in Revelations. They have come out and said that you are Satan's pawn and have prevented them from returning to their home in heaven."

She summarizes another article about anti-American activists who claim the Invaders were sent to exact revenge for American tyranny. Then another about white supremacists who swear they are descended from the "white" Invaders. I never realized so many people would be unhappy with someone who saved their world, whether or not it happened in a video game. I guess the game never shows what happens after the credits.

Max comes back into the room. Ignoring me and Paige he says to Driver, "They will be here at ten."

# CHAPTER TWENTY-EIGHT

At 9:45 DRIVER goes down to the lobby to wait for the crew member from The Daily Donna show and escort them to the apartment. At 10:05 there is a knock at the door and Max lets the two of them in. Driver is with a short woman who looks to be in her mid-thirties, built thick, with shoulder length brown hair. Her red-rimmed glasses come to a point at her temples. Before the door can even close Max has led her to the kitchen, set her hands on the counter and begins to pat her down.

"Look through her bag," Max says to Driver.

"I already did in the lobby," Driver says.

"Do it again."

Driver unzips her bag and searches its contents.

The woman scans the room around her with squinted eyes as Max pats her left leg. These are the people who have threatened to expose her affair.

She introduces herself to me as Sarah. "I recognize your face from the broadcast," she says.

"And I recognize your name from all the emails you send me," I reply.

"Funny, I don't remember you responding to a single one," Sarah says, her tone sharp.

"That's because I didn't."

She looks at me with suspicious eyes.

"My name is Paige," Paige says to Sarah who shakes her outstretched hand. "Do you want something to drink?

"No, thank you," Sarah says. "Let's get started shall we?"

She pulls a circular camera from her bag which reminds me of Driver's holo generator and clips it on top of a purple tripod three feet tall. She places the combination on the counter before she turns around and looks at the balcony. "Let's set up so we face the light," she suggests.

I move a stool to the coffee table, opposite the love seat, and sit down. The tripod isn't tall enough on the coffee table to get the camera to the height Sarah wants. "Can you grab me one of those boxes?" she asks Driver pointing to the boxes against the wall. She puts her tripod on the box and adjusts the angle of her camera to point at my face.

Returning to the kitchen, Sarah pulls a computer from her bag, and sets it on the box next to the tripod. She types on her computer and a woman's face shows up on the screen. I recognize Daily Donna from interviews on her show that I catch from time to time.

"So, who exactly am I supposed to interview today?" Donna says to Sarah as she scans the faces in the room.

"Corvus Okada," Sarah says.

"Who?"

"The man who blew up the ship." Sarah rummages through her bag on the island counter.

"He blew up a ship? Is he a terrorist?"

"No, he isn't a terrorist. Remember the alien ship that was above Bodalís? He blew it up and saved the world. We are the first to get an interview with him." Sarah pops a piece of gum into her mouth.

"Alien ships? Are you high?"

Sarah turns to me. "Excuse her," she says.

"No problem," I say.

Donna has no idea what I did in the game! She isn't an android. Well, if she is, her data hasn't been corrupted yet. I need to talk to her. I stay seated on my stool, unsure of how to get her to talk to me without interference from the others. She isn't receptive of the fact that everyone around me believes I saved the world.

The last thing I hear Donna say is "waste of time" before Sarah turns down the volume on her computer.

"Can I talk to her?" I say.

"Corvus wants to talk to you," Sarah says to her computer.

Donna responds but I can't hear what she says.

Sarah moves the computer to the island kitchen. She puts both hands on the counter and tilts her head back. When she turns around I can see her computer screen is dark.

"I'm sorry about this," she says. "Donna wants to reschedule."

"Reschedule?" Paige says. "For when? Sounded to me like she doesn't want to do the interview at all."

"She gets this way sometimes," Sarah says. "Let me call her and try and talk some sense into her."

Sarah pulls a phone from her bag, places the call and paces in front of the boxes while she waits for Donna to pick up. After two laps she hangs up and tries again. Two more laps and she is still quiet. She pulls the phone away from her ear.

"She isn't answering," Sarah says. "Fuck. Does she know what I had to go through to get this interview?" Tears well up in her eyes. She looks at Max. "I keep my mouth shut and you guys won't tell my husband, right?"

Max stares at Sarah.

"That's right," Driver tells her. "Just forget you were here and nobody will ever know."

"Done," Sarah says. She unclips the camera and folds the tripod before she puts them both back in her bag. "This is such bullshit."

"Agreed," I say. I am glad the interview didn't happen, I never wanted to do it in the first place. But I am upset that I didn't get the chance to talk to Donna before she closed the chat with Sarah. I wanted to talk to somebody else who rejects the fact that I saved the world.

Why wouldn't she reject it? If she is a human she will have no clue why Sarah wanted to interview me. And if she has never played Invader Assault she would have no reason to know what the Invaders are.

I don't even know how I would have explained the situation if we had gotten the chance to speak.

"You don't think I saved the world?" I might say. "Great! What if I told you it was from a video game? The data from the game has leaked into androids all around me. Sarah is one of them. There may be more!"

Based on the conversation in my head I know there is no way she would listen to me. No rational person would. She would hang up on me faster than she hung up on Sarah.

Sarah zips her bag closed and slings it over her shoulder. She walks up to me and extends her hand. "I'm sorry we couldn't do the interview. It was nice meeting you. Thank you for saving Bodalís."

"Nice to meet you too." I feel like I should say more but no words come out.

"Walk her down," Max says to Driver.

Sarah and Driver leave the apartment. I move the stool back to the island and Max moves the box back onto the stack.

"That was a waste of time," Paige says to me.

"Don't do that again," I say. "No more interviews. Look at all the problems you caused."

Paige looks at me, her eyes wet, and swallows hard. She gets up, walks onto the balcony, and closes the door behind her.

# CHAPTER TWENTY-NINE

DENISE REPLIES to my email that afternoon. She tells me that Next Level Automation has found a large opportunity in healthcare. She said that their presence in offices and hospitals has led to a vast reduction in the number of doctors required since most problems have a set treatment protocol. The doctors are only needed for the unique cases that lie outside statistical likelihood.

The military also tested the androids but found they are only useful for administrative tasks. The decisions in the field are too complex and require a human mind in order to sort through the information and make a correct decision.

She tells me how, when she first began to work for the company, she lost her ability to believe those around her were humans and not androids. She says that, in time, she learned to trust in the existence of the people around her again because she decided that, even if they were androids, she couldn't cut herself off from the rest of the world forever.

I can't help but think that this reply could have been written by her Sim.

My phone rings at 17:45. I am on the couch with Max in the apartment. An action movie is on the monitor, noise as I wait for the day to end. I never bother to find out the name of the movie.

"Too busy to call your old man?" Dad says. His voice is strained and he grunts as he exhales.

"What's wrong?" I ask him.

"It's nothing. I just had to rearrange myself. Are you just getting home from work?" he asks.

"Normally I would be but I don't work for Decant anymore."

"You lost your job?" he says, his voice rising in surprise.

"Something like that," I say. "I don't live in the same apartment either."

"You had to move out? Couldn't afford the rent?" He grunts again, this time louder but I can tell he tries to suppress it.

"That's not it. It's a long story. Dad, are you sure everything is okay? It sounds like you're hurt."

"I'll be fine. I just fell."

I pull my legs off the coffee table and sit up. "You have to be careful! Did you break anything?"

"I don't think so. Got a good knot on my head though."

"You hit your head? What the hell is the matter with you?! You aren't a young man anymore."

I pull the phone away from my head and mute the microphone.

"Max, we need to go to Miraflores. My dad fell. He hit his head and I need to make sure he is alright."

"Is anyone else there?" Max says.

"No, he lives by himself."

"I'll send Driver to go take him to the hospital," Max says.

After a nod from Max, Driver gets up from the stool next to the counter and puts on his dual chest holster.

I unmute the phone and begin to stand up. "Don't move, we are on the way to take you to the hospital," I say to Dad.

Max doesn't move his legs from where they rest on the coffee table and blocks my path to the door. "You aren't going anywhere," he says.

"What are you talking about? He needs to go to the hospital!"

"And he will. Driver will take him." Max turns back to the movie on the screen. Driver leaves the apartment.

"This is an emergency. You're telling me I can't go help him?"

"Pretty much. You can't just leave whenever you want. Plans need to be made, support needs to be put in place. These things take time."

I don't even know what to say. I stare at him as he stares at the screen.

"Fuck you," I say to the side of Max's face before I sit back down.

"What's that about?" I hear Dad say on the phone.

"I'm not allowed to leave the apartment. Driver is on the way to take you to the hospital," I tell him.

"Who's Driver? And who says you can't leave?"

I tell him about the last couple of days I have had. About how Eliana, who is the head of Blackwatch, who is also the Preacher, has blackmailed me because she has footage of me in the Phoenix Decant before the altercation with the old man. I leave out the part where they all believe I saved the world.

Somehow, through all of this, he only hears I haven't gotten a lawyer yet.

"If you had gotten a lawyer when I told you none of this would have happened!" he tells me.

I'm not in the mood to argue. "If you say so."

"Why do you live in a new apartment?"

I tell him about the assassination attempt in the parking garage underneath my old building.

"Somebody tried to kill you?" he says, surprised.

"Yes, Alpha team saved my life," I say, grateful to Max but still upset that I am his prisoner.

"Are you still seeing Paige?" Dad asks me.

"She works for me now. She went home earlier to study."

"Works for you huh?" His voice drips with sarcasm.

"As my manager," I say.

I get up from the couch and grab a beer from the refrigerator. As I pop the bottle cap off he asks me if I have told anyone about the *androids*. I tell him about the conversation I had with Paige in the car after I walked away from my job. He isn't surprised when I tell him that I needed to be alone that night.

"You've always been like that," he says. "Hell bent on figuring everything out yourself."

Instead of a response I take a long sip of beer and set the bottle on the counter.

"You ever think about getting a tattoo?" he asks me.

I know what he is about to say. His chest is covered in dark black ink. His armor. I have heard about the armor for years now. The tattoos that heal wounds. They use body heat as a catalyst to bind the tattooed skin back together.

"My armor is the reason I wasn't shot!" he says. I imagine his index finger is pushing into his chest on his side of the phone call. "The other guys didn't want to waste their bullets on me! The ink was experimental back then, it has to be even better now."

"That was fifteen years ago. It is better now, you can get any design you want these days. They use skin-colored ink between the black."

"There you go! It might not be a bad idea to look into with people out there trying to kill you," he says.

I take a minute to think it over.

"What happens if I want to leave and get a tattoo?" I say to Max.

He turns on the couch to look at me. "Same protocol applies, we need to get another team here for support. And we need to plan the trip. But, at the end of the day, we will need to get Eliana to approve of the trip."

"Does she need to approve of me going to the hospital to visit my dad?"

"She does. But I can't imagine that would be a problem. A tattoo on the other hand... Personally, I don't see the point. Odds are her opinion won't be any different." An explosion in the movie pulls Max's attention back to the monitor.

Dad has been listening to me talk to Max through the phone. "If she has been paying these guys to keep you alive she should be able to see that it is worth it to get you some of those tattoos," he says.

"They wouldn't be normal tattoos," I say to Max. "They would be the self-healing kind. In case I ever got shot."

"Why would you get shot?" Max says, eyes on the screen ahead. "That's what I'm here for, to make sure it doesn't happen."

"In *case* I do."

"You won't. And if you do I'll take the blame for it," Max says.

"What'd he say?" Dad says on the phone.

"He said I have to get permission from Eliana. Such bullshit."

"You can't leave to take me to the hospital, not surprising you can't leave to get a tattoo," Dad says.

I stay on the phone with him until Driver gets to his house. The trip takes almost thirty minutes.

"Tell your dad that Drone has remotely unlocked the door

and Driver is about to walk into the house. Don't want him to have a heart attack too!" Max says with a chuckle.

I don't find it funny.

"Dad, Driver is about to come in and take you to the hospital. Let me know when you find out how bad it is."

The rest of the evening is a blur while I wait for news. Driver calls Max after eleven o'clock.

"Your dad is asleep," Max tells me when he gets off the phone. "Turns out he fractured his tibia and got a concussion. Since he had a stroke last year they want to keep him until the swelling goes down. He fell asleep right after they gave him a room, that's why Driver called instead of him."

"Okay. Thanks for letting me know. Any chance I can visit him tomorrow?"

"Let me call Prime Team."

# CHAPTER THIRTY

I wake up the next morning when I hear Paige in my apartment. I check the time on my phone: 8:15. Same time as yesterday. I appreciate her consistency. Lets me know what to expect.

As I try to fall back asleep I wonder how Dad is. Was he able to sleep through the night? What have they given him for the pain? Will the swelling in his brain cause him to have another stroke?

Dad taught me to drive back before the driverless revolution, when the ability to drive was still a necessity. He once warned me about the most dangerous drivers on the road. "The indecisive ones," he used to say, "the ones who half-ass their decisions. As long as you stick to what you intend to do other drivers can react accordingly." I feel like that's why I appreciate Paige's consistency. It lets me react accordingly.

Sleep won't be easy to come by today. I throw the covers off and stare at the ceiling. After a big breath I roll out of bed. My feet hit the cold tile floor, my foot arches, and my toes curl up like the legs of a dead spider. I take a hot shower and grab the same clothes I had on yesterday from my open bag at the foot of the bed. "Not like I did anything in them," I tell myself in the mirror before I pull the shirt over my head. Dressed, I go downstairs.

Max is on the balcony. His hands are on the railing as he looks out over the city in the morning light.

Driver is already here sitting at the opposite side of the island to Paige. Steam rises from mugs in front of each of them.

Paige looks up from her phone when she notices me. "Morning. Want some coffee?"

"Sure," I say.

"You know, if you had kept Arcana on, all we would have to do is tell her to make the coffee. It's easy for them," Driver says, taking a sip from his mug.

I look sideways at Driver. "It's too early to be a smartass," I say. He laughs.

"Sorry to hear about your dad." Paige pours and hands me a cup of coffee.

"Thanks." I turn to Driver "Has there been any news?"

"Nothing. When I left last night, he was fast asleep. They said he should be fine, keeping him in is just a precaution."

"No news is good news," says Paige.

The three of us escape into our coffee and our phones. I open the reading app and continue reading my book.

Amanda continued to experiment on herself once she found out that memories were stored in synaptic noise. In one of her experiments she had her team measure which synapses fired when she performed a golf swing. She had the team fire these synapses with the synaptic noise left in. As the virtual avatar swung the golf club, Amanda became immersed in the memory of her first day of work at a lumber yard when she was a teenager. She could smell the fresh cut pine. The memory didn't last long, maybe a few seconds, but each time the synapses to swing the club were fired she could smell the pine. Her team continued to perform random physical activities and measure which synapses fired. They would fire those synapses with the noise left in to see which memories surfaced, to try and find a pattern to explain which memories would surface. They never found a correlation.

The door to the balcony slides open and Max comes inside. "Morning," he says to me. He slides the door closed, sits on the couch, and turns on the news.

Paige finishes her coffee, sets her phone on the counter and goes to the bathroom.

I glance at her screen and see my name buried in a block of text. I reach to my left and swipe down on her screen to see the title. "Coping with PTSD: *An unreal world?*" I read the first paragraph and realize the article is about me. About how I saved the world and have rejected my new reality as a result of the near-death experience. I scroll down to the bottom, to try and see the conclusion she has come to, and find that the essay is unfinished. I scroll back to where she had left her screen right before she comes back from the bathroom and sits back down.

Why would an android try to analyze human thoughts? To understand in order to manipulate? She doesn't know she is an android.

What if I am an android and don't know it? My vision shrinks to a point as the thought grips my mind.

How would I deal with an android who rejected their reality? I would keep them quarantined from the world and try to get them to remember through trusted peers. I am quarantined and Paige has earned my trust. Had earned my trust. This could all be part of some grand scheme to try and get me to remember the events of the game.

*If* I am an android, that is. If I am not, and I don't think that I am, what should I do about the essay Paige has written about me?

The room around me returns to focus, becomes clearer than

I ever thought possible. The edges of objects become more distinct, the colors more vivid – as if I have put on glasses and can now see the world around me with fresh eyes.

The doorbell rings and my thoughts are interrupted. Driver opens the door to a man dressed in the same tactical outfit as himself and Max.

"Prime, I want you to meet Corvus," Max says.

"Ah, Corvus. The man who saved the world," Prime says as we shake hands. Prime is Hispanic, stocky, and about a head shorter than Max. He carries a perpetual smirk, as if he always has a joke on the tip of his tongue.

"Where are the other two?" Driver asks Prime.

"Left them back at HQ. We don't have room for Duds in the car and Eliana figured Tek could help Drone," Prime says.

"Drone lives in that basement," Max explains. He turns to me and says, "The two of them will keep an eye on us through the city's cameras."

We get ready to go. Paige rests her hand on her chin as she watches me get dressed me in the living room. I put on the typical Blackwatch outfit: black tactical sweater, khaki cargo pants, black military boots. Prime slides a bulletproof vest over my head and Max insists I wear sunglasses and a black baseball cap. I hesitate before I put the hat on because I don't want to mess up my hair, but I put it on anyway.

Driver must have snuck upstairs while I got dressed as he walks down the stairs in one of my outfits.

"He will be your body double while we travel," Max says.

"What's up Decoy!" Prime says with a laugh, slapping Driver on the back.

The members of Blackwatch are alert as we get ready to leave which makes me anxious. Is it a bad idea for me to risk the trip? Now that I have their uniform on it all feels so rushed. Have they had enough time to prepare? All of these precautions make me think about the President and all that she must go through before she travels. This already feels like a lot and she must go through orders of magnitude more.

"You look good in that uniform," Paige says to me, her head still planted in her hand.

I give her a thin-lipped smile, disappointed that I have allowed her to integrate into so many facets of my life.

# CHAPTER THIRTY-ONE

THE HOSPITAL in Miraflores is an hour and ten minutes from
the apartment with traffic. The traffic is caused by a drizzle of
morning rain causing drivers to be cautious. It happens every
time the weather isn't pristine. Miraflores is just outside the city
limits of Bodalís to the north. It's a cheap town, covered with
strip malls and potholed roads. Every bus stop along Route 4 on
our way out of the city provides shelter for a homeless person,
sometimes two.

Driver turns into the large parking lot of the hospital, a lazy
ambulance passing us as we pull in. The asphalt is jet black and
the parking space lines are bright yellow. Neither of them look
like they belong next to the crumbled streets of Route 4. Max
drops us off at the front entrance before he chooses a spot close
by. He joins us in front of the hospital and together the five of us
head inside.

The smell of disinfectant and sickness hits me on its way out
the door bringing back the dread I feel every time I go into
hospitals. There is a heaviness in the air that reminds me of the
weight of the decisions the doctors and nurses here make
every day.

Driver leads us past the front desk. "He's on the fourth floor," he says as we approach the elevator. The security guard behind the desk watches our group as we walk past. It looks like he wants to say something before he decides against it.

On the fourth floor I approach the front desk and ask which room my dad is in. "Let me check for you," the nurse behind the counter says as she taps her computer. She has gauged piercings in both earlobes and piercings up the sides of her ears. Her hair which is shaved at the sides of her head is dyed green. Three vertical dots are tattooed on the outside of each of her eyes. "Third door on the left, but the doctor is with him now. Please have a seat and I'll let you know when you can go back," she tells us.

The five of us take a seat in the waiting area around a coffee table. The floors are all polished white linoleum and the walls are white to match. Posters remind us to wash our hands and to make sure we get our flu shot every year. There are two other people in the waiting area who have made sure two empty seats are between them.

Paige types on her phone while we wait. I can't shake the thought that her essay gets longer with each keystroke. I close my eyes and try to ignore her but when I open them again she continues to type.

"Why are you writing about me?" I ask her.

"I'm not writing about you," Paige says, looking at me sideways through lowered eyes.

"I saw the essay this morning."

"I'm messaging my mom if you must know," she says.

"Well now I am asking about the essay I saw on your phone this morning. Why are you writing about me?" I repeat.

She takes a moment before she speaks. The members of Blackwatch are stone faced. Each of them looks around the room, at anything other than us.

Paige sets her phone down on her lap. "First off, why are you looking through my phone. Second, I have been looking for a topic for my dissertation" she says, "and I think I've found it in you. I think your brush with death caused you to reject your reality."

"I looked because I saw my name. You wrote it without asking me. You don't think it's important to tell somebody you are writing about them before you do something like that?"

"It hasn't been *written* yet. I am *writing* it. And I was waiting for the right time to bring it up," she says.

"Is this the reason we spent the day together after we landed in Bodalís? So you could analyze me?" It bothers me that I care if an android has ulterior motives. It bothers me that a small part of me is hurt.

"No! I wanted to spend the day with you. But once I spent time with you I realized there is much more beneath the surface!"

"What if people read it? Everyone would think I was crazy!"

Why do I care what people think?

"I was going to take your name out!" she says. She lowers her head. Then, in a whisper above her breath, she says, "I should've asked you. I'm sorry."

"Yes, you should have." I want to continue the discussion but can't bring myself to stay upset. I wish we were alone.

I open my mouth to resolve our disagreement when the nurse at the front desk calls out, "You can go back now. Third door on the left."

Paige says she will stay in the lobby. Max nods to Driver and Prime and they stay seated while Max gets up and accompanies me.

Dad's room smells like bleach and cheap laundry detergent. The floors are the same white linoleum that is in the lobby.

Across from the doorway is a window half-covered by white blinds. On the left of his bed, which is in the center of the room, is a padded chair covered in fake purple plastic, the kind of chair easy to wipe down and disinfect. The TV on the wall has on an old game show but the sound has been muted.

"How do you feel?" I ask him, sitting down on the chair next to his bed. Max stands just inside the door.

"I feel fine, no reason I can't go home. The doctor is being soft. I fell, that's all. Once the doc casted my leg, I should've been allowed to go home."

"Shouldn't have had a stroke last year," I say.

"Yeah, well, too late now."

"You just been watching TV all morning?"

"It's on but I haven't been paying attention." We all look at the TV. The contestant whose turn it is guesses a letter and, when it isn't present in the mystery phrase, the next person gets their chance to guess.

"Who knows?" Dad says to me, turning his attention away from the TV and back to me. "Have you thought about getting a tattoo?"

"I've thought about it, yes, but they tell me I can't," I say with a nod to Max.

"Who are they to tell you what to do?" he asks, indignant.

"It's not worth the argument," I tell him, "and don't get upset over it. It's my problem, you are still free to do what you want."

"Not really. I am stuck here, aren't I?"

"Very true."

We spend the next half hour talking about the random bull-shit parents and kids talk about when the conversation is only because of shared proximity. When the conversation dies out and neither of us makes any real effort to revive it, I get up and tap Dad on the leg twice. "I'm out of here. Give me a call later and let me know how you're doing."

"I'll see you later, Corvus." He looks at Max and picks up an arm to say goodbye. "Take care," he says.

"Have a good one," Max says as he opens the door for me to lead the way out of the room.

Paige puts her phone back into her bag when she sees us return. "How is he?" she says. There is a trace of timidity in her voice.

"He's good, pissed the doctors kept him here, but fine otherwise."

"I'm glad," Paige says with a weak smile.

"Let's go," Max says with a nod to the other agents. He looks out the window to the parking lot below. "We've been here for too long already."

In the front lobby, Max brings the five of us in for a team huddle.

"I will walk out first," he says and points to me, "and you will be behind me. Driver will follow in your clothes and Prime will bring up the rear."

"Does it matter when I leave?" Paige says.

Max takes a second to think it over.

"Might as well have her walk next to Driver," says Prime. "It will look like they are a couple, sandwiched between security."

"That's what I was thinking," Max says. He stands up, pulls out his phone and, swipes the screen a few times. "Car's on the way," he says.

An ambulance storms in and parks in front of the entrance. The sirens get turned off and the EMTs rush their patient through the automatic double doors. The SUV waits behind the ambulance.

"Shit," Max says. He walks through the automatic doors,

looks left and right, and gets into the driver's seat. He backs the car up and parks the SUV past the exit of the roundabout.

Prime pats me on both shoulders from behind. "Our turn," he says. "Lead the way."

The doors open for me as I walk through at the head of the group. A gunshot rings out when I am halfway to the SUV and I turn in time to see Driver stumble to his right and lean against the wall, his hands around his neck. Blood seeps through his fingers as he tries to hold the liquid in his body. He falls to the ground, face down, surrounded by the pool of blood that has already found its way to the sidewalk.

Paige is already face down on the concrete.

"Get up!" I yell to her. "We need to get to the car!" She doesn't move.

"Move!" yells Prime from behind me, pushing me towards the car.

I struggle to twist myself away from him. I need to go back and check on Paige. I see now that there is a hole where the left side of her face used to be.

"Let's go!" yells Prime. He grabs me with both hands and forces me to the SUV. The sound of another gunshot reverberates inside my head as both Prime and I get into the back seat. I try to get out the door on the other side, to go check on Paige, but the doors are locked.

"Why won't you let me help her!" I yell.

The tires screech against the asphalt as Max slams on the gas.

"There's nothing we can do," Prime says to me. "We're already at the hospital."

I know he's right but I can't help but wish he had worn my clothes instead of Driver.

# CHAPTER THIRTY-TWO

We whip onto Route 4. Prime climbs through the two front seats and sits in the passenger side, staring across the street at places where the shooter could be. None of us say a word. We pass slower cars as we weave in and out of lanes, often times on the wrong side of the street, in order to put as much distance between us and the bodies as possible.

Max looks in the rearview mirror often. He must not see anything important because we never stray from our path back into the city. His eyes meet mine in the glass. "Are you alright?" he asks.

"I'm fine," I lie. Confused, disturbed, even pissed would all be better words to describe how I feel. "What will happen if they are dead?"

"Preacher will send someone out," Prime says, pulling out his phone.

Paige's essay is still on her phone, unfinished. Some of the last words we spoke to each other were when I was upset about that damned essay. Part of me is happy the world will never see it. Why do I care so much if anyone does?

"Eliana," Prime says into the phone. "There was another

assassination attempt. They killed Ludwig and Paige... Paige, the manager." He talks like it was just another day at the office. Like he had to fill his boss in on the day's events.

"Right now, Max and I are en-route to the apartment with Corvus," Prime says. The calmness of his voice doesn't belong, like it is separate from our reality and has chosen this time to make itself known.

"Well, if we got some quality intel we wouldn't have to worry about assassination attempts. Drone and Tek didn't see anything?" Prime says.

"Yes, I know it's our job to protect him with or without the intel. All I'm saying is that those two were supposed to provide surveillance. That includes the tops of adjacent buildings." Prime hangs up the phone.

"I'm sure they did what they could," Max says to Prime. Ever the leader.

"I know. I didn't mean to throw them under the bus like that but she made it seem like it was our fault," Prime says.

"She's right. It was our fault. *Our*. Them included. We are a team," says Max. Silence fills the car again.

A sign marks the outer edge of the city limits but nothing along the sides of the street change. There would be no way for us to know we had crossed the line into the city if the sign wasn't there. Max runs a red light. Tires screech as a car on my right stops just before a direct collision. The car has no driver. Would a human have been able to slam their brakes in time?

On instinct I look around to see if there are any cops who have seen us run the red light. We speed down another block and no police lights come to life behind us. Does Blackwatch have to worry about cops? Have they struck some sort of deal with the police?

I look out the window. Nothing comes into focus as we race through more red lights.

I pull out my phone and see a message from Marvle.

It turns out Wonky does have a replication on the Death Server. Marvle traced one of his connections and it was tied to a physical location, meaning Wonky is real but has another version of himself. He offered to help the real Wonky protect the fact that he has a replicated mind on the death server from anyone else. At first Wonky was upset that Marvle had discovered his secret but he agreed it would be in his best interest to have Marvle help bury the secret even deeper after Marvle let him know that he has an illegal replication as well.

Wonky told Marvle that he has noticed something wrong with his replication. The data has been corrupted and believes the events of Invader Assault are the real world. "I don't know how it could have happened but it seems that his replication believes the Invaders exist," Marvle says, "and without going through the replication process again there is no way to update the version of his mind on the death server."

Marvle says the cloud has been flagging more and more corrupted minds on the death server, all of them obsessed with Invader Assault. There are even reports that people's Sims behave as if the Invaders were real. He hasn't been able to figure out how the Sims and the minds on the death server could share the same corruption.

I read the message twice to try and make sense of it. Marvle has a replication? Will Marvle be able to figure out it all started the day after I beat the game? Maybe the cloud believes I corrupted the minds on the death server on purpose and has blocked me in response. I can't decide whether or not I should tell Marvle my theories. It could help him in his search or he could think I was crazy.

My phone rings. I look at the screen. Dad. I push the button to answer.

"Too busy to call your old man?" he says.

"I just saw you. Someone tried to kill me as I was walking to the car," I say. "They killed one of the security team, the guy who was dressed in my clothes. And Paige," I say.

"The Society!" Dad yells. "They are pissed that you saved the world."

"Don't get worked up, Dad, you need your rest."

"Calm down? They tried to kill you! Is Max taking you home?"

"No, I'm on the way to the new apartment. It's all my fault. If hadn't come to visit you she would still be alive."

"She wouldn't be alive to begin with if you hadn't blown up the ship," he says.

How is this a reasonable response? I am upset and all he talks about is their shared delusion. "Well you know I didn't blow up the ship. They just think I did."

"What do you mean you didn't blow up the ship?"

"I mean I didn't blow up the ship. I thought the people who believe I did were androids but now I am not so sure. Remember?"

"Corvus what the hell are you talking about? You blew up the ship last Saturday, I watched the broadcast!"

I pull the phone away from my ear and stare at it in disbelief. No. Not him. Not Dad. It doesn't make sense. I just saw him! I end the call.

I lay my head back on the headrest and look up at the ceiling. Today's events have left me drained. My thoughts are clouded by a pervasive numbness and somehow are still able to spin out of control. I know for a fact Dad isn't an android. It must have been his Sim on the phone. His Sim, a version of my Dad built on data the cloud has collected for years, has been corrupted. Do the Sims switch in batches or one at a time? I know for a fact Dad has never played Invader Assault so how did the corruption finds its way to his Sim?

I open my phone and turn off data collection before my Sim can be affected by the corrupted Sims. The corruption is the real invader assault.

Anybody I meet could believe, or will believe, that I am the one who blew up the ship. Even my own family. What do they want from me? I know the Society wants me dead. But the rest? Who knows? Invader Assault never showed the world once the game was over. It turns out there are real consequences when you save people who don't want to be saved.

# CHAPTER THIRTY-THREE

Paige -

I have been in my apartment for weeks waiting to hear if Eliana has come to some sort of agreement with the Society of the Stars. They continue to be adamant about the fact that I must die. Prime has taken over for Driver full time on the security team. I think they reassigned the other two members of his team, but I don't know for sure.

Max and Prime are similar in many ways. They are both former soldiers. Both of them always have that military edge to their personality, like my dad. (Dad also thinks I blew up the ship. I haven't figured out how or why but he tries to convince me that it really happened. It reminds me of you.) They have both been with Blackwatch for so long that they have adopted the culture of the congregation into their everyday lives, in particular their reverence for Eliana. Or, as they call her amongst themselves, the Preacher. I still call her Eliana and they don't seem to care either way. Max is more comfortable with silence than Prime. He is able to leave me alone and always has the news on. Whenever Max and I talk, I am the one who engages him in conversation. Prime prefers to chat to pass the time. He will often try to continue a conversation even after it is over and I am ready to spend time in silence. I often wonder if he can't tell that I am done talking or if he just doesn't care.

Max receives updates from Eliana about the progress of negotiations with the Society. He fills me in after each one but each update is the same as the last. For one, it seems they are terrible at communicating. Days go by without any new developments from them. They are insistent on my death each and every time.

I found out last week that the cable guy outside my apartment was a private investigator hired by the Society. His job was to find out when I entered and exited the building. Blackwatch interrogated him back at HQ and he had no idea why his client wanted the information. That's how they found us in the parking garage. I often wonder if they know I am in this building. Do they have someone outside? If so, they must be bored because I haven't left my apartment for so long. It kind of makes me feel good these contractors are still able to collect a paycheck from the Society for doing nothing.

Sometimes, when I think about my current situation, I get upset that people recognize me for what I did in a video game. A game I spent a lot of time playing until it stopped connecting. Video games are something I have always done with my team. Away from people who don't understand. Now it feels like there is this private part of me exposed to the world. Not just exposed, but lauded. It feels like everybody is mocking me. But why would they carry on the joke this long? It bothers me that I even care.

I know you think it was real but I'm telling you it wasn't.

It would be nice if Invader Assault would work. I guess I could play Ronin but I never feel like it. Every time I try to turn on Invader Assault it still says it cannot connect to the server. There is no sign of when it will connect again. I try to keep track of any news involving Invader Assault, specifically looking for any mention of down servers. Apparently, I am the only one who has any problems connecting because there hasn't been any mention of the game not working for anyone else. The page on the gamer blog about Invader Assault normally posts something new every day but the newest content was posted two weeks ago. The page about Ronin is still updated daily and that game is much older. It doesn't make sense.

Before all of this, spending all day at home never bothered me, even if it was all weekend. I preferred to binge on junk TV or play Invader Assault on my days off instead of going outside or hanging out with friends. Now that I am stuck here for the foreseeable future, not by choice, I feel like I should make the best of the situation and learn something new. I have been cooking a lot. I find new recipes online and try them out in the evenings. Even when they don't come out quite right they have still been edible. I am still waiting for one to be so bad that I have to throw it away.

When I am not cooking, I pass the time reading and playing older video games. I finished the biography of Amanda West. It's amazing how she was able to figure out how to upload consciousness. Rumor has it her mind lives on the death servers. I have started to read The Brothers Karamazov. It's an old book but they say it's a classic. We will see how long it takes me to get through. I have a new-found appreciation for music as well. Jazz, classical, and blues. Music I had never taken the time to appreciate. Anything to take my mind off the awareness of my situation helps. Existing in my skin while I am stuck here has started to become uncomfortable. Losing time is key. Between cooking, reading, and music I have found my own prescription to maintain my sanity.

I feel like you have been with me in the apartment. You remind me of what having a cat would be like. Content in coexisting, communication optional. Silence doesn't bother you does it? It mustn't, you have been silent the whole time we have been here. You read a lot to pass the time, more often than I do. I like that about you. It inspires me to make myself a better person. Did you know that? I haven't told you yet, so how could you know? But I am telling you now. You have been great company and I thank you for that.

Were you pretending to get along so well with me so that you could analyze me? Because you believed I was the one who blew up the ship? Did you see fame and glory in your future once you published your paper? Please let me know when you are ready. Which may be never but I am okay with that because your silence is a part of you.

I know how serious my situation is but it still doesn't feel real. I do know your death was real. Which means the guns are real. The numbers in my bank account are real. This has all been taken too far to be one big, elaborate joke. The change in reality has taken everything from me. My game, my job, my freedom, and you.

-Corvus

# CHAPTER THIRTY-FOUR

Max is on the couch and the news is on the monitor when I walk downstairs in the morning. Last night, after the grocery delivery, I put a pound of bacon into the refrigerator. The bacon was in my dream last night. I might as well fry the whole package now. Max might want to eat whatever I can't finish. If he doesn't want it, I can just save the rest for later today or tomorrow.

The tile floors in the kitchen are cold on my bare feet. I still wear the sweatpants and t-shirt that I slept in last night. It has been almost two weeks since I decided to ignore my morning routine of shower, brush, dress, though I still brush my teeth first thing in the morning from fear of the dentist.

The frying pan is hot on the stove. I lay the strips of bacon down one by one. The meat sizzles and the fat begins its slow creep until it covers the entirety of the pan. The fat begins to bubble and pop on the surface. It reminds me of a documentary I watched last week about fish in the Amazon. They jumped from the water, frenzied and aggressive, in search of food. Instead of food they found the floor of boats that passed by, full of tourists. I turn the strips over with a fork, mesmerized by the fat. A drop leaps from the surface in search of food and lands on my arm. It burns but I don't pull away.

The pain is gone in a flash but now my two arms are unbalanced. The right one has been burnt but the left is still untouched. I look down at my left forearm. Should I let it hover over the pan until a drop of fat leaps up to feed? It is important that I re-establish equilibrium, but what happens if two drops of fat decide to leap at the same time and land on my left arm? Then I would need to burn my right arm again and I could get caught in a balance loop of pain that ends with my hand in the fat, palm down.

The bacon is crispy on the edges before I can make up my mind on whether or not to pain balance my arms. I pull a plate from the cabinet and cover it with paper towels to soak up the grease before I take the strips of bacon from the pan and lay them one by one on the plate. I pour some of the fat from the pan into a styrofoam cup that is on the counter from either Max or Prime and fry four eggs. The eggs sizzle and crack as soon as they hit the hot pan. It takes no time for the eggs to cook which leaves me no time to decide whether or not to burn myself. Once the eggs are done and onto a separate plate I look down at the hot pan and decide it will be okay if I am unbalanced. It was just a flash anyways.

I put four strips of bacon onto the plate with my four eggs. I slide the plate with the rest of the bacon across the counter. "You want some?" I say to Max.

"Sure," he says. He gets up from the couch, pulls out a barstool, and sits down with me while I eat my breakfast. After his second piece of bacon his phone rings. "Preacher," he says to me after he checks who the call is from. He answers the phone on his way onto the balcony.

I finish my food and begin to clean the kitchen. Max comes back inside just as I finish the dishes.

"We need to go down to HQ," he says. "No rush though. There have been some developments Preacher wants to go over with you in person."

"Let me wipe the stove and I will get dressed," I say. This will be the first time I have left the apartment since the day that Paige was killed over three weeks ago. Max and Prime are the only two people I have seen this whole time but, if they didn't have to be here, I would have preferred to be alone.

It takes me half an hour to shower and get dressed by which time Prime has arrived at the apartment.

There is no traffic at 11:00 on a Sunday. I get a message from Marvle while we are in the car. The championships are today, downtown at the convention center. "Will you be there?" he asks. I didn't even realize what day it was.

I lean over and turn to Max. "Could we go to the convention center after the meeting with Eliana?" I ask him.

"The convention center? No way. The Society is still trying to kill you. You could ask the Preacher but I am sure she will agree with me," Max replies.

"I'll ask her," I say. The first thing I care to do in three weeks and they have to remind me that I am their prisoner. Eliana is the warden, they are just the guards.

We pull up to HQ, the gate opens, and we drive up through the manicured lawn. Two guards, the same two as the last time I was here, escort me out of the car and upstairs into Eliana's office. They seem to be more relaxed this time around.

Max and Prime come into the room and stand behind me. Goosebumps originate on the crown of my head and run the length my spine when I see the chair Paige sat in the last time I was here.

Eliana walks in five minutes later. It must be part of her

routine to make her guests wait. She walks around to her side of the desk and stands in front of the window that overlooks the lawn.

"How have you been?" she says, shaking my hand.

"I've been good. Holed up in the apartment but I'm sure you already knew that," I say.

"Yes, I did know. I am sorry for your loss," she says.

I am not sure what reaction she expects so I say nothing. She stares at me with dull eyes. Both of her hands rest on her desk, palm down, fingers splayed. Her nails are painted a red so dark at first glance it appears black.

Eliana clears her throat. "We have come to an agreement with the Society. They will stop trying to kill you," she says.

"What made them change their mind?" I ask.

"We assured them that we plan to let the Invaders decide what to do with you once they return. We had told them before but they didn't believe us," she says.

"You will offer me as a sacrifice is what you mean. And what am I supposed to do until then? Wait in the apartment until the Invaders return? This is ridiculous. I have been in there for weeks now. What about Paige's death? And Driver's? Aren't you going to make them pay?"

"We killed one of theirs already in the parking garage. Plus, revenge isn't always the best solution. We saw a way to stop the assassination attempts and took it. Simple as that." She walks over to a mini-fridge disguised as a cabinet in the far corner of the room, pulls out a bottle of water and holds it in my direction. "Water?"

"No. I don't want water. I want the Society to pay for killing Paige. And I want my life back." I point with my thumb to the two agents behind me. "I am tired of having them with me all the time!"

"You could wait in prison," Eliana says, as cold as the water in her hand. "We still have the video of you in Phoenix. I will make sure they throw you behind bars if that's where you prefer to wait."

I squeeze my fists so tight I can feel my fingernails dig into my palms. I don't need to look at my hands to know my knuckles are white. I exhale and relax my hands. "I don't want that," I say, defeated.

"Didn't think so," Eliana says. She sits back down in her chair. The sky outside the window behind her is a bright blue, not a cloud in sight.

I look at Eliana. "I have a request," I say. "The championships are today, at the convention center in downtown Bodalís. Since the Society has stopped trying to kill me do you think I could go?"

"Not possible," she says. She leans forward, folds her hands together, and rests her interlocked digits on her desk.

I lean forward in my chair as well. "Look, I have done everything you have asked. You can ask these two, how much easier could their job be? It would only be for a little bit. Plus, you said the Society agreed to stop the assassination attempts. What's the big deal? Alpha Team can protect me."

Eliana looks past me to Max and Prime. I don't know the information that passes between them but, when she looks at me again, she nods in consent.

"One hour," she says. "Then you go back to the apartment."

A nicer way to say that I have to go back to house arrest. "One hour." I rise from my chair. "Let's go," I say to Max and Prime as I walk out of the room.

Two thoughts run through my head:

One, how can she even trust the deal with the Society? What if they agreed to the terms so that I would leave the apartment? It could be a trap. They could still want me dead.

Two, if they do still want me dead, can I even trust Blackwatch to protect me? Paige was killed on their watch. Their own member was killed on their watch. I could do better on my own.

# CHAPTER THIRTY-FIVE

THE LINE TO drop off passengers in front of the convention center is dozens of cars long. We take our place at the end of the line as Max wants us dropped us off as close to the entrance as possible. I watch the people in the park on my left through the tinted car window. Children play soccer and frisbee on the lawn. Parents sit on benches underneath trees that line the outside of the lawn. There is a playground packed with children who traverse the monkey bars and wait for their turn on the slide. I have never understood the appeal of the outdoors. Some people crave it. Why be exposed to the elements? Why be outside when I could stay in comfortable, climate-controlled buildings? I am glad the families can enjoy it but the outdoors was never for me.

Players from last year's championship team walk by on my right, bunched together. Every last one of them has headphones on. Even if I didn't recognize their faces it is easy to recognize their maroon sweat jackets. Each team is assigned a different color jacket by the committee that organizes the event where they can put their logo on the back, and they are careful not to walk too close to the team in front who wear yellow. I still have last year's black jacket which *should* be in a box near the bathroom in the new apartment. Even if I had known where it was I wouldn't wear it. I don't want to act like I am on the team when I haven't played with them for weeks now. Plus, I don't know if we were assigned the same color as last year.

It is our turn to be dropped off.

"Do we need to get tickets?" says Prime as we head towards the entrance to the convention center.

"Yeah, we will need to swing by the ticket counter on our way in," I tell him. We walk through a set of glass double doors into the center.

The railings on the edge of each of the four floors are visible as soon as we walk inside. The ground floor is twice the height of each of the other levels and is covered by short blue carpet. Large blue pillars, connected to the edge of each level, run from the ground to the ceiling above the fourth floor. Escalators on our left and right rise between the levels on the outside edge of each. The moving railings of another escalator that descends into the floor below is in front of us. A large vertical banner hangs from the second-floor railing. "Welcome to the Invader Assault Championships!" The sign has an arrow that points down. Stepping off the escalator we buy our tickets, get red spectator bands around our wrists, and are waved through.

Past the counter is a series of booths that reminds me of a marketplace. Booths of all sizes offer different types of Invader Assault gear. T-shirts, banners, posters, and Exo Suits are all on display. I have seen this all before and know that none of it is worth the money. "Have you seen anything like this before?" I turn and say to Max and Prime as we walk through to the warm up area on the other side.

They both say no. People stare at me as I walk by but the sight of Max and Prime is enough to make sure nobody approaches me.

"My team should be in the warm up room right now. I have to find a way to pass security and get inside," I say.

"*We* have to find a way to get in there," Max says. "You can't go in without us."

"Why not? It's not like I can do anything back there," I say. "Besides, there's no way they will let *you* in. You don't know the etiquette. Your presence would throw the players off their game."

"Doesn't matter," says Prime. "Where you go, we go."

"Fine," I say.

We go through the marketplace and find the warm up room. I begin to walk past the lone security guard like I belong there but he sticks his arm out to block my path. The two agents behind me make it difficult to walk by without any extra attention.

"Credentials?" he says. I get the feeling that he recognizes me.

I look down and act surprised when there isn't a badge around my neck. I point into the warm up room. "I must have left it back there," I say.

"Can't come in then," the guard tells me. He looks away from me and stares at the wall ahead of him.

We don't move.

"You can't stand here either. Have one of your crew bring it out for you," the guard says.

I walk down the hall, further away from the booths, and sit down on the floor. I pull out my phone and message Marvle. I tell him I am outside the warm up area and that I want to say hi.

Marvle comes out two minutes later. He looks towards the booths before he turns in my direction. I get up from the floor as he walks towards me.

"Raven! How have you been, man? It's been a while," he says.

We greet each other and I introduce him to Max and Prime.

"Too bad you aren't playing with us this year," he says.

"Yea, I haven't been able to connect to Invader Assault for so long I forget what it feels like to play."

"Invader Assault? What's that?"

"The game? This *is* the championships," I say. "What did you think you were here to play, Tetris?"

"Ronin..." says Marvle. He looks as confused as I feel. "Look, I just wanted to come out and say hi. The match is in fifteen minutes. Let's talk later. Meet me in the coffee shop on the ground floor in forty-five."

"Sounds good. Good luck, man," I say.

Marvle turns to go back into the warm up room. I call to him, "Marvle, one last thing." He turns around. I point to a poster on the wall with the cover of Invader Assault, a black and white picture of a spaceship over a city skyline. "What is on that poster?"

"The special edition cover of Ronin." He flashes his credentials to the security guard and walks back in. The guard looks at me with a smug look on his face.

Fuck. Marvle is an android. His data has been corrupted. How many people here are androids and see Ronin instead of Invader Assault? If Invader Assault had never existed then this *would* be the weekend for the Ronin championships.

Max and Prime are behind me. Their faces scan the crowd while I am confused about which game everyone is here to see. I point to the poster on the wall. "What do you see on that poster?" I say to them.

"Excuse me?" Max says.

"What do you see on the poster?"

"Is this a trick? It is a samurai in the ready position. Hair covers his face. Lightning in the background," says Max.

I turn to Prime. "And you see the same thing?"

He nods.

Am I the only one here for Invader Assault? I want to run through the marketplace, ask every person if they are here to watch Ronin, but I am scared to find out that the answer is yes and they are all androids.

# CHAPTER THIRTY-SIX

Max, Prime, and I take a seat in the middle of the dark auditorium to watch Marvle's match. The auditorium was built for E-sports and I read on the plaque outside that it can seat just over five thousand people. The dimness in the auditorium reminds me of a large movie theater before the main feature begins. There is another, more informal, area down the hall to watch the action. It is well lit and has aluminum stadium seats. Dad preferred to watch our match from in there last year. He enjoyed the beer vendor that walked up and down the aisles and yelled "Beer here!" the way it's done at baseball games.

A dull glow fills the room when the blank, white screen in front comes to life. Applause rings out as the two teams of four stream in. Their profiles are illuminated by the white screen before they take their seats. Each of them has their own monitor in front of them. The large screen in front is for the audience. The players remove any hats or headphones they have on and put on the headsets that will allow them to communicate with their team.

The countdown begins. "3... 2... 1... GO!"

The screen turns red. The death screen.

I look at the crowd around me. All of them are androids, enthralled by whatever it is they see on screen. Their eyes dart from left to right as they try and follow the action that exists for them and not for me.

I lean to my right. "See anything?" I say to Max.

"Are you going to ask me this all day?" he says. "There are a bunch of guys running around with swords."

Ronin. Of course. The crowd gasps and then cheers. One of the players up front stomps his foot in disappointment.

All I see is red.

I scan the crowd again. I am the only one not focused on the action up front. It feels like I am the lone tall person in a crowd and can see over and past what everyone else can. They aren't aware of the true nature of reality.

I don't want to stick around and stare at the death screen for the length of an entire match. "Let's go," I say to the two agents. The three of us get up from our seats and leave the auditorium. The people we have to pass on our way to the aisle get annoyed with us for the interruption when the game has just started. Some of them don't even move their knees. Each person leans to the side before and after we pass so they don't miss a second of the action.

We walk back through the marketplace to the escalator that takes us up to the ground floor. I watch people nudge their friends when they see me walk by. They must recognize me as the man who blew up the ship but Max and Prime are enough of a deterrent to keep them away. When we get to the ground floor, I ask one of the workers to point us in the direction of the coffee shop. It turns out the coffee shop Marvle wants to meet in is a Decant store on the right side of the aisle. I haven't been inside a Decant since I left the company.

The store has a gate that wasn't rolled all the way into the ceiling. My place in line leaves me underneath the gate. The tile floor in front of the service counter covers just enough area to accommodate a few snack displays. They don't have any mugs or whole bean coffee for sale. All of the seats are part of the convention center, on the carpeted floor outside the gate above me.

I get to the register and order my usual – medium iced coffee, black – before moving to the other side of the counter.

The same drink I ordered in Phoenix. I think about the one punch that killed the old man. Why did I do that? Eliana would have nothing to blackmail me with if I never punched him. I look at Max and Prime as they order. I wouldn't have to deal with these two all the time. On the other hand, Alpha Team has saved my life twice now. The four dead bodies I have seen flash before my eyes. The old man, the assassin in the parking garage, Driver, and Paige. Why did she have to analyze me?

The barista hands us our drinks. Max and Prime both got small black coffees. We find open seats and sit down in three of four available cushioned chairs around an empty coffee table. I pull out my phone and open the reading app to kill the time until Marvle gets here. I can't find any focus on the words in The Brothers Karamazov. All I think about is the four dead bodies. Before I witnessed them, I had never even seen one dead body. Well, I did once. At the funeral for my grandma. But that's it. And that was different. She was dressed up and made up to hide the fact she was dead. I think the blood is what bothers me. I didn't just see their dead bodies. I was there when they died. Hell, I even killed the first one.

I re-read the same paragraph three times before I decide to give up. I open the news and try to read that instead.

A hand touches my shoulder while I read an article about new drugs that minimize synapse degradation in the years prior to upload onto the death server. The contact startles me. I pull my shoulder down out of instinct and turn to see who it is that thinks they can touch me. Marvle moves his hand to the back of my chair.

"Hey, man," he says. "It's just me. I'm going to grab a drink, I'll be right back."

Max and Prime watch him like a hawk as he walks away.

Marvle comes back with a hot drink in his hand. He stands next to my chair. "Did you win?" I ask him.

"Yeah. It was an easy match, only our second of the day." Max and Prime are on each side of me and the only open chair is across from me. I can tell that Marvle doesn't want to sit there. He doesn't know these two and I know that authority figures make him wary because of what he does on the side with the Onslaught Agency.

There is an open table right behind me. I point to it with my chin. "Want to sit there?" I ask him.

Marvle nods and pulls out a seat at the table. I get up and join him.

Max also gets up but he sits in the empty chair that faces the table so he can keep his eyes on me.

Marvle puts his backpack on the ground. "Were you able to find anything out about why I can't connect?" I ask him. Does he even remember the message he sent me?

"Connect to what?" he says.

"Invader Assault."

A confused look creeps onto his face. He doesn't remember.

"You mentioned that before," he says. "I don't know what that is."

Should I explain the whole situation to him? "Do you think I blew up the ship?" I say.

"The whole world watched the broadcast," he says.

"So, is that a yes?"

"Yes, I watched you blow up the ship. What are you getting at?"

"You wouldn't believe me if I told you. Do you have your computer?"

"It's in my backpack." He reaches down and pulls it out.

"Can you look up the last messages we sent to each other?" I say.

He types onto his computer and turns the screen to face me. "Here."

I see the message he sent to me about the Wonky's replication. I point to the message. "That one."

"What about it?"

"That's the last one you sent me. At the end you said you would try to figure out why the Sims and the minds on the death server share the same corruption. You were going to let me know if it had anything to do with my inability to connect to the game."

"That message is about team practice. The one you didn't show up to," Marvle says.

We both see a different message. This will get me nowhere.

"Never mind, it isn't important."

"No, tell me," Marvle says. He turns the screen back to face himself.

"Okay, but you won't believe me." I take a second to decide where to start. Before I can begin two teenage girls walk up and stand next to our table. They don't say a word until one nudges the other forward with her elbow.

"You're Corvus Okada aren't you?" the girl says.

I look at her and nod.

"Can we have your autograph?"

"Now? Can't you see I'm in the middle of something?" I say.

Their faces drop and I feel a pang of guilt. I change my mind. "Fine. Do you have marker? What do you want me to sign?"

They each pull out an Invader Assault poster and the first

girl hands me a marker. I have a feeling they both see Ronin posters. "Ronin?" I ask them. They both nod yes.

Marvle leans forward. "Want my autograph too?" he says to the two girls.

"Who are you?" the girl who pushed her friend says. The two teenagers look at each other and shrug their shoulders.

"Never mind," Marvle says and gets up from his chair. "Watch my computer, I'm going to the bathroom," he says to me. I get a glimpse of how red his face is before he walks away.

"There you go," I say to the two girls. "See you around."

"Thanks!" the two of them say between giggles as they scurry away.

I take the opportunity to take a look at the messages on Marvle's computer. All of our messages about my inability to connect to Invader Assault are there. The message about Wonky. The messages he can no longer see.

There is a bundle of files about Invader Assault. These have no doubt been lost to him as well. One of the files tracks the number of corrupted Sims over time. The numbers are displayed on a list and have increased each time they are measured once per day. There are now over three million corrupted Sims. There is a tab to display the numbers on a graph. I click it and am stunned to recognize an exponential function. I look at a calendar and realize it's been 28 days since I beat the game. Some quick math to find the $28^{th}$ root of three million spits out a two with multiple zeroes after the decimal point. The corruption has increased at a rate of $2^n$, where n is the number of days since I beat the game.

Another quick calculation and I find that, if the trend continues, the entire world will have their Sims corrupted on the $33^{rd}$ day.

"What the hell are you doing man?" Marvle yells. He has

come back from the bathroom. I close out of the Invader Assault bundle just before he grabs his computer away from me.

He types on his computer while he stares at me over the top of the screen. "I saw you typing," he says. "Why does it say there weren't any keystrokes?"

How do I explain the fact the files I looked at don't exist for him? "Beats me," I say.

"What were you looking at?" he demands.

"I just read our past messages. That's all."

He slams his computer shut and looks at me like he doesn't believe me.

"Stop!" Prime yells behind me. I turn around and see him draw his gun. I look where he aims at a man who runs towards me. He has something in his hand. Prime shoots, the man falls, and the explosion overwhelms all of my senses.

My ears feel like they have been drilled into and whoever has done it is trying to pull the drill bit straight out against the threads. I roll over, prop myself on my elbow, and look around. Pain blurs my vision. Marvle was between me and the blast. His body is thrown over the table in an unnatural position, limbs bent in weird angles. There is a hole in the side of his shirt that exposes tattered skin and flesh.

Max and Prime are both on the ground. They didn't have a body in front of them to shield them from the blast. They begin to stir as I get on one knee.

The blast flipped the table over. The computer pokes out from underneath, slightly open. The screen is cracked but I can still see the thread of messages. I grab the computer and stand up. I try to take a step forward, stumble, and catch myself before I fall. Before the two agents can get to their feet I run, as best I can, with the computer, towards the back of the convention center.

# CHAPTER THIRTY-SEVEN

OUTSIDE THE BACK of the convention center, I pull out my phone and order a car to pick me up two blocks away. My plan is for the car to be there before me so that I can open the door and jump right in. A street runs along the length of the building and traffic is at a standstill as hundreds of people stream away from the convention center. It will be tough for the authorities to get here with this much traffic.

My chest burns and I look down to find blood down the front of my shirt. I poke my chest and wince. After I search with my index finger I know that none of the wounds are too deep but there are a lot of them. In any other situation I would go straight to the hospital.

The car isn't at the corner where I told it to pick me up. Traffic is at a standstill here as well as two blocks away so I pull out my phone and check the status of the car. It says that it is three minutes away. I decide to wait for the car to arrive. Nobody pays attention to me and my blood-covered shirt. People around me still try to put as much distance as possible between themselves and the convention center and people in vehicles are more worried about the traffic. Cars honk and the sound seems like it was created underwater. Three minutes pass. Then five minutes. I check the status of the car and it still says three minutes away. Traffic hasn't budged. I cancel the car from my phone and walk away from the convention center with the rest of the crowd.

Did the blast kill Marvle? If he is still alive he will be upset when he finds out I took his computer. Or maybe he will be happy I took it. It's better that I have his computer instead of the authorities.

A clothing store called Parallax is on my right. The glass windows look like nobody has bothered to remove years of hard water buildup and are difficult to see through. I can't decide if the look is on purpose or not. I need to change out of this blood-stained shirt before anybody asks any questions. A small bell jingles when I walk through the door and into the store.

"Help," I say. I try to sound much more injured than I am. I am bent over, one hand on my stomach and the other holds the computer. "Help."

Piles of clothes are on tables around the store. They are all arranged by size and folded with crisp lines. I spot the table full of men's medium shirts. Every color is represented but there is no discernible pattern to which color is where. The table of pants is arranged by waist sizes with rows of different lengths. Doesn't look like there is any pattern to the color or style on this table either. It reminds me of the way a thrift store will throw similar sizes together and let treasure hunters comb through to find a gem among the piles. For all I know this could be a thrift store I have never heard of.

An associate emerges from behind a pile of large women sweaters and walks towards me. He is a young man, hispanic, both arms covered with tattoo sleeves and shorter than most. He has an unfolded red sweater in his hand. As soon as he sees me he puts the sweater on a pile of kids shorts. It doesn't belong there. "Oh my god, are you alright?"

"There was an explosion at the convention center," I tell him.

"Let me call for help!" He pulls out his phone.

I pick my chest up and pretend to have just seen the blood on my shirt. "Do you have paper towels in the back?" I say.

"Yes, I do. Let me grab them." The young man runs to the back.

I grab a black t-shirt and a black hooded jacket from two separate tables and leave the store. I don't think I have ever stolen before but I don't want Drone to trace the transactions from my card. Has he started to look through the street cameras to find me yet? There are still enough people, enough of a commotion, for me to get lost in the crowd outside the store.

The crowd begins to thin after I cross the street a block away. I turn around and see the young sales associate outside front door of the clothing store. He looks left and right but can't find me. I hope he doesn't get in trouble for the theft that happened on his shift but I don't see how they could have an accurate inventory of the piles of clothes. I turn right and there are three other people who walk the sidewalk on the block with me. No more than I would expect if this was a random Sunday. I walk one block further and turn into an alley to take off my shirt and inspect the damage the blast did to my chest. The edges of the cuts are jagged and the blood has already begun to clot at the edges. The middle of the wound is still wide open. I probably need stitches. I put the new shirt on, zip up the jacket over top and throw the bloody shirt into a dumpster.

Back on the street I can see the cars move along the roads, unaffected this far from the convention center. I turn to the left and see a group of people who wait to cross the intersection. They don't seem to be in a rush. When I was closer to the convention center everyone ignored the traffic signals in an effort to put as much distance as possible between them and the explosion. The effects of the blast don't reach this far away.

The Society will come for me again. The explosion had to be them. Who else would it be? I knew the deal with Eliana was a trap, they just wanted to get me to leave the apartment. How upset is Eliana right now? Does she even get upset? If I had to guess, she is the type of person who internalizes their rage and formulates their revenge.

Now I have to worry about Blackwatch *and* the Society as they try to find me. I feel exposed without Max and Prime next to me but the two agents always seem to draw unwanted attention. Maybe the fact that I am alone will make it easier to disappear, to stay under the radar.

I sit down on the sidewalk, set the computer on the ground, and lean against the building. There is nowhere for me to go. I won't go back to the apartment, I've had enough of the two agents with me all the time. A part of me wants to go back home but I can't go back to my old apartment either. I could go to Dad's house but that is another place they will look right away. If Paige was still alive I would go to her place. To tell her goodbye, to let her know I will have to hide out and that she won't hear from me for a while. I'm sure they would look for me at her place if she were alive. But she isn't so it doesn't matter.

This would be a good time to call on a friend if I had any. All of my friends are online and most of them were back at the convention center. Marvle was the guy I would have called in a pinch and odds are he is dead. There has to be someone I can call, someone I can rely on in my time of need.

There isn't. I am alone. I need to figure this out the same

way I figure everything else out: on my own. Across the street from me is a park. What if I just sleep outside? Homeless people do it all the time. I think about the homeless people who hang out in my favorite Decant. Should I become one of them and live my life off the grid?

I pull my phone out to look up the location of the closest Decant. Before I search a thought hits me like a ton of bricks. My phone can be traced! My pulse quickens. What if it has already been traced and they know where I am right now? I stand up and throw my phone against the concrete as hard as I can. I stomp on it, as if it were on fire, until it shatters into dozens of tiny pieces.

I pick up the computer and search the streets, looking for a black SUV, even though I don't even know what kind of car the Society provides for their agents. I grab the computer from the ground and begin to run. I need to put as much distance between myself and the shattered phone as possible. Each breath causes the wounds on my chest to split open and pull the corners of skin further apart.

I stop when my lungs tell me I can't run anymore. This area looks familiar. Trees line the streets and solar panels cover the houses. Some of the panels have been allowed to collect pollen and leaves and others are immaculate. This is the same part of town where I had lunch with Paige after the flight back from Phoenix. I couldn't say which house holds the restaurant, or if the restaurant is even on this block, but this has to be the same part of town. I find a sign for the underground station close by and catch my breath as I walk there. Chances are there is a Decant close to the station, the company tries to make itself available to morning commuters. The skin on my chest tightens now that it isn't stretched with large breaths.

Outside the station I ask a passing woman where the closest

Decant is. "Two blocks that way," she says as she points towards the sun. Her eyes are glued to my shirt.

I look down and see my jacket has become unzipped. Flecks of blood have seeped through my shirt. For all she knows it could be sweat. "Thanks," I say, zipping up my jacket and walking the two blocks to Decant.

# CHAPTER THIRTY-EIGHT

THERE IS an open seat in the back of Decant. I sit down and exhale, grateful for the familiarity. The usual smell of coffee and caramel, the usual jazz, even the usual sounds of the grinder and the chatter of people who spend the afternoon with friends; all take the edge off and help me find my center.

I set the computer on the table and open the screen, careful not to do any further damage. I am surprised to find there is no password protection. I know Marvle and it is a complete fluke his computer even works without some sort of security. The blast must have caused the computer to stay unlocked. I navigate through the menus on the cracked screen until I find the graph that displays the number of corrupted Sims in the world. Three million. I stare at the screen and try to make sense of the situation. I glance at the power levels and realize I don't have the charger with me. I turn the brightness of the display down to zero even though there is still 56% battery. I don't want to shut the screen. If I do it could trigger the computer to turn on the password protection, but if I keep the screen on it could run out of juice before I am able to finish my research into what Marvle has found out. I can't catch a break today. Even though, now that I think about it, the fact that I was able to survive the explosion and get away from not one but two Blackwatch agents with a computer that should be locked but isn't has been a phenomenal stroke of luck.

Over three million. What is the population of Bodalís? I have no idea. If I had my phone I would look it up. Have all the Sims in Bodalís been corrupted? If I wanted to take the chance I could always use Marvle's computer. But is it worth it? No, it's not. I think back to the people I have come into contact with since the night I beat the game. Every one of them believed the events had happened in the real world. Except Daily Donna. She had never heard of me or the Invaders. Does she still not know me as the one who blew up the ship? Let me message her and find out.

I turn the brightness back up and send a message through her website. In the message I ask her to sit down and talk with me. "Could you meet tomorrow?" I say. Why will she listen to me if she doesn't know who I am? I offer her the real story about what happened in the convention center. "I was there, I have the scars to prove it," I tell her. I can feel the wound on my chest. No way it will turn into a scar by the time we meet, if she can, tomorrow morning.

I push send and turn the brightness on the computer back down to zero. I need her to log onto Invader Assault so I can communicate with Marvle's replication. If it hasn't been corrupted it would have no idea I blew up the ship and could help me shed some light on the situation. I hope it knows about the corrupted Sims. Will it believe that his android had been corrupted? Would it know if his android was killed in the blast?

"Excuse me. We are about to close," a woman's voice says. I wake up with puffy eyes, confused and in a haze. The store is empty except for the employees. The sky is dark outside.

"What time is it?" I ask the employee, a young African woman who wears a black hijab.

"Almost nine," she says.

I rub the sleep from my eyes before I stand up. I must have been asleep for hours. I am surprised but grateful they left me alone, it is against company policy to let people sleep in the store. I close the computer, pick it up, and leave.

Outside, my hand goes under my shirt to feel the wounds on my chest. The edges have scabbed over but the center is still moist.

The nights in Bodalís are always mild. It never gets below sixty degrees, cool but not unbearable. I put my hood over my head and begin to walk with no particular destination. I should have asked the woman in the hijab where the closest park is so I can find a bench to spend the night on. As it stands I have nowhere to spend the next eight hours until Decant opens back up. This is bullshit. I can't believe I have to spend the night outside like an animal. I avoid the outdoors like the plague and here I am, about to spend eight long hours in the dark, exposed to the elements.

Have I ever been camping before? I can't remember a single time when I spent the night outside. I doubt I will get any sleep tonight. Are homeless people nocturnal? It has to be difficult to relax enough to get any rest without a roof over your head.

The streets are lit by street lamps, small globes atop black posts. I walk for five blocks in search of somewhere I can settle down for the night. There is an office park with outdoor stairs. Each office door has floodlights above them so the whole park is well lit. I pass by before I think about the ground under the bottom set of stairs and turn around. Seems like a good place to pass the time until dawn.

Someone has chained their bike under the stairs. I lay the computer in the deepest corner, where the stairs meet the ground, and lay on my side with my back to the computer. I move the bike to cover the front of my body. I keep my hood on and lay my head on my folded hands. The concrete is cold against the right side of my body. It will be a long night. The sun can't come back soon enough.

It doesn't take long for me to drift into a fitful sleep. I dream about the sequel to Invader Assault.

My Exo Suit is on and the heads up display on the outside edges of my vision tells me my health and ammo levels. I am on an empty intersection between four skyscrapers and look up at the second Invader ship as it hovers above Bodalís. They are here for their revenge. The ship is larger than the first and, from years of video game experience, I know it is more powerful. The ship is jet black at first glance. As I stare at the ship colored bands begin to move on the surface like an oil slick as it reflects the morning sun. I look down at the pistol in my right hand and know this isn't enough firepower to blow up the ship for a second time. Max and Prime are dead on the ground, one body on each side of me. I am alone.

Or so I think. There is another person ahead of me, outside the intersection but in the middle of the empty street. They are surrounded by a dense haze taken from above the river Styx. I walk towards them. Each footstep in my Exo Suit rings out against the buildings around me. The person doesn't move but the distance between us never changes. When I run as fast as the Exo Suit allows I am able to make my way through the viscous space. After what feels like a marathon I get close enough to touch the person. Their back is to me. Through heavy breaths I reach out my arm and grab their shoulder. I twist them around and get a glimpse of Paige, her eye sockets covered with taught skin, before she punches me in the face and the dream ends.

# CHAPTER THIRTY-NINE

Heavy footsteps stomp above me and my eyes jerk open. The noise startles me and I can feel my heart race. It takes me a second to realize where I am, that the noise is from someone as they walk up the stairs. It's Monday and somebody is on their way to work. Did they see me through the lower spaces between the stairs? If not, the shadows made themselves useful and hid me from view. I inch forward from my corner under the stairs and turn around to grab the computer. A deep chill is in my bones and my neck is stiff. What time is it?

On the sidewalk in front of the office park I fold over and arch back to stretch out the kinks. The sun peeks up over the tops of the buildings in the east and provides a back drop for the skyline. I retrace the path I took last night, through the shadows cast by the buildings on the far side of the street, back to Decant. My stomach grumbles. How long has it been since my last meal? I should get food but I can't use my card. Maybe at Decant? I still have store credit that I can use. How secure is Decant's payment system? They use the retinal scan but could the Society or Blackwatch be able to still trace the payment?

These considerations fill my head the entire walk back to

the coffee shop. In the end I decide it is worth the risk. I need to eat. Back in the store, I look in the display case. There are donuts and Danish pastries but I am not in the mood for anything sweet. Four kinds of lunch sandwiches are already on display in the refrigerator next to the pastries: roast beef and provolone, peanut butter & jelly, B.L.T., and Reuben. I reach down and grab a BLT. This morning is not a Reuben morning.

After I take a look at the drink menu and nothing catches me eye I order my usual. "Medium iced coffee, black, and this," I say putting the sandwich on the counter. The barista, an elderly woman with curly grey hair held back with a black head-band covered with white roses, smiles at me then rings up the two items. "Good morning," she says. The way she greets me seems to be a reprimand for my lack of manners.

"Morning," I reply and hold my face up to the scanner to pay. I hope that Drone isn't able to track this transaction. My nerves get the best of me and I blink.

"Keep them open," the barista reminds me.

I hold my eyes open and my identity is confirmed by my retina.

"Good to go," the barista says.

I grab my sandwich from the counter and look for some-where to sit. There are no other customers in the store this early in the morning on a weekend and all nine of the tables in the lobby are still empty. I choose the same table in the back of the store I fell asleep at yesterday and set my sandwich and computer down.

All of a sudden, I realize the computer is closed. It must have been shut since I left the store last night! This has saved the battery but if I can't get in because of a password... The computer creaks as I open the screen. It stays black. I hit the space bar a few times to see if the computer will turn on. Nothing.

"MEDIUM ICED COFFEE," the barista yells.

Frustrated, I go to pick up my drink from the counter. When I get back to my table I sit in front of the black screen and unwrap my B.L.T. The sandwich disappears in a few big bites that I wash down with iced coffee. With my stomach full I stare at the black screen in front of me. Then it hits me. Last night I turned the brightness down to save the battery. I reach out a finger, hold the button down to turn the brightness up, and the screen comes back to life.

My fingers fly as I log onto my email account to see if Daily Donna has replied to my message. She has, there is a message from her sent late last night. In the message she says that she is available to meet this morning and asks me to call her. I would except for my phone is in pieces on the other side of downtown. I memorize her number, turn the brightness on the screen back down to zero, and walk to the front counter. I ask the elderly barista if I can use the store phone. She tilts her head for a split second before she goes to the back. She comes back out and hands me the phone.

I call the number. A woman answers, "This is Donna," she says. I don't recognize her voice on the phone even though I have heard her talk numerous times before, in her videos online and on the computer in my apartment when we were supposed to do the interview.

"This is Corvus. I sent you a message yesterday about the explosion in the convention center."

"Good morning! I have some questions for you. Are you still available to meet today? I will come to you," she says.

"I am still available. I am at a Decant downtown." I put my hand over the receiver. "What is the address of this place?" I ask the barista.

"2776 Orchid Road," she says.

I repeat the address to Daily Donna.

After a moment she says, "I can be there in an hour."

"I'll be here,' I say and hang up. I hand the phone back to the barista and go back to my spot in the back of the store.

The old man in Phoenix sat in the back of the store as well. Was he a regular? Did he wait for the store to open so he could be there first thing in the morning? Did he ever switch which seat he sat in?

Eliana still has the video of me in Decant with him. How long until she releases it? It's been less than twenty-four hours since I ditched the two agents. As soon as she releases that video I will have to worry about the police as well, not just the Society and Blackwatch. My head spins when I try to trace the steps that have gotten me into this mess. Part of me thinks it would be better to be locked up in prison. At least I would have a roof over my head and three meals a day. Plus I could settle into a routine. I would know exactly when it is time to eat, time to go outside. They let you read in prison, right? I could finish all the books on my list and then some. It might not be that bad.

Donna said she will be here in an hour. What to do until then? I need to save the battery so I can't use the computer. I look around the room. There is a rack of newspapers near the front door. There is only one newspaper left in print, the Bodalís Daily, and Decant gives it away for free. I get up, grab one from the top of the stack, and sit back down. The paper feels awkward in my hands when I open the pages. I haven't had to read from physical paper since I was in high school and that was almost fifteen years ago. A section about high school sports includes the results from Friday night's football games and the schedule for next Friday's games. Another section has a page dedicated to an arts festival in the west village. On the backside of this page is a small informational box about the Invader Assault Championships held at the convention center. It says Invader Assault to me but the rest of the people that were at the convention center would see that the Ronin championships were this weekend instead. Every page has a scannable link and directs the reader to find out more information online.

There is no mention of the explosion at the convention center. I look at the front page. This is the Sunday edition. The explosion hadn't happened when the paper was delivered yesterday morning.

I finish my coffee and stand in line to get a refill. The store has started to get busy with people who look like they are on their way to work. Once I get my refill I sit back down and watch the people rush in to get their drinks and leave. If any of them were to take the time to look at me in the back of the store would they recognize me? Not one of them even give me a second glance. I think about how different their lives are from mine. Is Decant a part of their morning routine? Will my routine ever look like theirs again? Do I even have a routine anymore?

# CHAPTER FORTY

DONNA WALKS into the store and stands in line to order. I recognize her from her videos online. It has been almost two hours since we talked on the phone. She has short blonde hair, the sides of her head are shaved, and she wears dark purple lipstick. Her face and neck are thin but I am surprised to see that her hips and legs are thick and she is bottom-heavy. I watch her as she looks around the store. She glances at me but I can tell she isn't quite sure I am the one she is here to meet. She orders her drink and goes to the other side of the counter to wait for the barista to hand it off. When I see her look around again I raise my hand and motion to the seat in front of me. She nods and, after she picks up her drink, comes to my table.

"Corvus?" she says. She has a hot drink in her hand.

"That's me." She knows my name but doesn't seem to recognize me as the person who blew up the ship. A good sign.

Donna pulls the chair out and takes a seat. She wraps both hands around her drink and looks at my face. Still no sign of recognition.

"You were at the convention center yesterday? Tell me what happened," she says.

"Before I tell you anything I need you to do something for me," I say. I open the computer like it is a wet piece of paper that could tear at any moment and log onto my Janus console that should still be connected at the apartment. I type in the password and choose Invader Assault from the menu. Under normal circumstances I would use a controller through the remote connection to navigate the menu but, needless to say, I don't have a controller with me.

The death screen comes up. Red covers the cracked computer screen.

I turn the screen around and show it to Donna. She has a puzzled look on her face. "What's going on?" she says.

"This will only take a moment," I say. "What do you see?"

"A red screen," she says. Good. She doesn't see Ronin.

"Can you log onto the cloud?" I say.

"Why? So you can save my login information on the computer?"

"The computer has a retinal scan, you don't have to type in your password."

She takes the computer and, after the camera scans her retina, logs on to the cloud.

"Do me a favor: go to the games section and find Invader Assault."

"What does this have to do with anything?" she says. "Were you at the convention center yesterday or not?"

"I was but I am looking for another player who was there with me. He... ran away. He is always online though."

She looks at me with skepticism in her eyes.

"I need your help to find him. Can you click on the search bar?" I say.

"Why don't you just do it yourself?" she says.

"Click it."

She reaches out her arm towards the point on the screen

where the friends list should be. I reach out and knock her hand away from the screen just before she makes contact.

"Don't touch the screen. See the cracks? You could make it worse. Use the pad."

She uses the pad to click on the search bar.

"Now search for Marvle. M-A-R-V-L-E."

She types the letters and scrolls down. I peek over the back of the computer and see that she is in the menu.

"Found him," she says.

"Open up a chat with him," I say.

She clicks the name and moves the mouse. In my mind I can see the drop down menu she navigates.

"Alright, what do you want me to say," she says.

"Tell him that you are with Raven." I wait for her to type. She looks at me like I am crazy. "Tell him that before his android was destroyed it had believed I blew up the ship."

Donna stares at me. "What are you talking about? Are you high?" she says. She pushes away from the table and begins to stand up.

I lean forward in my chair. "Please," I say. "I will tell you everything you need to know about the explosion yesterday but first I need to make sure my friend is okay."

She pulls her chair back up to the table and types the message.

"He says that you haven't been online for a while," Donna says.

I wait for a moment to see if there is more. "That's it?" I say.

"He hasn't said anything else," Donna tells me. Another moment goes by, one where I try and come up with a way to make him understand what has happened. Is the replication aware of the fact he had an android?

"Hold on, it says he is typing," Donna says. She reads from the screen. "He says that there are fewer uncorrupted members of the death server every day. He is worried the corruption will spread to him. He traced it back to Wonky. The corruption was able to spread to the Sims not on the death server after Wonky used the same Sim for his replication and for his human."

I lean my head back against the wall behind me and stare at the ceiling.

"Do you want me to say anything back to him?" Donna says.

"Tell him something must have happened when I beat the game and all of the death server minds that were in my game must have been permanently altered. I think that's when the corruption began." Donna's fingers fly over the keyboard as she types out my words.

She sends the message and we wait. It amazes me that she is able to connect to the game when all I see is the death screen.

"He wants to know why he can't detect your character in the game," Donna says. She looks exasperated.

"Tell him that it is because the cloud has locked my Sim out of my character."

She stares at me like I am crazy before she types and sends the message. Minutes go by as we wait for his reply. Nothing.

"Can you tell me what this is all about?" Donna says.

"Where do I begin?" I say. "Have you noticed people acting strange?"

"Yes."

"They are all androids."

"You're definitely high." She pushed her chair back and tries to leave again.

"No, listen to me."

Donna takes a moment to consider the situation and slides back up to the table.

I explain the convention in Phoenix and tell her about Next Level Automation, about how they take data from the game to teach their androids natural human language. Somehow, the minds on the death server got corrupted when I beat the game. That corruption spread to other minds on the death server, both expired minds and Wonky's replication.

"Sims that control androids that have been planted in the world around us," I say. "The people who I meet in person that believe I saved the world have to be androids but I hold out hope that there are humans who have only had their Sim corrupted on the cloud. The last time I talked to my dad he believed I had saved the world and there is no way he is an android."

Donna nods. "So you think there are androids all around us? How did this happen?"

"I think they were placed in the world for testing purposes."

"Okay. And where does Marvle fit into all of this?"

"You just communicated with an illegal replication of him. The real Marvle, or the one who I thought was real, probably was killed by the explosion. I found out he was an android at the championships."

"Tell me more about the explosion," Donna says.

I turn the computer back around towards me, turn the brightness down, and tell her about yesterday. I begin at the part when I was in front of Decant with Marvle and tell her about the man who ran towards me before he got shot by a security guard. I leave out the fact that the security guard was *my* security guard. I tell her about the grenade that went off and how I ran once I got the chance. I leave out the part about how there is a good chance Marvle is dead, at least in our reality.

She takes notes on her phone the entire time. Once I am finished with the story of yesterday's events I turn the brightness on the computer back up and turn the screen around to face her.

"Did Marvle say anything else?" I say to Donna.

"Nothing," she says. She reaches forward and logs out of her account. She pushes her chair back and stands up. "Thanks for the story," she says. "There have been rumors of the gunshots that went off before the explosion but I haven't been able to get anyone on record saying if or when they happened. I must say, this has to be one of the weirdest exchanges I have ever had. Glad we could help each other out."

"Do you believe me?" I ask.

"About the explosion? Yes. About the androids? Not one bit."

She extends a hand to me, we shake, and she leaves.

It hits me like a ton of bricks that Drone has the ability to see that somebody logged onto my console in the new apartment. It is only a matter of time before he discovers it was me and where I am. I close the computer, grab it, and rush out of the store.

# CHAPTER FORTY-ONE

THE SUN IS BRIGHT OVERHEAD. There is nowhere for me to go and I begin to walk towards the river. After two blocks sweat begins to stick my jacket to my arms. Too bad I don't have my sunglasses with me. Did the store I stole the shirt and jacket from have sunglasses? I think back but the picture in my mind stays cloudy, underdeveloped. Another store around here must have sunglasses. I can't pay for them without a traceable transaction but I could steal again. The thought of another theft makes me realize how bad of a taste the last one left in my mouth. That's not who I am. I can make do without the sunglasses. I make sure to stay close to the buildings to take advantage of any shade they offer.

Is Drone able to see me right now? Is there a program he can run that would find my face in a field of faces through the city cameras? I pull my hood up to cover my face even though I am already too hot. At least it helps keep the sun out of my eyes. I pass by the office park where I spent last night under the staircase. The rest of the walk to the river is all residential. Rows and rows of single family houses are covered with solar panels. There are enough trees along the street that I don't have to worry about the sun in my eyes anymore but I still keep the hood up as I walk to block my face from the view of any cameras that might be around.

The river turns out to be twelve blocks away from Decant. I have been to the waterfront at the Heart of Downtown but the waterfront this far away is new to me. At the Heart, concrete covers the flat space on the shore and goes all the way into the water. Fountains are surrounded by benches that are never empty. Here there is a thin line of trees, maybe twenty feet wide, that separates the river from an asphalt footpath. The rest of the area past the path is an open park and covered with grass. Large rocks and patches of tress dot the landscape. The grass is kept short, right up to edge of the rocks and tree trunks. If I hadn't found my spot under the staircase this wouldn't have been a bad place to spend the night.

A large flat rock underneath a tree invites me to sit down. I set the computer down first and climb up. I spend the afternoon there, in the shade on the rock. People walk or cycle by on the asphalt path throughout the day. When I need to go to the bathroom I walk down to the trees by the river.

The thought of food creeps into my mind late in the afternoon. What do I want to eat? A Reuben? I remember my trip to Phoenix and the sandwich I had with Brianne. I wonder what her reaction would be if she knew I had spent last night and most of the day today outside. I imagine she would say "good one!" in between fits of laughter. I doubt anybody I have ever known would believe me if I told them. Except Paige. For some reason I have a feeling she would believe me. I like to think she believed I could do anything. What if she acted that way so that I would expose more of myself for her to analyze? It would provide her with more information for her paper.

The desire to eat becomes unbearable. I get up, grab the computer, and walk towards the Heart. There are a few small restaurants where I could get food but I want to make sure anybody that traces the transaction doesn't find out where I am. I find a McDonalds and get a burger, fries, and a coke. If anyone traces the transaction they could show up at any moment.

I get my food and walk back to my rock fast as I can. I think about the people who want to find me. Does Eliana have any other teams involved in the search? Are the police involved yet? How many people does the Society have on my trail?

How close are Max and Prime? Have they found my smashed phone? Do they know which Decant I visited? I spent a lot of time with them. Enough time to get somewhat comfortable. Would we have been friends under different circumstances? Maybe Prime but Max seems way too serious. It isn't hard for me to imagine being friends with Prime. We could watch the game together over a few beers. For some reason he reminds me of my elementary school friend, Richard. They share the same mischievous quality. Rich and I fought the first time we met but, once the fight was out of the way, we were inseparable. Until he moved across the country two years later. I never had a closer friend.

I shake my head to clear my mind and refocus. It doesn't do any good to think of Max and Prime as people. They are on the hunt for me and won't stop until I am found. Eliana has made it her mission to keep me around until she can offer me to the Invaders. The two agents have to do the job their precious Preacher asks them to do.

My rock is just the way I left it. The sun has shifted while I was away and now the whole rock is bathed in sunlight. I reach my hand out and touch the heated rock. Too hot to sit on. Not that I would sit in the sun anyways. I sit down on the grass in the shade of the tree instead and devour my food.

It begins to drizzle as the last rays of sunlight disappear over the horizon. At first, because of my stubbornness, I want to wait it out. This only lasts until I realize I have the computer with me and it could get damaged by the rain. With the cracks caused by the explosion even a little bit of water could fry the thing. I pick up the computer and hold it inside my jacket, close to my body, until the drizzle sticks around long enough to make me find shelter. I get up and begin the walk back to my staircase.

The computer stays under my jacket the entire walk away from the river. For some reason I get the urge to feel the rain on my face. If I put my hood down water could run down the front of my face onto the computer against my chest. Plus, if Drone has a facial identification program, the camera would have a full view of my face. I keep my hood up the rest of the way.

I get to my staircase and set myself up the same way as the night before. I try to sleep but I wake up multiple times throughout the night. The night seems to last an eternity. The sound of car horns wakes me up.

I crawl out from under the stairs with the computer under my arm. Cars are lined up bumper to bumper on the street. Today is Tuesday. People should be on their way to work. There should be morning traffic but not this much. Something doesn't feel right.

I look at the office park. None of the offices are open yet. Maybe it is still too early for anyone to be here.

Decant opens early so I walk the five blocks to the store. The store is empty when I get there and the door is locked. This doesn't make any sense. I bang on the glass door and a lone employee, the same grey-haired lady from yesterday, walks through the empty store to the front. She opens the door wide enough to talk to me.

"Why aren't you open?" I say.

""I can't open the store by myself and nobody else will come in," she says.

Makes sense. That's company policy.

I point to the streets full of driverless cars. "What's with all the traffic?" I say.

She points a crooked finger to the sky above downtown.

"I don't see anything," I say.

"You don't see the huge ship? The Invaders. They've come back," she says with a shaky voice.

# CHAPTER FORTY-TWO

"Wait a minute," the grey-haired barista says. Her eyes get wide. "I know who you are. You're Corvus Okada! You blew up the ship! I saw your face on the news this morning. Everyone is looking for you." She pulls out her phone.

I use my hand to block her screen. "Please don't tell anyone you've seen me," I say. Her eyes meet mine and something she sees in them sends a worried look over her face.

"Why not? We need you to blow up the ship!" She looks me over from head to toe. She has to know from my disheveled hair and stale odor that I spent the night outside. That I am in no position to blow up the ship. How could I save the world when I can't even take care of myself?

"I need more time to come up with a plan," I say to placate her. "Once I have a plan I will take care of the ship."

A moment passes before her lips crack into a smile and she slides the phone into her pocket. "Do you want anything? I'll go grab it for you. On the house," she says.

I breathe a sigh of relief and ask if she has any Reuben sandwiches left. She locks the door, walks into the store, and comes back with a sandwich in hand. She unlocks the door and hands it to me. "Here you go. Good luck!" she says.

"Thanks," I say. I leave the barista in the doorway and, with nowhere else to go, walk back towards my rock at the river. I guarantee she pulled out her phone after I walked away.

The city bustles with activity. It seems everyone is awake and they all have the same thought: to leave the city as fast as possible. The cars stuck in traffic crawl forward slower than my walk. Traffic signals are pointless in both directions.

As I walk past the houses between Decant and the river I see families load their cars with luggage. Some of the cars even have extra storage space attached to their roofs. Dads balance on the threshold of car doors in order to load more luggage before they flee the city. Moms shepherd sleepy children from the front door to the car in a rush to sit in traffic.

All of these people see a ship that doesn't even exist? The whole city must be populated with androids! They all see the threat overhead that arrived overnight. Any of the people who aren't androids and still leave the city are sheep who follow the herd.

I could get lost in the mass of bodies and go to Dad's house north of the city. To get there I would have to hop on the train from the station at the Heart of Downtown. Dad would want me to be with him if he believes the city is about to be razed and I want to see him one last time before I begin a life on the run.

Multiples tracks intersect at the Heart station. It must already be packed with people on their way out of the city. They could be a problem. What if one of them recognizes me? The barista already said my face is all over the news. They could also expect me to blow up the second Invader ship.

Linda from Decant told me about a wireless charging lobby at the station a few months ago. It seems so long ago that we worked together at the corporate office. She said that she sat there with her friend and, as they caught up with each other over a cup of coffee, her phone had charged. I could spend some time there before I get on the train so the computer can charge. Without a charger, what other choice do I have?

With my hood up, I think I could sit alone and go unnoticed long enough for the computer to get some juice. I turn and walk towards the Heart.

The station sits in the middle of expansive parking lots. The grey concrete structure looms large in front of me. The building alone covers an entire block. Lines of people are bunched up around the station doors. I keep my hood up and my head down as I join the group and wait to get inside. After a few minutes we move a foot closer. This foot makes it possible for me to see inside the doors. The ticket machines are what causes everyone to wait in line. I will worry about my ticket later, first I want to charge the computer. I force my way to the front of the crowd and through one set of double doors.

Inside the station it is easy to separate myself from the people who wait for their chance to buy tickets. The station has a high glass ceiling that filters natural light down onto the avenue of shops below. The floors are off-white tile, dull from years of high foot traffic. Hooked lamps of ornate dark brown metal hang from the walls between each pair of stores. I walk through the shops on my way to the center of the station.

The charging lobby is a square in the middle of the rotunda marked off with black velvet ropes attached to golden stands on the tile floor. There is a cylindrical cone, jet black and four feet tall, in the middle of the square with tables and chairs situated all around. There are no empty seats. I climb over one of the velvet ropes and lean against one of the golden stands careful to avoid eye contact. It feels weird to stand still, alone, with no way to know if the computer is charging but I don't have a phone to play with and I don't want to open the computer with so many people around.

I do my best to make sure nobody sees my face. It goes well, for about twenty minutes or so, before a young boy recognizes me. He isn't more than ten years old, with black hair and asian features. He points at me with one hand and pulls on his mother's arm with the other. She sits in a chair at a table next to where I stand alone. She ignores him at first but then he gets her attention when he says, "isn't he the guy from the news?" His small finger points at my face.

She turns to look at me. From her position in the chair she is able to see my face under the hood. Her jaw drops.

"You're Corvus Okada!" she says. The heads of people around her turn at the sound of my name.

"Who?" I ask her. I know it was a mistake the second I say the word. I can't pretend that I don't know the name. Everybody here knows the name. They wouldn't be on their way out of the city if they didn't believe in the Invaders.

My response doesn't seem to register with her. "Everyone is looking for you!" she says. "We need you to blow up the ship!"

"Blow up the ship? You're crazy," I say. I turn and climb back over the velvet rope. There are too many people around for me to walk away. They close in around me and I can feel my breath quicken. Their voices are indistinguishable but they all ask me to save them in some way or another.

"I don't know how!" I yell to them in response.

"You did it once you can do it again!" the Asian mother says behind me.

I can't even see the ship they want me to blow up! I need to get out of here. Their hands grope my jacket. One hand hits my computer and I have to throw my other hand across my body to hold onto it. I stand up on my toes to try and find a way out. Two policewomen next to the last shops in the lane have taken an interest in the commotion and are on their way towards me. I push the people next to me out of the way and run the opposite direction.

I barrel towards the exit with no regard for the people around me. When I try to squeeze through a line of people who wait for the bathroom the computer gets knocked out of my hand. There is a large crack as the computer hits the tile floor. I turn and stare, speechless, as the computer bounces in slow motion before it settles on its final spot on the floor. I go back to pick it up and am tackled when I bend over.

The officers tie my hands behind my back while I lie on my chest. They leave me on the floor and both stand up. One of them calls for back up.

They know about the old man in Phoenix. Eliana must have released the tape.

An officer searches my pockets and finds my wallet. She pulls the hood down and kneels down to look at my face.

"Mr. Okada! We are so sorry. We didn't know it was you! You shouldn't have run from us," the officer says.

The restraints are taken off and I am stood up. I don't know what to say so I keep quiet. People have made a circle around us.

The officer who stood me up has short black hair and there is a feather tattooed on her neck.

The other officer, a middle-aged woman with feathered blonde hair, says in a serious tone, "You need to come with us. We have orders to bring you in. It can be with or without the cuffs, your choice."

I bend down to pick up the computer. Whispers fly through the crowd around us like a plague.

"Let's go," I say.

# CHAPTER FORTY-THREE

THE WHISPERS FOLLOW the three of us outside. We pass through the doors and are greeted by more people who wait to get inside the station. All seem to recognize me and turn to watch me walk past. Some of them have a curious look on their face. They must wonder why I have a police escort or maybe why I am so far away from the ship.

"When are you going to take care of the ship?" a woman yells.

A man tries to force the two officers out of the way to get near me. He reminds me of the man I shared a cab with back in Phoenix. "You have to save the city," the man says. He falls to his knees.

The middle-aged officer pulls out her baton and threatens him with it. "Stay back!" she roars.

He leans back too far and falls backwards. The crowd swallows him as we press forward.

The officers lead me off to the side of the building once we are clear of the crowds. Six cop cars are parked along the curb. They are all white with a thick red stripe that runs the length of the car. I try and guess which one will be my ride. The black-haired officer pulls me past all six to a cement bench.

"Sit," she says.

I sit down and place the computer next to me on the bench. I open the computer, see that the battery has been charged to 72%, and close the screen. I'm surprised the station worked in that short amount of time. The two officers stand with their backs turned to me. The black-haired officer calls for transport. Should I make a break for it? I size the two of them up. I could outrun them. Then I look at the line of cop cars next to the curb. If I do run, with enough cops in the area to warrant the six cars, I am bound to run into one of them. If I get caught again I would be forced to wear the restraints. I would rather stay seated on the bench and keep my hands free.

The concrete bench sucks the heat from my legs. It highlights how cool the temperature is in the shade of the station. I shiver even with my jacket on. How much warmer would it be in the sunlight? The sun reflects off the windows of the skyscraper across the street and sends streaks of light to the ground below. The parking lot between myself and the skyscraper is full of cars left behind by people who decided to take the train out of the city. The street between the parking lot and the skyscraper might as well be a parking lot too since none of the cars have moved through two consecutive green lights.

The two officers are silent. They both stare, mouths open and frozen in place, at the sky to the right of the skyscraper.

"The ship?" I say to them.

They both nod. The middle-aged officer turns back to me. "Blow it up again."

"It can't happen the same way again," I say to her. I don't need to see the ship to know that. Video games never end the same way twice.

A van with police lights and Bodalís Police Department

written on the side pulls up and parks next to the cop car first in line.

"Here's your ride," the black-haired officer says to me. I don't know how we will get anywhere with traffic the way it is.

The two of them lead me to the rear of the van. They open the double doors for me and make sure I get inside. The interior is made of one large piece of white plastic. Metal hoops poke through holes between each pair of seats to attach restraints. I take a seat on the right side of the van, in the middle, and set the computer on the seat to my left.

"Good luck," the black-haired officer says before she slams the double doors shut. There are no handles inside the doors. Two loud knocks on the side and the van begins to move.

The sirens come to life. The sound drills into my mind and I do my best to ignore it. The van travels in fits and starts. At first, I try and keep track of the direction we are headed. Not that I have the streets memorized but I want to get a general feel for the part of the city I will end up in. I lose track after the first two turns.

We stop and the sirens continue to scream. The window between the plastic seats and the front cab slides open.

"Traffic is a bitch," I hear a voice say.

The voice sounds familiar but I can't place it.

"Where have you been? The city needs you," the driver says. It almost sounds like he is taunting me. "Everyone has been looking for you."

I am a little taken aback by the familiarity. I didn't expect the driver to be so conversational.

"I went camping," I say.

The driver laughs. "Camping! At a time like this? Never expected that from you."

From me? He acts like he knows me. "Trust me, neither did I," I say.

"You aren't tied down, are you? Slide forward and look through the front here," the driver tells me.

I move from my seat and look through the small window. All I can see through the plastic grate is the middle of the front windshield to the traffic in front of the van. The rearview mirror has been turned down. Why is there even a rearview mirror in a van like this? There is no rear window to look through.

The driver turns the mirror up to show me his reflection. Prime. He smiles wide and I see both rows of teeth.

I chuckle to myself. "It would be you," I say.

"Yes, it would. You surprised us when you ran out of the convention center! Preacher was mad as hell."

"I saw the chance and I took it," I say. "We going back to her?"

"Yup. Can't blame you for that! The explosion got both me and Max pretty good. But that couldn't keep us down!"

So, Max is alive too. "What happened to Marvle?" I say.

"Your friend? He died. Torn to pieces. He took the majority of the blast. Sorry, bud."

Prime's phone rings and he answers it. His words are indistinct but it sounds like he says the name of an intersection.

"Max is almost here," he says. "Where'd you go after the convention center?"

No reason to keep where I was a secret so I tell him about the past two days. Right before I get to the part about my trip to the station I hear the passenger door open.

Max sticks his face in front of the plastic grate. "What the hell is the matter with you?!" he yells. His words all rush out, one after the other. "The Society could have killed you! Preacher is pissed as hell at them for breaking the agreement. When she realized we would survive the blast she almost killed us herself!"

"Good to see you too, Max," I say when I get the chance.

The two of them begin to talk to each other about the best way to get to HQ with this much traffic and I go back to my seat.

Eliana will make sure that I don't get away again. I wouldn't be surprised if there are multiple teams with me from now on. She has whipped her followers into a frenzy about the best way to deal with the Invaders and it starts with my sacrifice. But the Invaders don't exist for me. I haven't been able to connect with their reality. What will happen when they do try to sacrifice me?

I never thought I would feel this way but I would rather be back on the streets than deal with this headache. On the streets all I have to figure out is a place to sleep and find food to eat. These seem easy compared to the Invader situation. The wait to find out what will happen gives me more anxiety than a homeless life ever could.

## CHAPTER FORTY-FOUR

TIME PLAYS tricks on me while I sit alone in the back of the van. The minutes pass by in fits and starts, the same way we move along the streets. It could have been hours or could have been less than one, there's no way for me to be sure. Twice, when the van stops for a moment in traffic, I attempt to escape. I throw my weight against the back doors until my shoulder aches and feels like my arm might separate from my body. The van stops just as I am ready to ignore the pain and try for a third time. The vehicle turns off and I hear one door, then the other, slam shut. I get up and look through the small window to see how bad the traffic is we are stuck in now. Not a single car is in front of us. Instead, there is a dark black driveway that curls away to the left. It is lined with trees whose leaves have bright yellow tips.

We have made it to HQ.

"Prime?" I say.

Silence.

"Max?"

Still nothing.

My heartbeat begins to rise. Are they going to leave me? Is it getting hot in here?

All self-driving cars are required to have sensors to detect if there are any creatures, human or animal, alive in the car. If it was summer, and the temperature began to rise inside, the car opens a window and unlocks the doors. No way a police van is outfitted with the same technology but I get up and push against the back doors anyways. The doors still have to be opened from the outside.

I sit back down in my seat and feel the panic begin to rise from deep within my stomach. I close my eyes and count backwards from ten, with an exhale at every number. I get to seven on my fourth set of tens before the double doors are thrown open.

The van takes it's turn to exhale and releases the stale air into the atmosphere. I grab the computer and climb down from the van. The sun is bright. Through squinted eyes I see the outlines of the guards around me. None of them have the shape of Max or Prime.

There are close to ten security guards around the entrance instead of the usual two. All of them carry an automatic weapon, ready in their hands, instead of slung over their shoulder. I use my hand to block the sun and look up. The sun reflects off the large window that marks the location of Eliana's office. Higher up, the ends of long guns peak over the edge of the roof. More security. Must be their job to make sure there isn't a repeat of the incident outside of the hospital.

I turn and look over the large lawn. It is a nice lawn, to be sure, but I can't help but think how much better it would be if it was dotted with trees and large rocks. A river in the background for good measure. I miss the waterfront.

Security escorts me into the building, through a hall on our right, and to a set of stairs which lead me to a small, windowless room. The room has concrete walls and a solitary black metal desk with one black metal chair on each side. They pull out the chair closest to the door and tell me to sit down, back to the door, before they leave. A few minutes later, the door opens and Max and Prime come into the room and stand behind me. Part of me wants to believe they are here to support me but I know their allegiance lies with their Preacher. Eliana doesn't make me wait much longer before she storms in and slams the door shut behind her. She walks behind the desk but doesn't sit down.

"What the hell were you thinking?" she yells. She leans over and places her hands on the black desk. "The Society could have killed you!"

"Why do you say it like you care if I am alive or dead?" I reply, taking care to keep my voice level. "You want to give me to the Invaders anyways."

"And how can I do that if you are dead?" she says.

"All you care about is your stupid agenda," I say.

"You're right. All I care about is my agenda," Eliana says. "My agenda includes making sure the Invaders don't come to kill us all! Which includes everyone you know and your family. It's like you don't care at all about everyone else in this city, on this planet. What happens if the Invaders decide to take their revenge on the entire human population because you blew up their ship? Did you ever think of that?"

"Not when I was playing a game," I say.

"So this is all a game to you?"

"It isn't even real!" I exclaim. I lean forward, put my elbows on the table, and put my head in my hands.

"Oh, it's real Corvus. It's real." Her tone is somber, exasperated. "And now I have to figure out the best way to save my congregation and, if I can, the rest of the world."

I am glad that the threat of the ship has worn her down.

"Plus, the Society has declared that I should be killed for

getting their leader thrown in jail," she says, her voice trailing off.

I pick my head up and out of my hands. "Do you think I should feel sorry for you? Welcome to my life." I take a moment and watch her response. She sits down without a word.

I continue, "Are they surprised? They broke the agreement."

"According to them, the explosion was the work of a lone agent who couldn't believe the agreement was made in the first place. It didn't matter to me. He was part of their organization so the blame still fell on them and ultimately their leader," she says.

"How did you get them thrown in jail?"

"The Police Commissioner is a member of my congregation. She made sure unregistered weapons were found during a routine traffic stop."

I lean back in my chair. "So, the cops work for you," I say.

"I am the one who suggested they keep officers on patrol in every underground station to make sure you couldn't use the trains to leave the city," she says.

"What if I drove?" I say.

"Well, we know you don't have a car. That's why you use the train to get around the city. It seemed the most likely and looks like I was right."

Prime clears his throat. "We should have kept an eye on Decant stores as well. He was telling me how he spent a lot of time in one of their locations."

Eliana turns an icy eye towards him. "We? You mean you. The two of you spent more time with him than anyone. Those are the types of things the two of you should have realized and followed up on."

I turn around in time to see Max glare at Prime, annoyed.

I turn back around and Eliana continues talking to me.

"Now that you are working with us again I want to get this taken care of. Nobody has been able to figure out how to communicate with the ship. Tomorrow we will take you directly underneath and hopefully the Invaders will get the idea."

"Tomorrow morning?" I say. "Why wait?"

"We could go right now but I want to be there. The teams need time to set up the proper security around the perimeter."

"Oh you don't want to be killed? Neither do I," I say.

"I am thinking about more than just your life here. Try to understand," Eliana says. Her voice almost sounds maternal.

Max moves to stand on the right side of the desk. "We will take him to a different safe house for tonight, just to be safe. We have been in the Edenroc long enough."

"Makes sense," Eliana says from her chair. "You two take care of it. I will see you tomorrow morning."

"Why don't I just stay here?" I say.

"The congregation will be here tonight and I don't want you in the building," Eliana says.

"Why not?"

"I don't have to explain myself to you," Eliana says. She pulls a small disk from an out of sight pocket and places it on the desk. She then turns her attention to her phone. A hologram pops up from the holo generator, a log in screen for her cloud account. She has her eyes on me while I stare at the hologram. I look at her and she uses her chin to point to the door.

I stand up and turn around. Max and Prime motion for me to walk in front of them. At the door I turn around and see Eliana finish entering her password before she presses enter. The hologram changes and another screen comes up.

Cannot connect to server.

# CHAPTER FORTY-FIVE

PRIME TAKES THE HIGHWAY NORTH, out of the city and into the suburbs. We drive for half an hour before we get off the exit for Pítal, a small town I have only heard of from its exit sign on the highway. We pass a gas station and a grocery store before we turn off the main road. Over the next fifteen minutes we wind our way up mountain roads until we pull into a short, steep sloped driveway. At first I think we need to turn around but Prime drives to the end of the driveway, puts the car in park, and makes sure to engage the parking brake before Max and Prime both get out of the car.

The house is surrounded by deciduous trees. Whoever made the house didn't bother to clear space for a lawn and the ground is covered with small plants that will soon be covered by fallen leaves. I get out of the car and follow the two agents into the house.

The house is split with two staircases right inside the front door that lead up and down. I follow the two men upstairs. The appliances and tile floors in the kitchen at the top of the stairs are the same as the apartment in the Edenroc where I spent most of the last month. I walk through the hallways, living room, and dining room and recognize the same beige carpet from the apartment covers the floors. That apartment never felt like home, and this place feels foreign, but there is a certain measure of comfort from the similarities between the two spaces.

"Welcome Corvus," a synthetic voice says from nowhere and everywhere. Arcana.

"Drone must have let the system know we were coming," Prime says.

"Let me know if you would like anything," Arcana says. "I will be listening."

She will be listening? These words cause a knot to form in my stomach. There is not a shred of privacy in my life. I just want to be left alone.

I sit down at the kitchen table and set the computer down. I open the screen and am relieved to see there aren't any new cracks. The old ones don't seem to have gotten any worse either. I turn it on. Password protection still hasn't been enabled. I am beginning to think Marvle never had a password on to begin with. The battery has dropped to 61%.

The graph showing how many corrupted Sims are on the cloud is the first thing that pops up. The number has continued to climb since the last time I saw the data. There are now more than a billion and a half. On a whim, I change the graph to display how many Sims are *not* corrupted. Just over 4 billion. I add the two numbers together and get the total number of Sims on the cloud to be somewhere just over 5.5 billion, about the same as the population on earth for the past decade. No surprise, they have always claimed to have made a second world online.

If my math is correct and Sims continue to change based on the function $2^n$, there are two more days until everyone's Sim has been corrupted.

I close the computer, grab a glass, go to the sink, and pour myself a glass of water. I sit back down at the table and try to organize my thoughts about my current situation.

Has my Sim been corrupted by the others on the cloud? Maybe it won't be affected since all of this seems to have started when I beat the game. Then again, it could just be the last one to be corrupted. If all of the Sims on the cloud believe I saved the world my Sim might get corrupted by the sheer fact that the rest of the world believes in a different version of reality.

What if everyone in the world is an android? If I am the last person to know that I didn't blow up the Invader's ship then I would have to keep the secret to myself. As Dad would say, I don't want everyone to think I am crazy.

What if this is how people earn their crazy label? Not because anything is wrong with them but because the world around them decided to descend to another reality, a reality that is closed off to them. They seem crazy to everyone else because they open their mouths about their situation even though they are the ones who see reality for what it really is. For some reason, perhaps altruism, they try to convince those around them that the world isn't what it seems. They get labeled insane for their efforts.

I have to remember that I own fifty percent of my reality, despite what those around me may believe.

My head spins. Max offers me dinner from a pile of sandwich halves he has made. I eat without any recognition of what kind of sandwich it is or how many halves I eat. My thoughts are a distorted fog and all I can focus on is the possibility of what could happen once every Sim has been corrupted.

Later in the evening, still stuck in my head, I sit down on the couch with the other two agents in the living room. The monitor is on but I couldn't say what has been on the screen. My mouth hangs open while my mind is caught in a loop. I realize it is time to go to bed when my thoughts turn even more unsettling. What if my mind is on the death server in another players game? Even if I am does it really matter?

I lie down in bed with the lights off. The Sims believe the Invaders have returned. The Invaders could be above the city and, since I don't perceive them, they don't exist for me. Are there other entities that lie in wait for somebody to recognize their existence? Is there anything above me in this room? Could there be something that hovers above this house? Above the planet? They bide their time and wait for someone, anyone, to recognize their existence so they can make their mark, good or bad, on humanity.

# CHAPTER FORTY-SIX

My clothes are still on when I wake up to the sound of people down the hall. How many days has it been now where I have woken up in the same outfit? Today is the day of my sacrifice and I am dressed in the same clothes I have worn for the past three days. Shouldn't I wear something a bit nicer for the occasion? Even people in the casket are dressed well before they're sent off for their meeting with death.

I roll out of bed and go to the bathroom to empty my bladder. Finished with my business, I root through the drawers underneath the sink and find an unopened toothbrush and toothpaste. After the past few nights without running water I have a new-found appreciation for the ability to brush my teeth. While I brush I notice a window to my left. A tree's branches and multicolored leaves help block the brightest rays of sunlight from the bathroom. A small yellow bird flies down and lands on one of the branches. She sits down and cocks her head towards me. If I hadn't seen her fly down she would be easy to miss against the leaves that have already changed turned to match her plumage. I finish brushing my teeth and rinse my mouth. I look back outside the window just in time to see the bird fly away.

Once I am done in the bathroom I walk down the hall. Eliana's voice stops me just before I turn the corner into the kitchen. She is arguing with Max and Prime. I listen to their conversation from where I stand.

"All we are saying is that you should have had a team bring you here," Max says. "You know the Society wants you dead. You should have never come alone."

"I'm not alone," Eliana says. "I have the two of you to protect me."

"Now you do. But you didn't!" says Prime.

"Let's focus on the bigger issue. We need to get Corvus downtown, underneath the ship," Eliana says.

"And what is supposed to happen once he is there? Are they going to beam him up onto the ship?" says Prime.

I wonder the same thing.

"Drone and Tek are doing their best to communicate with the ship. Let's hope for the best," Eliana says.

I turn the corner and walk into the kitchen. "Good morning," I say to announce my presence. I don't look at any of them and go straight to the refrigerator.

"Morning," they say from where they sit around the kitchen table. Each of them has a mug in front of them. The computer is on the table next to them, closed, and I can't help but wonder how long it took for them to get Drone to access its contents. Not that I care, odds are we can't even see the same data.

Eliana looks like she hasn't slept since yesterday afternoon. Her eyes are sunken in and outlined with large dark circles. I don't remember what she wore yesterday but it wouldn't surprise me if she still has the same outfit on. Not that I am in a position to judge, I'm sure I don't look much better. I can't remember the last time I took a shower.

Max and Prime look the same as they always do. They both have on the standard Blackwatch uniform and they seem alert and ready for whatever today will bring.

An uncomfortable silence descends on the room. Nobody wants to be the one to mention that today is the day of my sacrifice to the Invaders.

Might as well own what is about to happen. "Today's the day," I say.

Eliana nods and the two agents look down at their coffee.

I open two cabinets before I find the one that holds the mugs. I turn and look for the coffee so I can pour myself one. Prime watches my search with a content smirk on his face.

"Where's the coffee?" I ask.

"Ask Arcana," Max says.

"Hold your mug under the faucet for coffee," Arcana's synthetic voice says.

"I hate that thing," I say. Eliana nods in agreement.

I walk over to the faucet and hold my mug underneath. A stream of hot black coffee pours out. The liquid stops an inch before the top of my cup. My mind is still exhausted from the laps it ran last night. Any other day and I would have to ask how Arcana knew how much coffee to pour. But today I don't have the mental energy to even care about anything besides what will happen when Eliana forces me to stand beneath the ship.

I sit down at the table with them and blow on my coffee.

"Is that what you want to wear today," asks Eliana.

"I don't have any other clothes," I tell her.

"Are you at least going to take a shower?" Max asks.

"I planned on it," Why does he care? "Trying to impress the Invaders?" I ask him.

"Not necessarily. You just always seemed to care about your appearance," Max says.

"You also haven't known me very long," I say.

I had planned to take a shower. A long shower at that, to enjoy some of my time before I find out what will happen under the ship. But now that he brought it up I don't think I mind the grime and decide against the shower.

Max, Prime, and Eliana begin to go over the plan for the day. I sit in silence and sip my coffee, content to listen while they discuss the various team's duties during our trip downtown. My mind wanders to my two nights under the stairs and the mornings in Decant. All of my energy was spent on what to eat and where to sleep. No room for thoughts to spin out of control about what could happen with aliens that don't even exist. Life was so much easier homeless and, given the choice between the two, I believe I would go back.

Eliana looks at her phone before she turns to me. "Done with your coffee?" Eliana asks.

I gulp down whatever I have left. "Now I am," I say.

"Good, let's go. The helicopter is overhead," she says.

"We're riding downtown in style?" Prime asks.

"No, it's just an escort," Max says. "It will be above us while we drive."

The four of us leave the mugs on the table and, after I grab the computer, walk out of the house. We get into the car. Prime is in the driver seat, Eliana rides passenger, and Max is in the back seat with me. We drive back down the mountain and get on the highway towards the city. Every few minutes, both Eliana and Max lean to the side and stare out the window at the sky above. Maybe to see if the helicopter is still above us, maybe to see if the ship is still above the city.

# CHAPTER FORTY-SEVEN

Two BLACK SUVs fall in line behind ours as soon as we pass into the city limits of Bodalís. At first I wonder if they are with the Society but, once I realize nobody else gives the two vehicles a second thought, it dawns on me they must be with us. No other cars are on the road.

Activity in the city has ground to a halt. A few city residents, the humans who decided to stay instead of follow the androids and evacuate, walk the streets, unsure of what to do. A few of the small family run stores are still open. Their lights are on and people flock to them like moths to flame. The large chain stores are all dark, unable to stay open without the manpower to run them. There has to be a point in the near future when even the smallest stores run out of products to sell and turn their lights off as well.

Fewer and fewer people are outside the closer we get to downtown. I imagine this is what the city feels like at night. Except now the empty streets have had the lights turned on and still need more time to adjust. We drive through traffic lights that flash for no one and pass the occasional abandoned car. All of the people who waited in traffic yesterday were able to get out of the city. It just took them all day to do it.

The only people left on the streets of downtown are bands of homeless people. Without anybody to beg from they have coalesced into small groups, each less than ten. Their makeshift shelters sprawl over the entire width of the sidewalk and leave no room for anyone to walk past. Cardboard, old tents, and plastic bins all come together to form random structures to offer their builders some protection from the elements. They should find an outdoor staircase in an office park, alone, and be done with it.

Prime parks the car in the middle of the street at a four-way intersection. There is a skyscraper on each corner of the four blocks. The lights ahead of us flash red. Prime, Eliana, and Max all lean to their respective sides and look straight up into the sky. The two cars behind us drive past and park sideways across the streets of the intersection on our right and left.

We stay in the car for three long minutes. A fourth SUV shows up across the intersection from where we sit. Its driver turns the car sideways and blocks off the fourth entrance to the intersection. Prime puts the car in drive and turns our vehicle ninety degrees before he parks it again. The intersection is blocked on all four sides.

Max puts his hand on the back of Eliana's seat and leans forward. "Snipers in place?" he says to Eliana.

"Confirming now," she says, looking at her phone. From where I sit I can see on her screen is a map of the four blocks around the intersection. Dozens of yellow circles turn to green. When the last circle turns green, Eliana says "Let's go."

Max opens the back door into the intersection. "Get out on this side," he says to me.

I slide across the back seat and follow him out of the car.

Prime leaves the engine running, gets out of the driver's side door, and walks around the car to join us in the intersection.

Three Blackwatch agents stand next to each vehicle inside the four sides of the intersection. Eliana raises a fist in the air and faces each of them in turn. One member of each team raises their fist in acknowledgment. After the third and final team has raised their fist to Eliana, she turns to me.

"Walk into the middle of the intersection," she commands.

It seems like more words should be exchanged between us. To say goodbye or to utter my last statement. I look at Max and Prime. They both look up at the sky, at the ship they must see above us. I follow their gaze and see clouds tickle the tops of the skyscrapers. Paige had said that the tops of the buildings were all blown off from the explosion of the last ship. I'm one hundred percent sure the members of Blackwatch would agree with Paige that the tops of the buildings are all gone. If I could get to the top of one of these buildings, to the roof that exists for me and not for them, would I be able to stay there unmolested by Blackwatch and the Society? I can't believe I hadn't thought of this before.

I put my hood up and walk into the intersection, still unsure of what will happen. If the Invaders do somehow exist will they be able to recognize me from my face? I stare at the ground below my feet.

I stand in the middle of the intersection and nothing happens.

"Take your hood off and look up at the ship," Eliana says from next to the SUV.

"No thanks," I say. I'm not superstitious by any means but, if everyone else believes the ship exists, no reason to take the chance.

"Take it off," she insists. I stare at her, defiant. She raises her phone to her lips and says something into the receiver.

A member of the team on the left walks forward into the intersection. He walks up to me and, before I know what happens, he is behind me with an arm around my neck. It is a struggle to breathe so I try to remain calm, to require less oxygen. He pulls my hood down and twists my head up to the sky. The clouds have full view of my face from where they sit among the tops of the skyscrapers.

Nothing happens.

The member of Blackwatch lets go of me after some time. Even without his arm around my neck I continue to stare at the sky.

I look back at Eliana and shrug my shoulders.

"Come back," she yells, turning around in disgust.

She is on the phone when I get back to where they stand next to the SUV. "We need to find a way to communicate with the ship!" she yells. "You and Tek know how important this is, figure it out!" She hangs up the phone in frustration and looks at Max. "You better figure out a way to get Drone to take this more seriously or else he will find himself kicked out of the congregation. Make sure he gets it done."

"I'm on it," Max says. He nudges me with his elbow. "This ship is much bigger than the first one," he says.

"Yeah," I say. I could've guessed. This is the reinforcement ship, it has to be bigger. In Invader Assault, the scout is sent forward to find an unclaimed point. Then, once the point has been located, the Maulers are sent in, the big guns, to secure the point. This second ship is the Mauler equivalent of the Invader armada.

I would explain all this to Max but it would be a waste of my time. It is already a waste of time to try and understand their hallucinations.

Eliana orders everyone back into their cars. Each team piles into their vehicle and drives away through the empty streets. One of the three vehicles follows us away from the intersection.

Of course nothing happened. Why would it? The Invaders don't exist. It was just a game! I am not surprised but when everyone around me is so certain of the ship's existence it is hard to maintain my tenuous clarity of the situation. Plus, in the rooftops of the skyscrapers, I might have found a place Blackwatch doesn't believe exists. A place out of their reality and one where I can hide from the people who try to kill me.

# CHAPTER FORTY-EIGHT

We drive on empty streets back to HQ.

"We were under the ship for too long," she says. "The Society had their eyes on us, looking for the chance to kill Corvus."

"And the chance to kill you," says Max. "They might want you dead even more. Without their leader who calls the shots? I know that our congregation would want revenge if anything happened to you."

Eliana nods and the thought simmers in her mind. "Let's figure out next steps when we get back to HQ. I'm going to talk to Drone myself and make sure he understands how important it is we establish communication with the ship," she says.

"Trust me, I think he knows," says Max.

The trip takes no time at all without other cars on the road. Eliana and Max get out of the car once the car is parked between the lawn and the front door. Prime stays in the driver's seat. I open the door to get out as well but Max waves me back into the car.

"Stay here, I will be right back," he says.

I climb back into the car and shut the door. Prime turns the radio on, latin jazz, and leans his head back against the headrest. Through the rearview mirror I can see his eyes are closed.

I wish I had my phone so I could read my book. Or to call my dad. I wonder how he has been. "Can I borrow your phone?" I ask Prime.

Prime doesn't move his head and reaches into his pocket. He holds his phone behind his head for me to grab.

"Can you turn it down?" I say.

He raises his right arm and turns down the volume from the steering wheel. "Anything else you need?" he says, eyes still closed.

"You could let me go," I say.

"Smartass," he says under his breath. His lips curl into a thin smile.

I dial Dad's number.

"Hello?"

"Dad. It's me."

"Corvus! Too busy to call your old man?" Dad says as soon as he hears my voice.

"I'm calling you now, aren't I?"

"You are. Where have you been? I've tried calling you dozens of times! Each time it goes straight to voicemail."

"I lost my phone," I say.

"Are you okay? The news said you were a person of interest and that if anybody saw you they should call the authorities immediately."

I tell him about the last few days, up to when the cops picked me up in the train station. "Did you leave the city?" I ask.

"Na, I wanted to be here in case you came home. There is nowhere I would go."

"I figured as much." I look at Prime in the rearview mirror. His eyes are closed but, somehow, I know he isn't asleep. I don't care if he hears what I have to say.

"Look, Dad, I need to tell you something." I don't know if it really is him on the phone with me or if it is his Sim.

"What is it?"

I take a deep breath and exhale. "You know how I play a lot of video games right?"

"Yeah," he says.

I tell him again how I believe this is all connected to the night I beat Invader Assault. "There were only a few androids that had confused video game data with reality at first," I tell him. "The last time I told you all this you told me to keep it to myself so the police wouldn't think I was crazy. Do you remember?"

"I remember you were in Phoenix," he says. I can tell from his voice that he doesn't follow.

"Well, you didn't believe that the ship was real then. You hadn't even heard of the Invaders, except from me. Then that changed too. You became one of the people who thought that I actually blew up an alien ship above Bodalís."

"You did, I saw the broadcast," he says, confused.

I haven't known him to hand me off to his Sim before and I doubt he would when we hadn't talked since the evacuation of the city. If this isn't his Sim, and he really does believe the ship is real, he must be an android. How could this have happened? And when?

"I didn't. That broadcast is from the game."

"So you're telling me that everyone is wrong and you alone know what really happened? How do you explain the ship above the city now?"

"There is no ship above the city."

"The giant ship above downtown. You don't see it?"

"No, I don't. Because it doesn't exist. It only exists to the people who experience the reality from the game. More and more experience the game reality each day. If I am right about how fast people switch, everyone will experience the game reality as real tomorrow."

"Corvus, do you know how crazy this all sounds?" He sounds worried.

"Yes I do. But it's the truth. I'm the only one I know who doesn't see the ship."

"I don't see the ship," Prime says from the front seat. My mouth drops. "Are you serious?" I say to him.

"What do you mean am I serious?" Dad says.

"Not you, Dad. One of the agents with me said he doesn't see the ship either!" I say.

"I'm serious," says Prime. His eyes never open and his head stays pinned to the headrest while he talks.

I don't know what to think. I lean forward between the two front seats. "You have to help me," I say to Prime.

"I don't have to do anything. The Preacher tells me where I'm needed. For the good of the congregation."

"Hold on, Dad," I say into the phone.

"You have been going along with her this whole time?" I say to Prime. "Why didn't you say anything?"

"You do know I work for her right? And am part of the congregation? What did you expect?" Prime says.

"I know but the Invaders don't exist for you either! Doesn't it bother you?"

"It's not my place to decide what exists and what doesn't. That's up to the Preacher. I just follow orders."

I explain to Prime how everyone believes the tops of the buildings got blown off when the first ship was blown up. How, if I can get to the top of one of the skyscrapers at the intersection, I can live in a space outside of the reality of those who can see the ship. His eyes stay closed the entire time.

"Can't help you," says Prime.

Frustrated, I go back to my phone conversation. "Dad, you still there?"

"Still here."

"Look, there's no reason to leave your house. Nothing will happen because the Invaders don't exist."

"If the Invaders decide to blow up the city I don't see how I could survive. I am fine with that. I have lived a good life. You have made me proud, Corvus."

"Don't talk like that. I stood right below where the ship should be and nothing happened," I say.

"You stood under the ship?" Dad says, surprised. "I was watching the news earlier. One of the guys interviewed said the Invaders didn't come back just to fly away and leave us alone. He was a scientist of some sort." I can hear him begin to choke on his words. "The guy tried to be optimistic but I know the end is coming soon. Will I be able to see you before it does?"

This conversation is pointless. I don't want to upset him any more than I already have. Time to pretend.

"I'll make sure of it," I say.

"I can come to you," he offers.

"Not possible, I'm busy figuring out a way to blow up the ship. I'll find a way to get to you."

"What if you die?" Dad says.

"Well, in that case, their revenge will be complete and they will leave the rest of the world in peace."

So much for not upsetting him. Words get caught in his throat and it takes an extra second for him to squeeze them out. "I'm proud of you," he says again.

"Thanks, Dad. I'll call you again tomorrow if I can."

"Let's hope," he says.

"Let's," I hang up the phone.

I hand the phone back to Prime, sit back in my seat, and stare out the window at nothing in particular until Max and

Eliana come out from the front doors of HQ. Max carries a bag that he places in the trunk.

"Where to?" Prime says.

"My house," Eliana replies.

# CHAPTER FORTY-NINE

ELIANA LIVES near the restaurant where Paige and I had lunch after our flight from Phoenix. She has a large house with just enough of a yard between the right and left side of the house and the fence for someone to walk through. Enough space between the house next to hers for the two of them to not be connected but not enough for the lawn to be very useful.

The exterior of the house is covered in black solar panels. Each panel is embedded with right-angled spiderwebs made of thin slivers of green. Similar to the panels at the restaurant but more dull, blacker than black. They absorb almost all of the light. Even if the city lost electricity her house should be fine with this many high-quality panels.

We pull into an empty three car garage.

"Where is he going?" I ask, as Prime leaves.

"To get food," Max tells me.

We go through a covered walkway from the garage to the main house. "Make yourself at home," Elaina says when we get inside. Seems like even she hasn't made herself at home. There are dark hardwood floors and dark wood furniture, all untouched. A model house that never got the chance to be lived in.

She walks up a wide flight of stairs with curved banisters on both sides. Max and I go into the kitchen. I put the computer on the counter.

"Does she live alone?" I say.

"As far as I know. She spends so much time at work I don't know when she would have time for anyone else." He puts his bag onto the counter. "Change into these, you smell awful," he says.

"Thanks for sugar coating it."

"There is a shower downstairs," Max says. "I'll show you."

In the basement is all the gym equipment one would need if they didn't want to step foot in a commercial gym again. Across from the home gym is a couch and large monitor, alone on the carpeted floors. The walls are bare.

I walk into the bathroom next to the gym find a toothbrush and toothpaste inside the bag. I brush my teeth before I shower and change into the clothes Max has brought for me. A Blackwatch uniform. I haven't worn one of these since I went to visit Dad in the hospital. I remember Paige's body on the ground but when I try to remember specific details the image won't bubble to the surface.

Max is on the couch, phone in hand, when I get out of the bathroom. "Making sure I didn't drown in there?" I say.

"Have to stay with you at all times. You ran away once, can't let it happen again," he says with a nod towards the back door.

I roll my eyes.

We go back to the main level and sit on the couch in Eliana's untouched living room. Max turns on the news. The coverage must be about the ship above the city because all I can see is the same familiar message: Cannot connect to server.

"Can we watch something else?" I say.

"Sure, what do you want?" Max asks, scrolling through the channels.

He passes by a documentary about ocean life on one of the nature channels. "Let's watch that," I say. Max turns on the documentary and puts the remote on the couch next to him. I have seen this documentary before, it was filmed almost a decade ago.

We watch this channel the entire afternoon.

Prime comes back before the last rays of sunlight disappear. He walks by the living room on his way to the kitchen with bags in both hands. Where did he find food? All of the stores I saw on the way over here were closed. I need to talk to him again about the ship, or the lack of a ship, but the opportunity hasn't yet presented itself.

An hour later Prime tells us that dinner is ready. He has prepared a simple meal, chicken and white rice. The three of us eat together at the kitchen table. Eliana pops downstairs long enough to make a plate before she takes her food back upstairs with her. I help myself to two plates full of food and debate whether or not to get a third. The decision takes long enough that my stomach has time to inform me that I have eaten enough.

I get up from the table and walk to the large bay window in the back of the kitchen. The last rays of daylight filter through the leaves of trees that surround the quaint back yard. Neat clusters of tulips are planted close to the window. There are two white pergolas on each side of an outdoor fire pit. Each of them has two sides covered with purple and white orchids on wooden lattice.

I look to the left and see a wall of books through the window of another room. The entrance to the room is on the far side of the kitchen, double doors I hadn't noticed before. Each door has eight panels of glass set between a wooden grid. Through the glass I can see a desk.

"Is that her office?" I say to the two Blackwatch members.

Prime follows my gaze to the room on the far side of the kitchen. "Yeah."

The door is unlocked. I go inside and look at the wall of books. Paper books. How did she get so many? Most of them are about military history. I look through the titles for a book that catches my eye. Towards the bottom, and one of the last books I see, is the Brothers Karamazov. I pull it from the shelf and go back to the couch in the living room. The monitor was left on and shows a documentary about nature in the tundra.

Prime and Max join me in the living room. Max sits on the couch next to me and Prime sits on a chair on the other side of Max. I try to read the book but I can't focus. Prime told me that he doesn't see the ship either. My thoughts get stuck on how to convince Prime to help me get to the top of a skyscraper.

I wake up still on the couch. The book is open on my chest. Both Max and Prime are asleep in the room with me. It must be the middle of the night. A nature documentary is still on the monitor, this one about the decline of the Amazon River.

For a second, I think about how I could run away from them again. I calculate how far I am from the office park, the one with my staircase. I lean forward on the couch, about to stand up, when Max opens his eyes and looks at me. I close the book, place it on the end table next to me, and lay my head back down on the couch.

Tomorrow is the day that the number of corrupted Sims will equal the population of Earth according to the data on the computer. Will my Sim get corrupted? If so, will it be the last one corrupted?

If we go back to the intersection, tomorrow is also the day I will get into one of the skyscrapers and make my way to the upper levels. They will have to shoot me if they want to stop me. They have worked so hard to keep me alive I doubt they would risk it all just to make sure I don't enter a building.

The smell of bacon greets me before my eyes open in the morning. Sunlight filters through the windows. Max and Prime are no longer in the room with me. I follow the scent into the kitchen. Prime has made breakfast, bacon and scrambled eggs. Max is at the table with an empty plate in front of him.

"Morning," I say.

The two men nod.

I go back to grab the book before I make a plate for myself. I read in silence while I eat breakfast. When my eggs are gone, but before I eat my last piece of bacon, I hear Eliana's footsteps come down the stairs. She walks into the kitchen already dressed in the Blackwatch uniform, ready for the day ahead.

She grabs two pieces of bacon and puts them on a plate. "Drone has detected a signal," she says, taking a bite of her food.

"Oh yeah?" Prime says. "From the ship?"

"Obviously," she says. "Nothing direct but it's a start. At a frequency in the terahertz gap. He hopes to be able to establish communication soon."

"Corvus," she says, her tone serious.

I look up from my book.

"Do you want something to drink? I have coffee, iced coffee, juice..." her voice trails off.

"Do you have green tea?" I say.

"I do." She nods at Prime and directs him to a cabinet next to the refrigerator.

Prime puts the tea bag into the mug and pours hot water from the tap. Steam rises from the mug he sets down in front of me.

There is a moment of silence in the room as Prime walks back around the counter after he sets down my drink in front of me. I set my book down, gather myself with an exhale, and look at Eliana. "You know the Invaders don't exist right?" I say.

"What are you talking about?" she says.

"They don't exist. There is no ship. It's all from a video game."

"I don't have time for this right now," Eliana says. She takes a bite of bacon.

"Ask Prime, he knows. He can't see the ship either," I say.

Prime glares at me from where he leans against the refrigerator. "I don't know what he is talking about," he says.

"Yes, you do. You said yesterday—"

"I didn't say anything yesterday. There is a ship above Bodalís. A ship full of Invaders that need to decide what to do with you if we are to have any hope of saving the world."

Max types into his phone and holds it up for me to see. "See?" he says.

"All I can see is that your phone cannot connect to the server," I say. "Tell me, did the tops of the buildings get blown off in the last explosion?"

Eliana and Max both look at me like I am crazy. "You know they did," Eliana says. I look at Prime and he avoids my gaze.

"No I don't. I told you, the Invaders don't exist. They never existed. How could something that doesn't exist affect a building?" I say.

"Then how'd you know to ask about the tops of the buildings?" Max says. He seems very pleased with himself that he found a hole in my logic.

"You're right," I say. "The upper levels of the tallest buildings are gone." I look at Prime and I could swear he nods.

"It doesn't matter what exists or doesn't exist," says Eliana. "The fact is we are about to leave."

"Where are we going?" I say.

"Back below the ship. Be ready to go in twenty minutes," Eliana says. She finishes the rest of the food on her plate in two quick bites and leaves the kitchen. Her footsteps echo off the hardwood floor and then the stairs.

"Let me run to the bathroom before we go," Max says. He gets up from the table and walks to the bathroom in the hall just outside the kitchen.

Prime and I are alone in the kitchen.

"You can tell when people switch can't you?" I say.

He nods. "Why did you throw me under the bus like that? What the hell is the matter with you?"

"She is willing to kill me for no reason," I say. "And you know it. You can live with that?"

"The decision is on her. I just do what I'm told." His eyes fall to the ground.

The muted sound of a toilet flush comes from the hall.

I rush to get my words out. "You have to help me get to the roof of one of those buildings."

Prime raises his head to look at me, a defiant look on his face. "I don't have to do anything," he says, his voice one level above a whisper.

How loyal is he to Eliana?

The sound of the water in the toilet gets louder when the bathroom door opens. Max comes back into the kitchen. I open my book and return to the letters on the page. My eyes see the words but my mind doesn't comprehend any of the sentences. All I can think about is Prime's stubbornness.

I get up, grab the computer from where it sits on the counter, and go back to my chair at the table. The screen's hinges creak as I open the screen. The monitor comes to life. There is twenty-three percent battery left. The number of corrupted Sims is still on display, over 5.3 billion. Not long until the Sim of every human in the world has been corrupted.

The sound of Eliana's footsteps enters the room before she does. "Let's go," she says.

## CHAPTER FIFTY

Max leads the way back to the garage. We all take our seats in the SUV, the same seats we sat in on the way here. The computer is next to me in the middle seat. Prime drives us back to the intersection below the ship.

The other three black SUVs all return to block the intersection from the other three sides.

Eliana waits for the yellow dots around the intersections to turn green before we get out of the car.

The four teams all stand next to their cars inside the intersection. Eliana raises her fist and one member of each team raises theirs in response.

"Corvus, are you ready?" says Prime. The tone of his voice is on the line of immiscibility between confidence and uncertainty. Like he has overstepped his bounds the second he opened his mouth and now has to live with the consequences.

I look at him sideways. "Ready for what?" I say. We both know the ship doesn't exist.

He crosses his arms and pulls out two pistols from his shoulder holsters. He points both of them at me.

"What are you doing?" screams Eliana.

"Yeah, what are you doing?" I say with squinted eyes. Has the Society convinced him to kill me?

"Something I should have done a long time ago," Prime says. He gives me a wink and turns the two weapons away from me. One points at Max and the other at Eliana.

"Run!" says Prime.

My legs carry me towards the building on my right before I have the chance to process what has happened. I am halfway there when a loud crack of gunfire rings out from behind me. Asphalt explodes on my left. The sound reverberates from the skyscrapers and lingers in the air. I urge my legs to run faster. I am almost to the sidewalk and I can see though glass doors to the lobby of the buildings ahead.

A second gunshot rings out and the concrete in front of my feet explodes. Small pieces of concrete hit my legs and fine white powder rises up and covers my black shirt.

I knew they would miss. They have to protect their investment.

The doors are looser on the hinges than expected and I almost fall backwards as I yank them open. I rush to the elevators and push the button to go up over and over again. The elevator doors can't open fast enough. I turn my head to look back outside in time to see Prime crumple to the ground. The sound of a sniper's gunshot follows.

Blackwatch agents usher Eliana around the back of the SUV. Without Prime to keep him in place, Max turns and begins an all out sprint towards me. It takes only three powerful strides for him to get to full speed. I rush into the elevator and push the button for 52, the highest floor in the building.

The "close door" button has most of its decal worn off but there is enough of it left for me to know the function. The doors begin to close and I hold the button down in case it is possible for them to close any faster. Max must enter the building just as the elevator doors are about to meet because I hear him yell "CORVUS!" before they shut and seal me inside.

The lights above the door that display which floor the car is on blink in quick succession. Even if Max was to find a staircase there is no way he could keep up with how fast the elevator passes by each floor. My reflection in the stainless steel doors stares back at me. I am in desperate need of a shave and my chest rises and falls as I pant. I can feel my heartbeat slow down and focus on each exhale in order to calm myself down.

The light for 40 passes by and I continue to rise. Above which floor does the building cease to exist for the androids?

The light for 50 blinks on and the elevator lurches to a halt. My heart begins to race in the space between two of its beats. I press the "door open" button dozens of times. This level probably doesn't exist for them but to be safe I can take the stairs to the $52^{nd}$ floor.

Nothing happens.

The elevator begins to descend. I watch in horror as the lights blink on for each floor as I go back down. Between the $24^{th}$ and $23^{rd}$ floor, after I press every button I can think of, I accept the fact that my attempt to escape is over and I will end up back on the ground floor. I move to the back of the car and lean against the wall. I close my eyes so I don't have to stare at my reflection.

If I had selected the $49^{th}$ floor I would have made it. Hell, I probably could've selected the $40^{th}$ floor and used the stairs to make it the rest of the way. Too late now.

The elevator stops. The mechanism to open the doors engages and they begin to open.

"Hello, Corvus," Max says.

I open my eyes and see his gun pointed at me, a satisfied grin pasted on his face. He holsters the weapon and steps back to let me off the elevator. He holds his hand up to his ear, thanks

Drone, and lets the rest of the channel know I am back in custody.

"Let's go," he says.

I walk off the elevator and turn to go back outside through the glass doors. I see the backs of four other agents as they walk away from the building to their respective sides of the intersection. Prime's lifeless body is on the ground next to the SUV.

"I don't know how you got him to help you," says Max behind me. "What was your plan, to hide in the building? You know we have enough agents to find you in here, right?"

I don't say a word as we walk back into the sunlight.

# CHAPTER FIFTY-ONE

Eliana rushes towards Prime's body from behind the SUV. She has a gun in her hand and stands above him for a moment before she begins to fire into his chest.

"Don't." Fire.

"Ever." Fire.

"Point." Fire.

"A." Fire.

"Gun." Fire.

"At." Fire.

"Me." Fire.

"Again." Fire.

She puts her gun in the front seat of the car and slams the door shut. Max stands next to her when we get back to the side of the SUV.

Prime lays on his back in the center of the street at a forty five degree angle over the double yellow lines. Blood fills each contour in the asphalt as it flows forward in every direction away from his body. The sniper's shot went clean through his bulletproof vest and left a large hole in his chest. No blood seeps from the numerous holes in his shirt where Eliana shot him in anger. All of her pistol's bullets were stopped by the vest. She had to get her frustration out but it didn't change his death sentence.

"March," Eliana says to me, pointing to the center of the intersection.

I walk where indicated and look straight up into the clouds overhead. Today isn't as cloudy as yesterday and spots of blue sky are visible through the clouds.

I stand there for minutes on end and nothing happens. I look at the top levels of the building on my right. I was almost free.

"Come back," yells Max. Eliana paces the length of the SUV while she is on the phone.

She has hung up the phone by the time I get back to the side of our SUV. Prime's blood seems to have stopped its progression away from his body. With the pool of blood around him and his limbs extended at strange angles he looks like a replica of the Vitruvian Man viewed from underwater.

I can't help but to be mad at Prime. Maybe if he had told me what was about to happen I could have stood closer to the building. Or I could have been more ready to run. I only needed a few extra moments. Now he has died for no reason and I am still in custody when I should be at the top of the skyscraper in a separate reality.

A homeless man has shown up to watch the sacrifice. He shuffles forward on the sidewalk and leans against the glass door of the building Max and I just came from. A large piece of cloth, one that looks like it could be a burlap sack that has been cut open, covers his body. The cloth is draped over his head and hides his face from view but I can tell from the way the fabric moves that he has picked his head up to investigate our group. Is he an android or is he still confused as to why the city has packed up and left him with nobody to beg from?

Eliana hangs up the phone and turns to Max. "That was Drone. He said that the signals from the ship spiked when the guns were fired. He wants us to fire more shots so we can get their attention."

The ship sent out signals because of the gunshots? Drone might have jumped to conclusions. What if the ship is able to measure loss of life? Maybe that's why the signals spiked when Prime was killed. I keep my theory to myself in case they get it in their heads to kill someone underneath the ship. I don't want more blood on my hands.

Eliana hands me a gun. "Shoot at the ship," she says. Out of the corner of my eye I can see that Max has stepped back from me and has his gun pointed at my head.

I stare at the hard plastic in my hand. In Invader Assault, with a quick combination of controls, I would be able to turn, fall to the ground, and shoot Max in one fluid motion. Then I could stand up and shoot Eliana before I sprint back to the glass doors of the building. The same doors that now have a homeless man in front of them. My hands perform the actions that would control my character as I go through them my head. The daydream evaporates when Eliana yells, "What are you waiting for?"

I raise the gun into the air and shoot the clouds above the middle of the intersection. The sound of gunfire echoes off the buildings but doesn't surround me the same way the sniper's shots did.

Eliana's phone rings. "Talk to me, Drone," she says as she brings the phone up next to her head. Her face remains flat as she listens.

"Hold on, I'm putting you on speaker. Repeat what you just said," she says.

"There were no signals from the ship after that last gunshot," I hear Drone say.

Eliana looks at Max. Her eyes ask him for his thoughts but he says nothing.

"Try again," she tells me.

I take two more shots.

"Nothing," says Drone.

"Maybe those shots aren't loud enough. Should we try a higher caliber?" Max says.

Eliana nods to him. Max types into his phone.

Three shots boom out from the building across the street in quick succession. The sound that reverberates off the skyscrapers digs into my bones and vibrates me from the inside out.

I look at the building with the glass doors. If I am going to run again it has to happen soon. The homeless man stands up, unstable, as if his legs aren't used to the weight of his body. He stands still and, even though his face is still hidden, part of me can tell he is focused on the three of us as we stand outside the SUV.

Drone's voice comes through the speaker. "Some small signals but not much. Try again."

Three more sniper shots ring out after Max types into his phone.

"Same thing, just a few weak signals," Drone says.

Eliana holds her hand out to me. "Give me the gun," she says.

I hand the gun back to her and Max puts his back in its holster. After the weapon is out of my hand I realize I should have made more of an effort to break for the building with a gun in hand. Max doesn't want me dead and wouldn't have killed me.

Eliana raises the gun to the clouds above the middle of the intersection. She fires off five shots in frustration.

I look at the teams around the intersection. They all have their eyes on the sky.

I look at Max and Eliana. They are focused on the sky as well. Everyone waits for Drone to tell us a signal has come from the ship. The silence is as loud as the gunshots that came from the building across the street.

Now is my chance. I turn towards the building and get ready to run.

The homeless man is no more than five feet from the SUV and continues to get closer. He moves forward in a slow shuffle. The fabric still covers his head but, now that he has stood up, his shoes peek out from the bottom. Worn-out black dress shoes. Why would a homeless man have shoes like this on?

He follows the gaze of Max and Eliana up to where the ship should be. He mumbles under his breath and throws the fabric off of his head. His eyes fall back down to earth to focus on me. The lines in his face run deep. He has seen hard years. He mumbles again, so low that if I didn't see his lips move I wouldn't have known that he mumbled at all.

I furrow my brow and look at him. My face asks the question for me, "What did you say?"

"Time to make this right," the old man says. There is a quality about him reminds me of the old man in Phoenix, like this is his ghost who has come back to haunt me.

"Get back," I hear Max say behind me. Max walks forward with his gun drawn and aimed at the homeless man.

"You can't hold back the storm," the old man says. He throws the fabric off his body. The white of his clerical collar stands in sharp contrast to his black cossack. His right hand is balled into a fist.

Max fires into his belly. The old man doubles over and falls to the ground.

"He will come again to judge the living and the dead," the

old man says in a weak voice. His hand peels opens. A small white ball rolls out of his hand towards me. Max pushes me away and the world goes black.

---

CHARRED white residue covers the side of the black SUV. The door is blown off. I can't feel any of my limbs. Human viscera covers the ground around me. From me, from Max, or from Eliana?

Each labored breath sends a sharp pain through my chest. The world around me is muted, like each of my senses are underwater. I try to roll over onto my side but my body can't or won't follow the signals sent by my mind. All I can control is my eyes. I look up, or, since I am on the ground, towards the front of the SUV. Eliana's phone is on the ground. The screen is cracked but I can still see the time: 9:00.

The world begins to spin and I close my eyes. The asphalt is warm against the side of my head. I can't tell whether the warmth comes from the sun or the blood. Footsteps close in around me.

# CHAPTER FIFTY-TWO

LIGHT FILTERS in through a crack in the blinds that cover my window. The room around me comes into focus. Through the dim light I recognize the layout of this room. I am back in my bedroom, in my apartment off Monocots. I throw the covers off and sit on the edge of the bed. I take a big breath, stand up, and flip the light switch. I look into the closet and see my suitcase on the floor. All of my clothes are where they should be and my shoes are organized the way I had them before Blackwatch made me move to the new apartment.

How did my clothes get back here? How did *I* get back here?

I grab my phone from the nightstand and check the time: 9:01. I used to wake up at seven to get ready for work. I check my bank account from my phone and see the money Eliana had transferred to my account is still there.

Confused, I go into the bathroom. I stand in front of the mirror and stare at myself. There are no scars from the blast. My stomach rolls into itself when I remember all that happened before I woke up in my bed. What happened after the explosion? The old man that dropped the bomb had to be from the

Society. Has it really only been minutes since the explosion at the intersection or is this a new day altogether?

I peek out into the living room and expect to see Max. The apartment is empty. I grab my phone off of the nightstand, scroll through my contacts, and can't find his phone number. I look at the phone in my hand. Where did it come from?

I walk, still naked, into the living room. The place is spotless. It even has the scent of the lemon cleaner I like to use before I leave on a trip. Even though all of my stuff is here, back from storage, the apartment doesn't feel like it belongs to me. It feels like it was built around me right before I woke up.

I lose track of time as I pace behind the couch dozens, hundreds, thousands of times. I don't know what to do with myself. The morning passes by in a blur. As the afternoon arrives I find myself on the couch with the news on the monitor but I haven't paid any attention in minutes, maybe hours.

My phone rings when I get a message from Marvle. DON'T FORGET ABOUT THE GAME TONIGHT.

Might as well try to log on, even just to make sure the death screen still pops up. I grab my gloves and lenses from the end table and put them on. I turn on the console and the system light comes to life. The console has power.

I navigate to the games section, prepared to see red. Invader Assault isn't listed. The first game on the list, the most popular, is Ronin. I take the gloves off and set them on the couch next to me.

The walls seem to close in around me. I need to get out of here. To take a walk and clear my head. Does the Society still want me dead? I don't care if they try to kill me again. I get dressed, grab a jacket, and go to the street outside.

The bodega is across the street. Cars are back in the city and make their way between the lights on Monocots Avenue. None of this feels any different than a normal day but it doesn't feel like the city I know either. The colors are more vivid, the small pieces of character the city had possessed have been scrubbed away. There is no litter on the ground, none of the trash cans are full. Even the homeless man seems to have just gotten out of the shower. It all feels so fresh, manufactured. Has my recent escape from death given me a new perspective? The thought does nothing to get rid of the knot in my stomach.

I get my bearings and look towards downtown, towards the intersection where I should have, where I may have, died. Where everyone was convinced the ship hovered above the city.

Far in the distance I see the ship just where everyone said it would be. It exists.

My arms feel weak as I lift them up and interlace my fingers behind my head.

The tops of the buildings have disappeared. All of the towers are jagged and shorter than they should be. Panic begins to creep in.

I am one of *them*. An android.

I rush back into the building and go back into my apartment.

I message Marvle and tell him to get online. I sit on the couch, put my lenses on, and wait in the Ronin lobby until he arrives.

"Does Invader Assault work for you?" I say as soon as he arrives in the chat.

"Invader Assault? What's that?" I hear Marvle say.

"The game? Ronin is the only option for me."

"We play it together all the time..." Marvle says as his voice trails off.

"No, we play Invader Assault! You don't remember? The game caused the Sims to be corrupted."

"If the game corrupted Sims the cloud would collapse it so androids won't be affected."

It wasn't just the androids who were affected, Marvle. You only exist on the death server.

"You knew about Invader Assault the last time we talked. I had to talk to your replication after the blast in the convention center. You don't remember?"

"Any replication I had on the death server would have been absorbed by my mind when my android time ended," Marvle says.

I stand up from the couch and begin to pace the room. "You know you had an android?" I say.

"Of course. Now I have to wait until it is my turn again."

"Wait your turn for what?"

"To get another android."

I can't handle this. "My mind feels like it is about to explode," I say.

"I remember the feeling. Happens to everyone when they lose their android."

"Happens to everyone?"

"Everyone. When one of us gets their android the connection to the rest of the death server is cut so they can connect to their Sim. Each mind doesn't know they once were connected to every other mind on the death server until the android gets destroyed. When the connection first comes back it feels like your mind will explode."

"My android has been corrupted. I see the ship outside," I say.

"I don't think you have an android anymore, bud. Check to see if you have a Sim."

I grab my phone and try to find the setting to turn my Sim back on but it isn't there.

"There isn't a place for me to turn it on," I say.

"Told you," says Marvle. "You lost your android. Now you

have to wait in the back of the line until you can get your next one."

"Wait in the back of the line? How many people are in line?"

"Well, there are 100 billion minds on the death server. There are only ever about five and a half billion androids at any one time. Don't worry, the time goes by quickly."

"Why are there only five and a half billion androids?"

"That was the population of the world in 2049, when the last mind was uploaded. Amanda West had figured out how to upload all the minds onto the death server and into androids but there was a storage problem. Both on the servers and on Earth. All of the minds wanted the chance to use their immortality so Amanda, on the death server, designed a queue for the minds to wait for their chance to occupy an android and live again."

"When was the last mind uploaded?" I say. My stomach knots up when I realize I don't want to know the answer.

"Funny you ask, your mind was the last one to be uploaded. Happened over two centuries ago."

# ABOUT THE AUTHOR

Marcos Antonio Hernandez is a lifelong athlete and avid reader of both fiction and non-fiction. His favorite authors are Haruki Murakami and Philip K. Dick -- in that order.

Marcos graduated from the University of Maryland, College Park with a degree in Chemical Engineering and a minor in physics. Since graduating, he has worked as a Barista, a Food Scientist, and a CrossFit Coach.

*The Hysteria of Bodalís* is Marcos's debut novel.

authormarcoshernandez.com

Made in the USA
San Bernardino, CA
27 June 2018